THE CITY WITHIN

A 2603 NOVEL

KORY M. SHRUM

All rights reserved.
ISBN: 978-1-949577-49-5
Copyright © 2020 by Kory M. Shrum
Cover design by Christian Bentulan
Editing by Toby Selwyn

THE CITY WITHIN

AN EXCLUSIVE OFFER FOR YOU

Connecting with my readers is the best part of my job as a writer. One way that I like to connect is by sending 2–3 newsletters a month with a subscribers-only giveaway for signed books.

If this sounds like something you're interested in, please look for the special offer in the back of this book.

Happy reading.

Kory M. Shrum

PART ONE

ONE

COMMOTION RUMBLED on the periphery of Grace Buteo's hearing. At first, she mistook this as the standard awakening of the precinct. It was now past starting time and officers were arriving in droves, reporting to their captains for their assignments and tasks.

And should their captains need something, they reported to their lieutenants. Should their lieutenants need something, only then would Grace, or her co-commander, Adams, be called upon.

But this wasn't a slow-building din flexing around her. A woman's high voice cut through the hive's low buzz.

"I *have* to speak to her!" she cried. "It *has* to be her. I'm telling you!"

Heron Jane pivoted in his seat, looking over his shoulder toward the door.

Grace lowered the opacity on her lenscape until her surrounding office came into view. Her eyes first snagged on Heron, reclined in his seat.

She stared at that notch on his throat for far too long

before she lowered the opacity of the office wall itself and gazed out into the precinct's reception area.

It bustled.

The desks lining the center walkway between the entrance and Grace's closed door were blocked with officers interviewing waiting citizens. Small clusters of junior inspectors took instructions from their superiors and more yet issued tasks for the day.

Sudden movement drew Grace's eye.

A woman in a short bamboo dress yanked her hand back. She was yelling at the officer, shrugging off his attempt to take her elbow and move her toward the waiting area.

It was Lore Duchovny, and he threw a worried glance over his shoulder at Grace's door.

The look of uncertainty on Duchovny's face, the consideration that perhaps she *should* be summoned, was enough to give Grace pause. She trusted his judgment.

"Shall I—?" Heron began, reaching for the door.

"Please," Grace said, so close to finishing her agenda. "One moment more."

Heron closed the door behind him. Through the opacity of the office wall, she watched him approach Duchovny and the woman. At the desk, he turned up the wattage of his smile.

Both relaxed at his appearance.

Grace felt a twinge of envy at that. She supposed the burn scars crowding the right side of her face made such charm impossible, but the social lubricant would've been useful.

Grace returned to her lenscape, organizing the remaining few tasks.

She'd just confirmed a 16:00 appointment with the constable when Heron knocked.

<<All good? Can we come in?>> Heron pinged, the message appearing in the lower side of her lenscape.

"Come in," she called, collapsing the appointment book from her vision.

Heron pushed open the door, allowing a petite woman with black hair and dark eyes to step into the office. Heron closed the door behind them.

"Commander Buteo," the woman said. The name escaped her lips as an exhalation, dripping with relief. "Please hear me out. *Please.*"

"Of course." Grace wasn't used to someone begging for an audience.

She motioned toward the seat across from her. Rather than taking the second seat, Heron chose to stand near the wall, one ankle crossed casually over the other.

Grace wasn't fooled.

Her lenscape pinged a second later, with a cache from heronjane1.

Grace accepted the file and saw the woman's collected details pour into her lenscape.

Lenorie Range, 34, unmarried. One child. Deceased.

Grace's heart stuttered at that.

One child, deceased.

That was true for Grace as well. In her mind, she saw the auto lifting off the pavement, blown upward by the force of the blast, and her son's widening eyes.

Mom! he'd screamed, before the auto and her life were consumed by flames.

Grace blinked. "Ms. Range, how can I help you?"

Her eyes flicked to the lenscape, absorbing the information available from Heron's cache as well as the woman's profile and bio signature.

"Are you reviewing my files?" the woman asked defiantly. She sat up taller in the seat. "It's fine. I've nothing to hide. And I guess after what's happened to you, you can't be too careful."

To be of such small stature, she had quite the force behind her. Every word and movement was charged with energy.

And, of course, she knew Grace was using her lenscape. Grace's eyes would be lit blue with the soft light of the embedded lens.

<<Accept private chat with heronjane1?>>

Grace accepted.

<<Would a woman with nothing to hide use such a strong face filter?>> Heron asked through the private chat.

Grace's embedded police programs meant that her lenscape removed all embellishments used by citizens. If Lenorie was using a strong face filter, Grace couldn't see it.

<<I'll take your word for it,>> she wrote back. <<And remind me we need to review your programs list later. You're missing some standard precinct software.>>

Heron's mouth tightened, his indignation apparent.

Grace almost smiled at that. Heron with his expensive booster ring and four processors would be upset to discover there were programs he lacked.

"This is not a *joke*," Lenorie cried, mistaking Grace's sly smile. "I need your help. My brother was kidnapped."

One living relative. Brother: Tristan Range, 38. Zone 2 residency.

"What makes you say that?" Grace asked, schooling her features. "Did you see him taken?"

"No," Lenorie said, pushing her sleek black hair back behind her right ear. "But he would never integrate with CyTown."

It had been a while, perhaps a year or more, since Grace had heard anyone mention the cyber city. It was a near-perfect replica of their own Zone 2, she'd been told.

Though it had removed all the flaws of living: disease, aging, pain.

It was called Utopia 2.0 for a reason. Husbands and sons weren't murdered there, for starters. And their living arrangements were much more extravagant than any found in the real Zone 2, where resource management reigned supreme.

"It's illegal to force someone into CyTown residency," Grace said. "Your brother would have had to enroll in the program and be approved by a city official before being intubated."

"I *know*," the woman huffed, now tucking the other side of her hair behind her ear. "That's why I'm here. He would *never* have done that. He had views on CyTown, okay?"

<<You're scowling,>> Heron pinged over their chat. <<You don't believe her?>>

No, she thought. But then again, months ago she hadn't believed many things were possible—things that were now very much her reality.

<<We need more information before I draw any conclusions,>> Grace replied.

She softened her features. "I'm sorry, Ms. Range. Perhaps you should start at the beginning for us. Walk us through what happened."

The woman squirmed in the seat, adjusting her posture. "My brother, Tristan, was kidnapped a week ago. That's the last time his building manager saw him."

"Who's his building manager?"

"Elinabeth Dose. She saw him coming home with his weekly library books last Monday. He always went to the library after work on Mondays and got new books. She saw him come home around nineteen hundred."

"Alone?"

"Yes, just him and the books."

"You haven't seen him since?"

"No, I came by his place Tuesday morning to bring him breakfast before he went to work. This would've been around six thirty, but he wasn't there. I opened his apartment with my key and called his name. No answer. The library books were on the bedside table, and his bed was rumpled like someone had dragged him out of it."

Speculation, Grace thought, but continued to record the details on the notepad along the right side of her lenscape.

"My brother *always* makes the bed, Commander. *I'm* the messy one. He would have never left his apartment with his bed unmade unless something was very, *very* wrong. I can promise you that."

<<A stickler for order. Sounds like your type, Gray,>> Heron pinged.

Grace ignored this.

Heron's body was at ease, his shoulders softly rounded against the wall. But his eyes were sharp and assessing. At least he looked like an inspector when he tried. Grace wondered what details he was absorbing that she wasn't.

"Did anyone see him leave?" he asked.

"No. He usually wakes up around six so that he can be at work by eight. We always breakfast together on Tuesday mornings when I'm in his part of town."

"And what do you do?" Grace asked.

"I'm a home carer, and it takes me all over the zone, depending on who I am scheduled to visit," Lenorie said, fidgeting in her seat again. "That's…that's how I know about you. Your mother told me I had to come see you."

Grace kept her eyes on Lenorie, trying to maintain an impassive face. "You are a home carer for my mother?"

"I am. I visit her and Henry twice a week."

Heron visibly reddened at this, a laugh pressing against his lips like it might erupt from him.

Grace threw him a cold glance. <<Don't you dare.>>

Her mother didn't need a carer. Her mother might be ninety-two, but she was perfectly fit. She was often mistaken for a woman in her fifties, and when she used filters, even younger.

But it was Zone 2's policy that all residents above eighty receive support from the home care network. And Grace was sure her mother liked the company. Caroline hadn't met a stranger in her life.

If Grace was honest with herself, her mother had been the most recent caretaker in their relationship. While Grace lay in the hospital healing burns all over her body and mourning the loss of her husband and son, it had been her mother who'd supported her. Her mother who'd gotten her home, who'd cleaned out Kaiden's room, and had packed Davion's things away.

Her mother who programmed her ChefMate to feed her ridiculous amounts of food so she wouldn't lose any more weight.

Grace felt a swell of affection for the woman.

"Henry?" Heron asked, smiling.

"It's Kitty's—" Lenorie stopped herself. "Miss Caroline's companion."

"Robot companion," Grace amended, and rushed on before her face turned any redder. "Why did my mother send you?"

Lenorie sat up straighter in her seat. "Because you exposed that corporation. They were doing terrible, terrible things and getting away with it! No one else had the gumption to take them on, but you did! And you *destroyed* them."

Grace thought of Viscosity, Inc.'s dark practice of

deleting employees from their register, nulling their Zone 2 citizenship. This act alone had driven thousands to live beneath a shipping warehouse. The company had broken hundreds of economic, citizenship, and human rights laws. Of course Grace had challenged them.

Honestly, she didn't understand. They were willing to ruin the lives of families and children for something as simple as a bottom line? All that suffering so they could expand their profit margin and avoid paying the petty environmental tax?

Disgusting.

She'd been frustrated that she'd only been able to prove Viscosity's guilt, when undoubtedly other corporations had done the same. She hoped that the threat of accountability would make them think twice.

"If CyTown is kidnapping people and forcing them to live in cyber space, you're the one who can bring them down," Lenorie went on, her chin set hard with determination.

<<She has a point,>> Heron agreed.

<<It wasn't just me,>> Grace said. <<You did more than your share in exposing Viscosity.>>

He perked up at this. <<I did well, didn't I?>>

So humble, she thought.

"You think your brother…" Grace wasn't sure how to finish.

"He was forced into it. I *swear*. It was because of his pamphlets. He pissed off the wrong person and they took him."

"Back up," Grace said, leaning her elbows on her desk. "He was an activist?"

"Yes, I told you. Tristan has *views* against cyber living. He published his rants in the *Daily Gazette* every week.

Someone must've wanted to shut him up. His following was large. He was causing quite the uprising."

More speculation, Grace thought. It would take time to separate Lenorie's emotions from the facts.

"Are you going to help or not?" the woman demanded.

"I'm not sure there's a case here," Grace said. "It would be very difficult to prove someone was forced into cyber living when there are airtight protocols in place for their protection. Forms have to be signed and medical examinations completed to ensure that the body can be integrated."

That doesn't mean someone isn't scamming the system, a voice said.

Davion's voice.

Even the most rule-book organizations exploit people when they can.

Her heart clenched.

Even four months after his death, his voice was enough to wind her.

Lenorie stood, her little mouth pressed into a rigid line. "Your mother said you would turn me down at first. That you weren't a…spontaneous person by nature."

Grace's eyebrow arched. "Did she?"

"She advised me to tell you to think on it. And that you'd come around." Lenorie pulled at her dress, smoothing invisible wrinkles. "So think about it."

"I will," she said, and wondered why in the world she would make such a promise.

Lenorie clearly approved. "Then get in touch with me when you're ready to begin."

With that, the woman marched out of the room without a backward glance.

Heron was trying not to laugh again.

"From what I understand about your mother," he began, "I can see why she'd like her."

Grace lowered the opacity on her office wall and watched the woman leave.

Neither she nor Heron moved or spoke until Lenorie walked past the officers' desks and through the precinct's double doors, out into the sunny morning.

"I don't think we have time for a conspiracy," Grace said, returning the wall to normal. With two flicks of her eyes, she sent the weekly agenda to Heron.

They were already ten minutes behind schedule. Grace's flesh crawled at the very thought of it.

"How do we know it's a conspiracy?" He patted his pockets, sensing their imminent departure. "She might be right. Something dark and sinister might be going on in CyTown Towers."

Only Heron would use those words, *dark* and *sinister*.

"Besides, you promised you'd consider the case," he pressed. "We have to *at least* check it out."

The threat of danger was enough to excite Heron into action.

"We'll check it out," Grace said, rearranging the morning to accommodate this unwelcome surprise. If she moved everything just so, they'd be back on schedule by lunchtime. "But first, I have questions."

"Where are we going?" Heron asked as they crossed the plaza surrounding the Zone 2 precinct and walked toward the auto stop on the corner. "You've cleared the agenda for the next hour but didn't fill it."

"To see my mother," Grace said with a sigh.

Heron's steps faltered. "Together?"

"Yes." She used her lenscape to summon an auto.

Then she checked the time. "She'll be at her condo in Westside."

A white auto slid into the designated queue and Grace waited for the automatic door to unfurl like a swan's wing and allow them entry.

The dark, cool interior was a relief from the warming day.

"Welcome to CityRide, Commander Buteo," the AI chirped. "We're glad you've chosen CityRide to serve your transportation needs today. My name is Honor. What is your destination today?"

She gave her mother's address, watching Heron fuss with the safety belt on the opposite bucket seat.

"That's a fourteen-minute ride by level-one transport, Commander Buteo. May I confirm your selection?"

Grace confirmed her selection, but that wasn't enough for the AI.

"You don't have any music saved, Commander Buteo. Would you like—"

"No," Grace said, always irritated by the AI's insistence to accommodate her. "I want silence, please. Just go."

The auto obliged, pulling away from the sidewalk and into traffic. This left Grace free to take in the city beyond its clear windows.

Tall rose-gold buildings lined both sides of the ten-lane boulevard that the white CityRide autos scuttled down like beetles through the morning haze. Grace's eyes caught snatches of green vegetation everywhere.

Already, a heat haze was forming on the upper levels. She suspected by the look of it that the air-quality rating would be lower today, and the UV risk elevated.

Grace enjoyed several minutes of blessed silence before she caught sight of Heron.

He looked…pained. As if he were unsure of where to put his hands or his eyes.

"What's wrong with you?" she asked.

He flicked his gaze up, pouting his lips. "Nothing."

"You sound suspicious, Heron. Why do you sound suspicious?"

"I'm not suspicious."

Grace arched a brow. "We made a deal, remember?"

And he'd better remember. It was the whole reason she'd agreed to keep him on as her assistant inspector even after he confessed to being a fraud.

They'd been sitting in a Low Town bar as he'd told her the story of his secret mission to fulfill her dead husband's last wish. How Davion, upon realizing he might "disappear" for his resistance work, had recruited his friend to aid Grace and their son any way he could—unaware that his actions would get their son killed, too.

Heron hadn't hesitated to forge a visa and sneak into the zone under the pretense of filling the inspector position at her very own precinct in case the people who killed her husband and son came back for her.

He was risking his life, banishment from civilization, and much more, simply because Davion had asked.

So she'd agreed to let him stay under one condition: no more pretending. No more lies.

Not with her.

Heron could fool anyone he wanted—anyone he needed to—but *not* her.

"We made a deal," she said again.

Heron sighed, laying his head back against the auto's dark seat. "Okay, but you won't like it, and I hate telling you things you won't like."

These words were enough to prickle the hair on the back of Grace's neck.

He raised his head and met Grace's eyes. "Remember when I tried to update your house last month, before we were real friends?"

"You mean when you hacked my house without telling me then said its security was garbage."

"Oh, it was. Really, Davion should've been ashamed of himself," he said, then seemed to catch himself. "Your house isn't the *only* residence you visit, so…"

Grace tilted her head, the heat in her face building.

"I mean, you have family in the city. I just thought I'd update your mother's system while I was at it, but we got to talking and—"

"What are you saying?" Her jaw flexed.

Heron fell back against the seat. "This is why it's hard to tell you things, Gray! You get so upset."

Grace, ruffled now, took a slow, deep breath. She ground out, "Finish."

"Arjun needed an apartment anyway, okay? Why *not* install him near your mom? And it was easy. Once we got him moved in, we visited her one day, brought some dessert, said hello, embedded a security tracker in your mother's home mainframe, and now we can monitor her at all times—"

"*What?*"

"We ate shortcake! Big deal!" He aimed for a nonchalant shrug, but it was far too tight.

Grace only blinked at him.

"This is a good thing. Arjun can keep an eye on things while we continue working on Davion's case."

On Davion's case.

Their investigation into Davion's murder was a case that didn't officially exist.

If one were to review the existing files, they'd learn that a radical extremist named Lix Richards, bent on destabilizing Zone 2, had infiltrated the precinct. It would say he was the one who placed two IEDs near the police precinct, hoping to destroy the police force and leave the zone vulnerable to seizure.

Grace had disarmed one bomb, but had missed the second placed in her personal vehicle. It was the second one that exploded, killing her husband and son, and nearly her.

Lix was apprehended and died by "suicide" days before he was set to be exiled on the Midnight Train.

But that wasn't what happened.

Davion and Kaiden died, but the blame didn't rest with radical extremists from the outer zones seeking to rob Zone 2 of its resources. Lix Richards had been innocent.

Davion was "disposed of" because he'd been forging visas, moving thousands of families from the worst zones into better ones.

Because relocation wasn't cheap, he'd been stealing from the wealthiest corporations in the zone to fund their travels. Until he was caught and someone decided to put an end to his work.

Davion's case, she thought again.

Part of her, a bitter part, thought Davion had gotten what was coming to him. He couldn't expect to go against the most powerful entities in one of the wealthiest zones without repercussions.

She would give anything to have him back. Anything to wrap her arms around him, but that changed nothing.

She was proud of him and angry with him. She understood he'd done what he'd done because he was a good, loving man who couldn't abide injustice any more than she could.

But Kaiden had been a child. *Her* child.

An innocent eight-year-old boy, and Davion had gotten him killed.

Grace wanted the head of whatever sick bastard who'd done it.

Heron was watching her war with herself. Grace exhaled until she felt steady again. "Do you have her under full twenty-four-hour surveillance, or do you just check-in?"

"We have sensors. We're alerted only when something is amiss."

"You *do* know what my mother does to her robot."

"We haven't turned your mother's condo into a porn house, Gray! Consent is very important!" Heron looked up at her through long lashes, his lower lip noticeably fuller than it'd been a moment before. "Tell me. What would you do if someone hurt your mother?"

"I'd be irrational and go after them."

"Exactly," Heron said, snapping his fingers as if his point had been made. But when he saw Grace's face, he deflated a bit. "It pays to be cautious."

"How long ago did you infiltrate my mother's house?"

"About three weeks."

"Right after we met."

"Hmm." He scratched his chin, clearly pretending to think it over. "Something like that."

"You're telling me this now because…"

"Because your mother is going to recognize me. I didn't want you to be surprised."

"Wait, why you? I thought Arjun was the undercover neighbor."

"I sleep over. Often." At this he wagged his eyebrows. "And I say hi to people. I'm not *rude*. Also, there was the shortcake."

Grace adjusted herself against the seat. "Can I ask you something?"

"Mint chip and rocky road."

"What?"

"My favorite ice cream flavors. Classic but stylish."

"Wait." Her eyebrows knit together. "How can you have *two* favorite flavors? The word *favorite* is used for *one* thing. Not two."

"Grace, you and all your rules. Of course I can have two."

She was trying to remember what she'd wanted to say before he'd distracted her with this nonsense.

"I love them both equally. But sometimes, I'm simply in the mood for one more than the other. Or sometimes I want them *both* at the *same* time, and then I get them both together and—"

"Stop." He was definitely not talking about ice cream. "I don't want to know about your preferences."

He pouted a little. "Oh, okay. Well, yours is vanilla, which apparently you eat by itself. How sad."

"How do you—?"

"Your mother."

Grace bit back the urge to scream. "Why did Arjun agree to come to Zone 2 with you?"

Heron glanced out the window.

"You uprooted your life and came here because Davion asked you to and he was your friend." *Supposedly.* She'd begun to wonder if they'd once been more. "But why would Arjun risk it?"

Heron forced a smile. "For *love*."

"Be serious."

He scoffed. "Excuse me. He *does* love me."

"I'm sure. But is that enough to risk what you're risking by being here?"

Heron met her gaze at last. "He goes where I go. He looks after me."

She thought, *Lucky for you. To still have someone like that.*

His smile softened. He made a wide, sweeping gesture toward the window. "You're looking out for everyone. Let us look out for you."

That was what she'd vowed to do when she accepted the position of co-commander. It was her job to keep the zone and its citizens safe from outside threats. But more and more lately, the threats seemed to be coming from within, much closer to home than she'd like.

All of this overlooked one blaring fact.

She'd failed.

She'd failed to save the two people who really mattered to her.

She was still learning to live with that.

TWO

THE AUTO ROLLED up to the gate outside the Gloryside Condos compound.

Grace waited for the sensor to read her metrics and open the gate once it confirmed her identity. Since her mother had moved to this singles condo, Grace had been registered as her guest.

"Welcome to Gloryside again, Mr. Jane," the sensor chirped.

When Grace scowled at him, Heron flashed a sheepish grin. "Sorry. I guess I come here more than you do."

A pang of guilt hit her. He wasn't wrong, exactly. It was true that her mother came to her home more often than she visited the condo.

If she was honest with herself, it was because of Henry. She'd never been entirely comfortable with her mother's AI companion.

Grace pinged her mother. <<I'm rolling up for a quick visit. Put on clothes.>>

There was always the danger that her mother was

naked and occupied. Despite her age, she was an energetic woman.

The auto rolled to a stop in front of 4323.

The door to the condo flew open before Grace had even fully exited the auto. "Gracie! What a lovely surprise!"

Caroline was a couple inches shorter than Grace, with her bleached hair pulled up in a high ponytail that fell coquettishly over one shoulder. The opposite shoulder was bare, the oversized shirt drooping on that side, revealing sharp collarbones.

Caroline opened her arms, ready to give Grace a warm reception. But then she saw Heron stepping out of the auto behind her and her face *really* lit up.

"Janie! It's *wonderful* to see you, handsome boy! I didn't realize you were working with Gracie."

"We *just* discovered the happenstance in the auto," Heron said.

At least Heron hadn't lied *only* to Grace. That improved her mood slightly.

It wasn't a lie, her mind corrected. *He didn't purposely deceive you. There'd been no need to divulge the information.*

If Grace was honest with herself, she suspected there was much about Heron Jane that he hadn't gotten around to telling her yet.

Something inside her unclenched at this, and a stir of something—excitement, maybe—rippled through her.

The hug Grace expected from her mother turned into a brief shoulder squeeze as the woman moved past her to clasp Heron's hands.

"Did you come by for a morning game of mahjong?" her mother asked, her eyes never leaving Heron's face.

"We aren't here for mahjong," Grace said stiffly. The

heat quadrupled as she stood in the direct sun. It was becoming difficult to think clearly. "We came to talk about Lenorie."

"That's my Gracie. Work, work, work," Caroline said to Heron with an air of conspiracy. She leaned in close and pretended to whisper, "One could hope your influence would loosen her up a bit."

She accompanied that innuendo with an elbow nudge into Heron's ribs.

"Mother!"

Caroline rolled her eyes. "All right, come in already. I made cherry-chip scones and I've got that Venetian blue tea you like, Janie."

Grace gestured toward the condo's open door. "After you, *Janie*."

"Don't mind her," her mother said. "She was an only child. She never learned how to share Mommy's affections."

The muscles in Grace's back tensed. She turned and threw a nervous look over her shoulder at the street around them. The shining white façades of the condos with their cheerful yellow trim beamed back at her. The white auto sped away toward the gate.

She saw no one. Then why did she feel like she was being watched?

"Gracie, do you want tea?" her mother called from the kitchen.

Grace reluctantly entered the condo and closed the door behind her. "No. I've already had a bullet and a half this morning."

Her mother groaned. "How can you drink that? Your father was the koffee drinker. You must have his stomach. If I drink anything that strong, it burns me alive from the inside."

Grace regarded the neat kitchen off to the left. Above the stove sat a dual-armed ChefMate resembling the one Grace had at home, the metallic arms suspended, waiting to fulfill their programmed menu at the designated time.

Her mother filled two mugs with hot water from the dispenser. Given the earthy, uneven quality to the mugs, she wondered if her mother had made them herself. The woman was always joining art classes, architecture classes, exercise classes—classes of all kinds, really. She seemed to have an insatiable appetite for hobbies and meeting new people.

Grace wanted to keep up with all her mother's hobbies, show an interest in her life, but asking her about anything was a dangerous game.

Her mother was a chatterbox.

She needed only the slightest invitation to fall into a hole of personal updates, gossip, and tangents that would carry them long into the evening.

Grace had budgeted only thirty minutes for this interlude.

Heron was already at the four-person table, settling in as if he'd spent many a night here.

Her mother presented him with a steaming mug, a wide smile, and a cherry-chip scone centered on a white plate. "Arjun, Heron, and I play mahjong on this table all the time. Henry is our fourth, but you could join us."

Grace's eyes swept the apartment, on the lookout for her mother's robot companion, but she didn't see him. She wondered if it was too much to hope he was at a repair shop or something.

"I'm not a very good player," Grace admitted. "I suspect the three of you would destroy me."

"Not at first," her mother said, taking a seat beside Heron and grinning mischievously over the rim of her mug. "We'd bolster your confidence first. Wait until you relax."

"How generous, Mother."

"Who did you think you got your generosity from?" she said. To Heron, she explained, "She's serious and a thinker like her father, but I've bestowed *many* amiable traits on her."

"Yes, I've noticed," Heron said, matching her flirtation for flirtation.

"Did you know that Heron's boyfriend is a sex worker?" her mother asked as casually as one says "It'll rain this evening."

"She's aware." Heron's smile twitched.

Grace arched a brow. "Sorry. Why is that relevant?"

She took the third seat at table.

"It means they're open to experimenting. You—"

"Mother, no. I've told you, discussing my sex life in front of *anyone* is inappropriate. Heron and I work together."

"Mother," she echoed, leaning toward Heron. "She only calls me Mother when she's angry."

"Mother."

"It's not inappropriate to talk about sex, it's *healthy*."

"Not when my subordinate is involved."

"Mm, subordinate," Heron repeated. "Careful, Gray. I find dominance play very satisfying."

Her mother giggled. "You need some release in your life."

"Davion just died."

"Four months ago, and he wouldn't care as long as you're happy."

Kaiden just died, she thought. But she refused to invoke her son's name in such a conversation.

"Arjun—or Heron—could show you a good time."

"Why not both of us?" Heron said, his grin wicked. "At the same time."

Her mother didn't hear this quip.

"It'd be no strings attached, and then you could relax a little more. Honey, I only want you to be happy."

Grace pinged Heron. <<Accept private chat from gracebuteo4?>>

<<Stop encouraging her,>> she wrote before Heron's text even appeared on the lenscape.

The text was redacted, and instead he wrote, <<All right, but your mother is hilarious!>>

To you, she thought. <<If you keep encouraging her, we'll never get the information we need. We are working here.>>

She could practically hear the resigned sigh across the lenscape.

<<Roger that, Commander.>>

"I don't see what's holding you back," Caroline said. "You're a beautiful young woman. Janie, tell her."

"Very beautiful," he said, and Grace saw the tinge of red highlight his cheeks.

"Mother, you might use sex to solve all of your problems, but I don't."

Caroline turned to Heron again. "Ouch. Vicious."

"Again, we're coworkers," Grace said patiently, forcing her leg to still under the table.

Her mother lit up. "Oh, speaking of coworkers, has Adams asked you out yet?"

Grace frowned. "No. Why would he?"

Heron visibly stiffened beside her. "Do you like him, Caroline?"

"He's very attractive, don't you think? He's tall and muscular like Arjun. I would think he'd be your type."

Heron squinted his eyes in consideration. He had the

face of someone trying to find a way to politely disagree. "He strikes me as a bit cold."

"Cold, not at all!" Caroline continued, unaware. "He visited Gracie every day that she was in the hospital."

She leaned toward Heron and fake-whispered, "I think he's loved her for a long time, but he was being respectful of Grace's marriage. Like Samuel in *Sailors & Starships*."

"God, I love that show," Heron said, lifting his tea to his lips.

"Adams and I are colleagues." Grace tried to imagine Adams as the pining sort. It was ridiculous.

Her mother arched a brow. "I have a sense about these things. He has plans for you, my love. Wait and see."

"Monogamy is overrated," Heron said. "Loyalty has very little to do with where you put your genitalia."

"Oh, agreed." Caroline nodded.

If Grace did not seize control of this conversation, they were going to waste their entire thirty minutes. She glanced at her lenscape clock. They had only eight minutes left.

"We need to talk about Lenorie," Grace interjected, sitting up straighter and using a tone that she hoped would focus her mother's flippant attention.

"Heavens, Gracie. We're having a nice teatime here."

"Tell us about Lenorie so that we can help her."

Her mother sighed. "Lenorie is a good girl. She comes every week to check on me, and we watch *Sailors & Starships* together. Such a great show."

"Do you think the duke will forgive Nadia?" Heron asked, his face a mask of horror.

"He has to. If he doesn't, what will happen to the district's supply chain?"

Heron looked ready to ask more but saw Grace's face. Instead, he took a bite of his cherry-chip scone.

Grace pressed on. "What did she tell you about her brother?"

"That he's gone missing. She suspects a government plot to silence him since he's been very vocal about his views on CyTown. I told her to contact you. I was *so* proud of you for the way you handled that organ company. *Vultures.*"

Her mother leaned forward and cupped her cheek.

Grace resisted the urge to pull away. When her mother finally released her, she asked, "Has Lenorie ever given you the impression that she's radical in any way?"

"Oh no." Caroline tilted her head. "She's just a girl. A rather silly one at that, but she means well. It's my impression that it's her brother who has all the views."

"You don't think she would lie or strive for attention?"

"No, I believe her," her mother replied. "That's why I told her it was best to talk to you. Your position is a little more secure than, say, Heron's."

<<She has no idea,>> Heron wrote.

Grace closed the chat, effectively kicking him off her lenscape. It was hard enough to focus on her mother without the second conversation scrolling along her window.

"All I can tell you about her is that she seems honest, hardworking, and loves her brother very much. It's only the two of them in the zone. The rest of her family is dead. I believe they died in the 2594 outbreak of C. auris."

Grace considered this.

"If she's in trouble, I really hope you'll help her. I'd hate to lose my *Sailors & Starships* companion." She caught Heron's eye. "Not you, dear, but you've been very busy."

"This is true," Heron conceded.

Grace realized that Heron must not talk about her to

Caroline. Whether this be from loyalty or practicality, she appreciated it. And a swell of affection rose in her.

Feet sounded on the stairs, causing the trio to look up.

There was Henry.

The robot looked perfectly human, as he was designed to do. His limbs probably felt as real as the arm Grace had replaced after the accident, synthetic flesh stretched over titanium bones.

But the brushed-back blond hair and blue eyes, paired with the vapid grin, made him look more like a Boi doll than ever.

There's not a single thought in that head, her father would have said.

Today the Boi wore only a tight pair of underwear.

Grace didn't understand why her mother insisted on keeping the doll naked or near naked all the time.

"Hello, Henry," Caroline said, greeting it with a smile. "We have guests."

The robot looked from face to face. "Hello, Grace. Hello, Heron. Nice to see you both again."

Grace forced a smile.

"I'm assuming you've finished cleaning upstairs?" Caroline asked, stroking the Boi's arm.

"Yes, Kitty. Shall I make bread?" Henry offered. "Something to go with your tea?"

"No, my love. We already have scones." Caroline grinned at Grace. "Kitty is my nickname. Isn't it *adorable*?"

"You're adorable," Henry said reflexively.

Grace could see the outline of the Boi's oversized penis in his speedo. She didn't find it remotely adorable.

She stood, pushing back her chair. "We should go. Heron, please order the auto. We'll wait outside."

"I got Grace a Boi," Caroline said. "Designed it myself."

"It's still in my storage closet," Grace said, *because I can't find anyone to take it.*

Apparently, the machines had to be disposed of properly, and Grace couldn't return it without a receipt to prove it wasn't a black-market edition. A receipt which her mother refused to hand over.

"That's a shame," Caroline lamented, rising from the table. She bent toward Heron's ear and whispered, "I got it fully loaded, if you get what I mean."

Heron pressed his lips together again.

"If you think of anything about Lenorie, message me, okay?"

Caroline caught up to her at the door. She slid a paper bag of scones into Grace's hands. "You're still too thin. Eat these. Don't give them away."

Grace accepted them. "Did you hear what I said about Lenorie? Anything. Anything at all."

"Yes, yes, my love. I heard you." She planted kisses on Grace's cheeks.

Henry came up behind her and placed an arm around *Kitty's* neck.

That was enough for Grace.

She kissed her mother's cheek and took off down the sunlit walkway toward the street.

Once they were in the auto, Grace looked up from the scone bag in her lap and swore.

"Such language!" Heron said, laughing. "I didn't know words like that could come from your mouth. Mine, certainly, but yours?"

Grace pressed her fingers into the wrinkles between her brows. "*That's* why it looks like you."

He arched a brow, waiting.

"That's why the Boi she gave me looks like *you*. Because she ordered it after meeting you. Damn it, Heron."

"I'm sorry." His face folded from recognition into unfettered laughter. "Who knew I was such an inspiration?"

THREE

GRACE HAD enough time to stop by the precinct cafeteria and grab another bullet and a half before their next appointment.

Heron agreed to wait by the auto stop and begin the preliminary research on CyTown and the Ranges. That would make catching an auto faster. If she timed it right, they'd meet their first appointment exactly on the hour. The possibility lightened something in her chest.

The cafeteria was large and nearly three stories high. Crystalline light poured through the glass ceiling, sparkling along the white stone floor as she crossed to the welcoming koffee stations. She saw an opening at one of the metal machines and made her move.

"Good morning, Commander," a voice called. "A moment, please?"

It was too good to be true, Grace thought. The very idea that she could get in and out of the precinct without interruption was ridiculous.

"Yes?" She turned and found Adams approaching her from an adjacent koffee station. A steaming cup rested in his right hand, and he seemed unsure what to do with his left. It hung in the air, suspended somewhere between a hug and a handshake. He settled for slipping it into his pocket.

"I came by your office this morning, but you'd already gone."

"Busy day." She mashed the buttons on the machine that would produce her preferred koffee.

"I'd heard there was a situation at Duchovny's desk."

Grace wanted to steer Adams away from Lenorie and the potential case until she had a chance to go over it herself. He had a habit of swooping in and applying a heavy hand prematurely. "Nothing I couldn't handle."

"I know," Adams said, his pride evident.

Grace hesitated, turning toward him.

He looked ready to burst.

"What is it?" she asked.

He pulled an object from his pocket with his free hand. "Close your eyes."

If he hadn't looked giddy, on the verge of pure delight, she might have mistaken this for a threat.

But because they were in the precinct cafeteria, in view of a thousand officers, and because it was hard to imagine something terrible happening in such a bright and cheerful place, she humored him. Closing her eyes, she heard fabric rustle. Then a surprising weight was pressed into her palm.

She opened her eyes and found a golden cylinder. She turned it in the light, the surface glittering.

"The ends twist open," he was saying, his excitement evident.

I remember, she thought, but stopped herself from saying so. Had she, it would've provoked a lot of questions.

She grasped each smooth disc and turned. The cylinder opened, and something rolled out into her hand.

It filled most of her palm, rolling along her bones, the surface as iridescent as its scroll-like case.

It was a golden egg, unblemished except for a crack along one side, giving the impression that something was about to erupt from the shell. An intentional effect, she was sure.

He chewed his lip. "Do you know what this is?"

"An Egg Island invitation," she said, unable to hide her surprise. *Why would they offer this to me?*

"*Yes*," he said, the word erupting from him. "You've been invited to join us. I'm proud of you, Grace. You'll be inducted on Friday."

The egg warmed as if pulling heat from her hand. "I'll be inducted?"

"Yes. This Friday."

"If I accept."

Adams stuttered. "*If* you accept? Why wouldn't you accept? This is an enormous honor."

She turned the egg over in her palm.

But why now? Why me?

She thought of Heron's stricken face when she'd shown him a cylinder just like this, taken from Getty Peters's desk. Getty Peters, CEO of Viscosity and the man who'd tried to plunge a lethal syringe into her throat.

You've taken down one of the largest corporations in the zone overnight, Heron had said. *If there is as much corruption here as I think there is, you're in danger. Serious danger. They will figure out how to get you under control. Or eliminate you.*

"I don't understand." Adams shuffled in place, bringing Grace back to the present. "They want to acknowledge your sacrifices and contributions to the safety of the zone."

She turned the scroll in the light and saw the scrawling script engraved there.

Flectere si nequeo superos, Acheronta movebo.

"What does this say?"

"If I cannot sway the heavens, then I shall move hell." He shifted, impatient. "What about the honor?"

It seemed hard to imagine that a bunch of the wealthy elite wanted to do something as casual as invite a police commander into their ranks. They'd already inducted Adams two years ago, shortly after he thwarted a nearly successful cyber takeover.

He ran a hand over his cropped hair. "I hope that you'll accept. Joining the organization changed my life."

She met his eyes. "Is that so?"

He seemed to weigh his words. "Wouldn't it be nice to be on the inside for once? To see this other side of the zone that we're not usually privy to? More will make sense to you once you're on the inside."

She arched a brow. "Do you think I don't have a handle on the zone now?"

"N-no," he stammered. "That's not what I meant."

"Do you think things are happening here that I don't see?"

He didn't look ready to imply she was ignorant. Not with his eyes raking over her scarred face and throat, no doubt calculating her other losses in his mind.

She threw a glance at the exit, wondering if she should ping Heron, ask him for help. She met Adams's eyes.

Getty Peters flashed in Grace's mind again. She saw his menacing face, the thick, unmanaged rage.

I made a mistake requesting you, he'd hissed the day Grace arrived to arrest him for fraud and crimes against the zone. *I thought I was asking for a shell-shocked, pathetic woman, but look at you. The other one would've done as he was told.*

The other one. Was Adams *the other one?* Grace had wondered ever since. If Adams was working at the beck and call of the city's wealthy, and not in the service of the people he'd sworn to protect—then what?

What would—could—she do about it? He'd been voted into his post the same as she.

You have no idea what you've done, Peters had warned. *They'll destroy you for this.*

And was this elite invitation into a secret society—a society that Peters himself had been part of—the first step toward that destruction?

"There's nothing wrong with having connections to people in power," he said, seeming to find his composure again. Grace envied that about him. He'd always been quicker to paste on a politician's smile and slick manner than she could. "Think about it. A personal line to any resource or ally you need. I thought you'd be thrilled. You could have anything you want with this kind of power."

"I don't want power," Grace said, frowning. Power seemed like a ridiculous thing to wish for. What could power save you from? Aging? Death? Pain? It protected you from nothing.

He bit his lip. "I just meant, think of what you could do on the zone's behalf if you accepted this."

She turned the egg in the light one more time before returning it to its cylinder and pocketing it.

She paid for the koffee with a flick of her wrist and moved to go.

"I hope you change your mind," Adams said. "I wanted to take you on Friday."

Grace stopped, turning back. "What?"

"I wanted to take you to the induction Friday." He licked his lips and stepped forward. "As your date."

She looked at his throat, noted the pulse visibly jumping.

"But if you don't want to go with me," he added,

returning his hand to his pocket, "I hope you'll still consider accepting the invitation. You deserve what they're offering you."

What did this man know about what she deserved? They'd been colleagues for years, but she didn't believe he understood the first thing about her.

What did he even see when he looked at her ruined face?

She registered a small glimmer of fear—and annoyance—nipping at the tips of her ears as she turned away from him.

She hated when her mother was right.

<<Coming out now,>> she pinged Heron. She pushed open the doors and stepped out into the open air, feeling eyes on her back. <<Get the auto.>>

At the stop outside, Heron waved her toward a waiting white auto. "Your chariot, sir."

She climbed into the dark interior, raising her hands so that the automatic belt could fasten across her chest and lap.

"We need to stop in Eastside first and touch base with the team at the medical clinic."

"Check," Heron said, a pleased grin on his face. "Then we can go by CyTown."

"Right. Afterwards, if we aren't satisfied by their answer, I'd like to have a look at Tristan's apartment and see if we can reconstruct what happened there."

"Absolutely. I have the perfect software for that."

"Illegal, I'm sure."

He clicked his tongue, looking up at her through long lashes. "You have little faith in me."

"So it's *very* illegal then?"

He grinned. "*Very.*"

"And—" Then it hit her. "The auto isn't talking."

Heron sat up, excited. "I figured out how to silence the programming. Apparently, there is a 'date' feature, sometimes called a 'surprise' feature. It's used if you don't want your companions to know where you're going. The auto communicates directly with my lenscape and not out loud."

"Thank you." Grace smiled. "Is this what happens when I leave you alone for five minutes? I might have to do it more often."

His grin only deepened at the praise. "You're welcome."

Date, she thought, and Adams returned to her mind, as well as the weight of the golden cylinder in her pocket.

"I saw Adams."

His smile vanished. "I leave *you* alone for five minutes…What did he want?"

Grace pulled the cylinder from her pocket, opening it to reveal the egg inside. She placed both in Heron's outstretched hands.

"Did you steal this from his desk or is this the one you took from Peters? I thought you'd returned that to evidence."

"I did. This is what Adams gave me. It's my invitation to join Egg Island."

He searched her face, looking between the gold cylinder and her gaze. Finally he muttered, "Shit."

"That isn't language befitting an assistant inspector," Grace said, sipping her koffee. "But yes. *Shit.*"

Heron turned it in the light through the windows. His frown only deepened. "I don't like it."

The auto's opacity was very low, so the walls were nearly transparent, the road and surrounding motorway whizzing past them.

She watched the egg roll in his palm. "Why not? It's very beautiful."

"I don't like the implications. Why are they giving you this now? Is it because you exposed Viscosity?"

"I wondered that too." The timing was interesting. It'd been four months since she'd thwarted the precinct attack. Almost six weeks since confronting Viscosity's CEO, Getty Peters, for fraud. "Perhaps they simply want to honor me for my recent work."

They met each other's eyes, neither believing any of it.

He handed the egg over. "What are you going to do?"

"I want to say yes," she said, her voice low, as if someone might hear her. "It could help with our case."

He was watching her face very closely. "That would be very dangerous. You're far too honest to be a double agent."

Her heart sped up at the idea. Keeping her seat grew difficult, but she didn't want to fidget in front of Heron. "Lix was framed, and whoever really murdered Davion and Kaiden had power and influence. Otherwise, it wouldn't have been tied up quite so nicely. I might be able to figure out who if I see who the members are, gauge who has the power and connections to pull off such an attack."

He relaxed against his seat. "It's not a bad idea. All of the board members and even the acting director of Trinity Trust are members of Egg Island."

Grace wasn't unsurprised to learn this. It was a large and powerful banking institution. More importantly, Trinity Trust was the company her husband had stolen money from to fund the illegal visas he'd forged, not to mention the travel expenses of the families he'd relocated.

In her mind, anyone connected to the company might be responsible for his death. And her son's.

Her son. She kept doing that, laying claim to Kaiden

as if Davion had forfeited his right to him the moment his actions got him killed. It wasn't good to let anger and resentment settle in a heart, but it wasn't easy to stop either.

"How do you know they're members? It's a secret society. Emphasis on the word *secret*."

Heron cocked his head, looking more like a bird than ever. "When has something as pathetic as secrecy stopped me?"

"This is an opportunity," she insisted, and here she did lean toward him, unable to contain her excitement at finding out the truth. "If not to find Davion and Kaiden's killer, at least to find out if others are abusing the system like Peters was."

He regarded her a long while, something serious passing over his face. He was quick to cover it with a smile. "Watch out, everyone. Commander Grace Buteo is coming for your coffers. Lock up your riches while you can!"

Grace found this amusing, since Heron was the richest person she'd ever met. Yet he seemed equally interested in challenging those in power.

He laced his fingers over his knee. "You're allowed a plus one for this engagement, I assume. I look *wonderful* in a tux."

"Adams already asked me."

Heron's jaw twitched. "I don't like him. Have I said?"

Grace smiled. Twice in a day.

"I've suspected so from the first time you stole his chair."

"He doesn't deserve such a nice chair."

"Deserve it or not, I'll accept his offer. We can't rule out the possibility that he understands the inner workings of Egg Island. If I can ask the right questions, I can set us on the right track."

His smile tightened. "You're terrifying me. But I appreciate your use of 'us'."

"Davion was your friend too," she said. "I know you want to find the person responsible as much as I do."

"I do." Heron glanced out the window, the humor gone.

"Then I'll go Friday and see what we can learn."

AT THE EASTSIDE MEDICAL CLINIC, Grace stood on the square at the building's entrance and let it scan her body.

"Welcome, Commander Grace Buteo," the AI said. "We've been expecting you. Please visit the ninth-floor records room, where your party awaits."

Grace waited inside the door for Heron to pass the bio-seal.

"Good morning, Inspector Heron Jane. We're happy to see you."

"Do you hear that?" Heron said. "She called me *Inspector*."

Grace humored him with a tight smile as she downloaded the building's map and made her way past the waiting rooms and offices to the elevators. On the ninth floor, she found four inspectors reviewing the clinic's internal system for malware and pilfering encryption.

Everyone straightened a bit when Grace stepped into the small office containing the main terminal.

"Good morning, Commander. Inspector," They chorused at their arrival.

Immediately, they folded Grace and Heron into the group lenscape, an excited review of stored data and the clinic's inner movements.

The team was trying to solve the mystery of stolen medical data. Someone was pretending to be several of the clinic's patients and doctors. Using various accounts, over a hundred prescriptions had been filled and sold. By hacking the billing AI, nearly a thousand fake bills were sent to patients to be paid. However, when the patients paid the money, it didn't go to the clinic, diverting instead to an invisible revolving account.

"How's it going?" Grace asked.

"We're stumped, sir," a young woman said. It was a junior inspector, Celebrity Smith. "We've looked over the hard components thoroughly, but we can't find any inter-ference boosters or foreign hardware."

<<I love it when they call you *sir*,>> Heron pinged. <<So authoritarian.>>

Grace ignored this and said aloud, "The forger could be accessing the data remotely."

"We considered that," Smith replied. "But it seems impossible that someone could be that familiar with the building's configuration, given that it is bio-sealed and the layout is private."

Grace frowned, stepping closer to the young man nearest her, Assistant Inspector Elijah Stone. "What do you mean?"

"The data bot we found in the system is an implosive 890DRT," he explained, his eyes lit blue with the lenscape's reflective light. "It had to be directly introduced into this system."

"We think it was done using this port," Smith added, pointing at a small slot in the control computer's northern wall panel.

"It's very intelligent, actually," Stone said, his irritation at Smith's interruption clear. "If the records had been accessed remotely, it would be easier for us to follow the trail to its source. In cyberspace, there are many digital trails to follow, through dummy accounts, etc. Something will eventually lead to a source. But because it was inserted manually, all the data trails are evaporating once the extractions are made. It's like they can't exist outside the internal frame."

Grace considered this, sipping her bullet and a half.

"That means we have two options for tracking," she said. "We can dye the whole system, encode every piece of data so that the next time the extraction is made, it will essentially stain the extractor's code and make them bioluminescent to our spyders."

<<Am I supposed to know what any of this means?>> Heron pinged, his face unreadable beside her.

<<Smile and look pretty,>> Grace replied.

<<This I can do.>> Heron unbuttoned his suit jacket and slipped a hand into his pocket.

Three of the junior inspectors flicked their eyes in his direction. Cheeks spiked with color.

Grace ignored this. "We can also investigate all persons with physical access to this room. It's possible that someone —patient or doctor—added the malware to the system. I would look closely at new patients who came for only one or two appointments in the last year. It's possible they targeted the clinic intentionally."

"Yes, sir."

"Any glitches in the mainframe, updates, computer outages, anything at all that would make this system vulnerable, check it out. If someone was called in to fix it or if it was fixed in-house. Complete our records."

"Yes, sir."

"All of this will be a monumental demand on your time," she acknowledged. "I'll have Officer Duchovny increase your team's support staff. Check with him by the end of the day. If you have concerns about what we set up for you, speak up."

"Yes, sir."

<<Careful, Commander. Celebrity likes your alpha voice,>> Heron teased.

Without meaning to, Grace cut her eyes to the junior investigator.

Immediately, Celebrity glanced away, but not before Grace saw the inspector bite her lip. Arousal or nervousness? It didn't matter.

<<Speculative and unprofessional,>> she warned Heron. Aloud, she added, "Good work, everyone. As you were. Ping me if something breaks."

The auto was already rolling up to the curb outside of the Eastside Medical Clinic when they stepped out into the sunlight.

The familiar *chirp, chirp, chirp* of an Informed Citizen bulletin sounded in Grace's ear as she slipped onto the dark seat.

On the pavement outside her window, people in all directions froze, standing suspended in place waiting for the bulletin to play.

As the seatbelt affixed itself to Grace's torso, her lenscape was overrun.

Dearest Citizens, please note that the UV rating for Zone 2 has risen from Orange-Elevated to Red-Risk. Please seek protection immediately. If you are seen without protection in any public area, you will be ticketed. Remember: Information is Liberation.

The bulletin dropped away, leaving Grace and Heron alone in the auto.

"I'm surprised you didn't tell me first," she admitted. Her gaze slid to the booster ring on his finger.

He shrugged. "We were getting in the auto. I planned to tell you before we got out at CyTown. Do you have a sunbrella?"

"I do." She said this absently, her lenscape already hard

at work creating an information cache and instruction packet for Officer Lore Duchovny, outlining the support that the Eastside team would need to investigate the identity theft.

"How long until we arrive at the Towers?" Grace felt a tinge of longing for the auto's bleating information.

"Six minutes. I can turn it back on if you want," Heron said.

"No," she said, surprised he'd seemed to read her mind. "I prefer the silence."

"Let me ruin it by asking you a question." He affected the wide-legged posture of a rogue.

"Sure," she said, sending her follow-up packet off to Lore.

"What are you doing for dinner tonight?"

She blinked at him.

"That meal that people have at the end of the day." When she didn't speak, he added, "You are going to eat?"

"I'll have whatever the ChefMate makes. It's set to random."

"If you're looking for something less adventurous, you could come over to my place and have dinner with me."

She hesitated. "I don't want to be a third wheel."

"You won't be," he said, picking at his nails. "Arjun is working tonight, and I don't like to eat alone. I could go to a bar and find someone to eat with, but I'd rather have dinner with you."

She searched his face, waiting for the smile or joke, given that was how he often punctuated heartfelt statements.

"If you don't," he went on, "I'll probably ask your mother. Then we both might end up at your place and—"

"I'll come over."

Heron straightened in his seat. "Excellent. It'll be nice. You haven't been to my place yet."

"I came over when I thought you were being murdered."

"Oh, that doesn't count. It was theatrics."

Her tone darkened. She still resented him for being tricked. "I remember."

"This time will be pleasant," he said. "I promise."

CyTown Towers slid into view, gold in the hazy light. High noon glinted off the solar-paneled surface as green tendrils waved from the buildings' roofs.

"And this way, I can say I dated you before Adams did."

Grace started. "I'm not dating Adams. Or you."

"No." The door opened, and Heron slipped out of his seatbelt. "*Not yet.*"

FOUR

<<WHY are we coming directly here again?>> Heron asked as they stepped into the open lobby of the cavernous building. Like the precinct's main hall, the ceilings were easily fifty or sixty feet high, giving the room a submerged feeling.

<<The easiest way to find out whether or not Tristan was forced into CyTown citizenship is to ask him, don't you think?>>

Heron's eyebrows rose. <<And they'll let us walk in here and ask?>>

<<They'll let me,>> she said. *Or they should.*

As Grace collapsed her sunbrella and slipped it back into her pocket, a young AI receptionist looked up at their approach. She stood from her desk and extended her hand toward them. Grace inhaled and accepted it, giving it a firm shake. It was cool to the touch, her body full of circuitry and wires rather than pumping blood.

So is yours, she reminded herself before her prejudice got the best of her. The auto blast that had taken Davion's and Kaiden's lives had also taken her arm. They'd replaced it and integrated the sensory detail with her lenscape so that it was impossible for her to tell it was a fake.

"Good morning, Commander Buteo," the AI chirped, only the slightest pause detected before Grace's name as it no doubt read her public profile. Then she turned to Heron. "Good morning, Commander Adams."

Grace scoffed, turning toward him.

He flashed his devilish smile. <<Nice trick, isn't it?>>

"Don't," she said aloud. <<Adams could martial you for impersonation.>>

Heron rolled his eyes. To the AI, he said, "I'm sorry, I think you're mistaken. Can you read my profile again?"

The AI met his gaze again and said, "I'm very sorry to have mistaken you for someone else, Inspector Heron Jane. It's wonderful to have you both here at CyTown Towers today. How can I help you?"

"I want to interview one of your residents," Grace said, her heart still skipping. "Tristan Range."

The AI seemed to consider this.

"I'm sorry, Commander. I cannot process this request. I've called for a specialist to assist you. Can you wait in the reception area, please?"

"Sure."

They found sofas in front of the glass windows offering views of the street beyond. Because the Towers were located in South Pendam, there wasn't much foot traffic. Apart from the Towers themselves and the waste lots of North Pendam, very little was located in this section of the zone.

Perhaps that added to the impression that CyTown was its own little world.

<<What do you want tonight? Are you in the mood for anything specific?>>

Grace searched his face for the double entendre but saw nothing. "Noodles."

He tilted his head "Noodles? Care to be any more specific? I have at least fifty noodle recipes."

A man in shiny black shoes and a tight white shirt marched across the lobby toward them.

"Surprise me," she said, rising.

The man tugged at the bottom of his shirt before offering Grace his hand. "Commander Buteo. I'm Abe Rise. It's lovely to meet you. What brings you to CyTown?"

Grace's lenscape registered the nervousness in his facial features.

It doesn't mean he's a criminal, she reminded herself. Plenty of people became nervous in the presence of law enforcement.

"We need to interview one of your residents."

"Please follow me." Pushing his glasses up on his face, he led them toward the elevators. "Is this your first time visiting the Towers?"

"Yes," Grace answered truthfully.

"Oh, you're in for a treat. I remember my first visit," he said wistfully, the pleasure evident on his face. "It's hard to beat the first time."

Heron's grin deepened, and Grace shot him a warning look. <<No jokes.>>

<<You know me too well,>> he lamented.

Abe Rise continued, unaware of the exchange. "It's hard to believe that there are over two million residents in CyTown. The entire population of Zone 2 is about twenty million. That means that nearly one in ten residents is a CyTown resident. Remarkable, don't you think?"

Grace ignored the implication that he thought her incapable of math and said, "Yes, it is."

"It's absolutely essential," he continued in his pedantic tone. "Given the ecological cost of living, virtual residence is far more sustainable. We project that we can accommodate nearly two hundred million CyTown residents at the same ecological cost of Zone 2's current population. Wouldn't it be an interesting world if the population ratio were reversed? Imagine if twenty million residents lived in CyTown and only two million in real-time."

When he saw Grace's face, Rise's expression faltered.

"It probably won't happen in our lifetime," he added nervously. "But it's an exciting possibility in case our planet's recovery options fail."

Heron pinged, <<You're giving him the murder glare.>>

Grace shifted her gaze toward the elevator doors and saw Rise visibly relax in her periphery.

"Would you like a short tour en route to my office?" Rise asked.

"Sure," Grace said, adding a lilt to her voice. She hoped to ease him. People were more generous with information when at ease.

"This building is mostly administration. It isn't as easy to coordinate the entire workings of a city, as you might imagine."

He seemed to realize who he was speaking to and grimaced.

"My apologies. I'm preaching to the choir here. You know all about running a city, don't you? What I meant is that this building is mostly offices, except for the upper fifteen floors, where we have the pods, simulation chambers, and visitors' chairs. You'll see them if we take a detour through level sixty-six."

Grace consulted her agenda. "We have forty-five minutes."

Rise lit up at that. "Excellent! It's plenty of time. It will be a short fifteen-minute detour at most."

<<Lies,>> Heron pinged. <<These tech guys get excited and lose entire days chatting up their gadgets.>>

Funny that. Heron had talked at her for almost an hour about the workings of his booster ring once. Grace had thought her nose was going to bleed. <<I'll rely on you to keep us on schedule then. We can't be late for our appointment with Ezra.>>

<<Who?>>

<<The constable.>>

The elevator doors opened, and they followed Rise into a long hallway. As they passed, the floor lit beneath their feet and the lights on the wall activated. Halfway down, a long white cylinder appeared on the right, and Rise ran a loving hand over it.

"This is our newest pod, the LiveRite 9000," he said with obvious awe.

His hand trailed up the glowing white surface until something activated at his touch. Then the frame of a window lit up and swung upward.

"State of the art," Rise said, his tone reverent. "It suspends the body in such a way that there's absolutely *zero* physical echo. Phenomenal."

"Physical echo?" Grace asked.

"Feedback from the body. The sensory detail sent from your body to your brain is what provides a sense of spatial orientation. In earlier models, it wasn't possible to interrupt this brain–body connection. People would be in CyTown but would feel what was happening to their body here. Bodies atrophy when unmoving. Aches develop. So, it's essential to stimulate them. We use gentle electrical currents through the pod's sensors to do this. Now that we've eliminated the echo, it no longer interrupts total immersion in the simulation."

"Really?" Heron asked. "They feel nothing at all?"

"A few beta testers reported a slight tingling in their limbs, as if their leg had fallen asleep, for example, but the sensation passes quickly and it doesn't disrupt the experience."

"Do all of your residents live in these?" Heron touched the edge of the pod. Its colors changed on contact.

"No," Rise said apologetically. "We have a range of models in the Towers, given the fact that some people have been residents longer than others. Our earliest model is the LiveRite 2000. It feels analog in comparison to this."

The technician's eyes cut nervously to Grace.

He added, quickly, "But we have an extensive plan in development for moving all residents to the updated pods without interrupting their residency."

"It looks cozy," Heron said. "May I?"

"Please." Rise looked thrilled, stepping back so that Heron could access the door.

<<Heron, what are you up to?>> Grace pinged.

It was Grace's experience—even in the short time they'd been together—that Heron was *always* up to something. This was especially true in moments like this, when he expressed sudden, unexplainable excitement.

He didn't answer her.

"Let me close the lid, and you can have the full experience," Rise said.

He closed the lid on Heron, and the lit window went dark.

A heartbeat passed. Two, three, four.

Panic began to rise in Grace. Rise was smiling, but it felt wrong.

"We need to get moving," she said, tapping the closed pod.

"All right." Rise pressed on the glass, and the window lit again, the hatch opening.

Heron sat up, smiling. "Very cozy in there. I felt like I was floating on air."

"It's amazing, isn't it?" Rise was obviously pleased with himself as he helped Heron from the pod. "We're very proud of the progress we've made in simulation living. In my opinion, it's the future. It could improve the living conditions of millions, and eliminate the overuse of resources."

The corridor ended in two closed rooms.

"This is one of our simulation rooms," Rise said, opening the door. "Here, potential residents can design their homes and their future CyTown lives."

Grace looked at the metallic walls and floor and saw nothing. But when Rise's eyes lit blue with the activation of his lenscape, the room came to life.

"Let's say you want to live in a mansion with a pool, servants, and the perfect spouse. Perhaps with a pack of dogs," Rise said with a little laugh. "You can design that life here."

Grace watched as the light in the room shifted around her.

The largest wall in front of her began to fill with shapes. Objects were dragged and dropped from the adjacent corners until an image began to form.

The outline of a grand house, a Spanish villa with a large courtyard and veranda, a fountain spewing water out front. From the right, a small white terrier trotted across the stones.

Then the front door opened and a beautiful woman stepped out. She smiled brightly upon seeing them, her lips painted dark red and her teeth white. Her bare feet made no sound on the stone as she moved toward them, shielding her eyes from the light with a hand.

"What are you doing out here?" she asked, her voice adjusting as she spoke until arriving at a sweet, inviting lilt. Her hyper-femininity landed somewhere between coquettish and childish. "Come inside and eat lunch with me."

<<He's really misread our interests, hasn't he?>> Heron pinged.

"This doesn't provide the full immersion experience," Rise said. "But people spend hundreds of hours in these rooms, crafting their dream lives before beginning their residence."

"I imagine it takes time to craft the perfect lover, job, house—" Heron said.

"And body," Rise added. "They design it all."

Grace frowned at the beautiful blonde beckoning her to lunch. "Do they know they're in a simulation? Do they remember once they go in?"

"Of course," Rise said. "Assuming they want to know. Many build such a life because they want to forget the one they've left behind. Or some want to reconstruct a life lost. We have many who duplicate the life they had before a spouse died, for example."

Grace's heart kicked. "But it wouldn't be real."

"It is to them." Rise shrugged, his displeasure obvious. "If you were fully immersed, you'd understand. There is no way to tell reality from fantasy once inside."

Heron was watching her with a strange expression on his face. "What about families who want to move in together?"

"It's not yet possible, I'm afraid. One of our last real

impediments. CyTown is a fully customized, individual experience. It isn't like InnerLife or another shared reality. It's also hampered by the Geneva Law of 2568 stating that it is inhuman to put children into VR space while underage."

His derision for this view was clear in his tight face and tone.

"Apparently, the right to a 'natural' childhood is a human right. What is a 'natural' childhood anyway, with all the VR and lenscape technology we have now?"

When neither Grace nor Heron echoed his humor, his laughter fell away.

"How many people sign up for this each year?" Grace asked.

"Around thirty thousand. Over seventy percent of CyTown residents are outer-zone immigrants. About fifteen percent from Zones 1 to 14."

Heron wrote, <<I imagine living an idyllic life, even if it is virtual, is preferable to starving to death in the outer zones.>>

"How many are actually Zone 2 transfers?" she pressed.

"It's less common," Rise conceded. "But it happens. I'd say less than five percent."

"We only have about twenty minutes left, Mr. Rise."

"Right!" Rise killed the simulation and turned on the lights. "I love this stuff. I could talk your ears off all day."

Grace breathed easier once they stepped from the dark simulation room into a brightly lit antechamber.

Beyond the window, she saw only the large, vacant waste lots of North Pendam. Piles of broken pots and unusable circuitry sat in their neatly marked squares, spreading out for miles as a few ant-like citizens roamed the remains, looking for items they might need. Free was quite the bargain, after all.

In the distance, Grace watched storm clouds dance on the horizon. The black-gray swellings pulsed and thrummed with lightning as large transformers darted in and out of the clouds, trying to capture and redirect all that energy into the grid.

"This way," Abe said, pointing down the hall. "I have an entry chair in my office. You can use it for your interview."

The entry chair looked like a white recliner with a headset attached to its top.

"How will this work?" Grace asked, eyeing the chair suspiciously.

"You'll sit in this recliner, and I'll attach the device to your head. It will temporarily integrate with your lenscape to help fill in the details. It won't be full immersion, but it will help flesh out the details of CyTown enough to prove navigable. You should be able to see each other clearly. I need the name of your interviewee again."

"Tristan Range."

He typed the name into the system. Paused. Then a look passed over his face. His expression tightened.

"Something wrong?"

"I'm sorry to say, you can't interview that resident."

Grace's stomach dropped. "Why not?"

"He's listed as declining."

"Which means?"

<<Accept scapeshare from aberise12?>>

Grace accepted and the file appeared in her vision. A picture of Range's face appeared on the left side of her lenscape, showing his narrow nose and gaunt cheeks resting beneath sharp blue eyes. On the right, superficial details—his name, age, address—but also a status report: declining. Class 3."

"A citizen will be listed as declining if their mind is in a fragile state for any reason. This can be trauma-induced or a medical symptom."

"Does it say which Range suffers from?"

Rise shook his head. "That information would be classified. You will need authorization from the constable to access it. Also, permission from his physician if the cause is medical or psychological."

Grace closed the file, copying it to her embedded folder, and met Rise's gaze again. "What does Class 3 mean exactly?"

He seemed reluctant to explain. "It's an evaluation system. One being the least severe. Three as most compromised. Class-3 residents are usually unaware that they're operating in VR space to begin with. Introducing the idea that they are living in a virtual reality often causes deep and lasting psychological distress, not to mention physical complications for the body as it begins to reject integration with our systems. We usually only integrate these residents if they have no desire to ever return to real-time."

When Grace didn't interrupt, Abe licked his lips.

"It says here that he was admitted by a physician. If that is true, it's likely Mr. Range agreed to this arrangement, expressly requesting it as part of his end-of-life plan."

"His end-of-life plan," Grace repeated. "He's only thirty-eight."

Rise gave another shrug. He seemed fond of shrugging. "You would have to speak to his physician for those details and possibly obtain authorization from the constable. I'm very sorry, Commander."

. . .

On the bright sidewalk outside, Grace took a deep breath.

"Feeling claustrophobic again?" Heron stood uncharacteristically somber beside her. Maybe he didn't like CyTown Towers any more than she did.

"A bit," she admitted. She let her eyes trace the long, wide boulevards, the expanse of the city stretching out ahead of her and the bright sky above, until something in her chest relaxed.

"It seems unlikely that a thirty-eight-year-old man would have cognitive decline so severe that his physician admitted him without even informing his family."

"Sounds underhanded to me," Heron agreed with a sharp nod. "And *few* things sound underhanded to me."

"Yes." Grace frowned at him. "You need to be more careful when we're in public. Hopefully, the system won't register that bio change. What did you do, hack Adams's profile?"

Heron shrugged, a perfect mimicry of Rise. "I'm experimenting with a new piece of software I'm designing."

"We have bio-seals to keep people and buildings safe. If you're making something that will hack bio-seals—"

"Relax." Heron sighed. "This is for my own personal use. It's not like I'm going to sell it to the highest bidder. I do have *some* morals. Besides, you don't know what we'll need in the fight against their murderers. It may require cleverness I've never used before."

Their murderers.

Grace regarded him. Heron liked to play the part of dashing rogue, certainly. He enjoyed bending rules to see how far they would bend until they broke. He often disregarded anything he felt was arbitrary.

But Grace would never say he was without morals.

"You'll need to pull out your sunbrella if we're to keep standing here like this," he said.

She pulled the pen-like stub of her sunbrella from her pocket and began extending it. "He's right, though. We'll need authorization from the constable to get those records. Good thing she's next on my list."

FIVE

CONSTABLE EZRA DANE was pacing their office when Grace and Heron arrived. Grace did a quick review of the constable's gender profile.

Today it was registered as *they*. Grace overwrote the present demifluid pronoun *jer* in her log and closed the door behind Heron.

The constable held up one finger, then pointed at the chairs opposite the bare desk. They sat and waited.

It was nearly five minutes before they turned their lit blue eyes on Grace. "Thank you for waiting. It was the Zone 8 mayor. I thought I was going to have to hang up on him."

Their gaze slid off Grace and landed on Heron.

"This is your new assistant?" they asked, humor in their face. "A pleasure."

Heron rose from his seat, extending his hand for a profile share. The constable accepted it, the backs of their hands brushing.

Grace adjusted herself in the seat. "I appreciate you taking the time to meet with us."

"It's good to see you." They clicked their tongue. "Don't make that face, I mean it. Scars and all. Now your outside matches your insides. Tough. Formidable."

Grace forced a gracious smile. "Thank you, Ezra. It's good to see you too."

And it was. They were short, gruff, and unpolished, but Grace loved these qualities. Often, Grace's position felt like a game, a show of decorum and diplomacy that she didn't enjoy. Her heart lay with the police work, with cases and investigation. She felt she had a kindred spirit in Ezra for this very reason.

Ezra rarely cared for the showmanship of politicking. They wanted to get to the bottom of things. To act. To do what needed to be done to move the issues forward.

"What do you have for me?" Ezra ran a hand up the back of their head. "Wait, one second."

Ezra's lenscape clicked on, and the walls lit blue. A gridlock proofing field extended to each corner, sealing the room top to bottom, side to side, from any recording devices or internal communication.

"There. Some privacy," Ezra said. "*Now*, what do you have for me?"

"We've several things. We're at an impasse with the Zone 3 and 4 mayors over the immigration numbers. They've reached a consensus on the quarter-two targets. However, our mayor wants more time to process our current census."

Ezra crossed their arms and leaned against their desk. "Yes, well that's your fault, isn't it?"

"Excuse me?"

Ezra's tone was brisk, but they were smiling. "If you hadn't found thousands of displaced citizens squatting under the city, we'd have a better handle on our numbers, wouldn't we?"

Grace couldn't help but smile. "Yes, I suppose that was my fault."

Ezra nodded. "Well done, by the way. I'd suspected for years there was corporate corruption, greedy bastards extorting our visa policy."

"Really?" Grace couldn't hide her surprise.

"Oh yes," Ezra said with a haughty laugh. "They think they're being sneaky. That all their little requests were innocuous and unnoticeable, but I'm not an idiot. Everything crosses my desk, and I do mean *everything*. Do they think I can't put together the connections or see the patterns? Then again, I'm a *mere* civil servant. Easily disregarded, overlooked."

Grace wasn't sure how to respond to this.

She hadn't considered herself a fool, let alone blind to what was going on around her, but she'd been blindsided by the Viscosity case. By the knowledge that Davion was having to secretly emigrate children and their parents from the dangerous outer zones while others lived comfortably away from all such suffering. That someone would have the audacity to murder her husband for such a thing—without proper trial or justice. That yet another innocent man had taken the fall and the bomber was yet to be apprehended.

All of this exposed the deep well of Grace's naïveté. And if she was being honest with herself, it stung like hell.

Ezra must've seen something on her face. "But it's hard for you, isn't it? To see us this way? First your family, and then Viscosity. This zone isn't how you imagined it."

Grace would've found this line of inquiry condescending, or at least annoying, if it had been anyone else. But the constable was at least twenty years older than Grace and had been doing their job for far longer. That knowledge was to be respected.

Grace's throat clicked. "No, it hasn't been easy."

The constable nodded, solemn. "You're adjusting in stride. Someone with half your grit would've fallen apart by now."

Grace considered her words carefully. "I'm doing my best."

What else could she say? That sometimes, a memory of her son would rise up so suddenly that her heart would clench, her throat would close, and tears would stream down her face? That at night, she replayed memories of her husband lying down beside her just so she could fall asleep?

That everything reminded her of them. *Everything*.

And there seemed no remedy for any of that except to stay busy, to keep pushing forward.

"Better than best, I'd say," the constable said. "As to your immigration concerns, I'll increase funds for our own census processing so that we can get up to speed more quickly. Put more hands on deck. I'll also have Alicia work up our new immigration numbers and targets. We can jump right into the applications once we're up and running. What else do you have for me?"

Grace ran down the short list of open investigations needing warrant approvals and the details that required examining. One of Ezra's prime duties was to decide if a police action overstepped the rights of the zone's citizens.

Ezra approved most of the requests instantly. For those with need for clarification, they asked a few follow-up questions, requiring addendums and compromises before accepting them.

Through all of this, Heron watched, curious, silent.

"Is that it?" Ezra asked, stretching. "If so, I'll take down the sound barrier. It makes my implant buzz."

Grace hesitated. "Actually, I've one more. Something that isn't officially an investigation."

Ezra must've heard something in Grace's tone. They arched a brow. "I'm curious. Go on."

"It's in its early stages of investigation but it carries quite a few similarities to the Viscosity case."

The second eyebrow rose to join the first. "I'll leave the barrier up then."

Grace outlined Lenorie Range's visit to the precinct, her claim that her brother had been forced into CyTown residency against his will. The suspiciousness of the notion that a thirty-eight-year-old man has degenerative mind issues and can't be interviewed.

"I want permission to inspect his residence for forced entry or theft. I'd also like access to his medical records to see if there is any history of trauma or a medical condition that could cause brain degeneration. Records regarding his end-of-life wishes would be helpful, too. There's only one catch."

Ezra's lips twitched. "Oh, only one?"

"I don't want anyone to know I've requested this information," Grace went on. It was possible that Rise might be suspicious of her visit, but Rise was only a technician. "If anyone notices that I'm digging around, they might destroy evidence or produce a convenient alibi. I only need some time to look around. Unimpeded. That's it."

Ezra leaned back in their chair, casting a glance at the ceiling.

Grace braced herself for rejection.

"Listen to me." The constable pushed off the desk and came to sit in the empty chair beside her. "I want to tell you something. Not as a constable to a commander. But as a friend."

Grace's skin rippled, the hairs on her arms rising. "I'm listening."

"I don't want to assume, but would you say that the

one thing you were most afraid of losing was your child? Or your husband?"

"Yes." Grace said this without hesitation.

"Right." Ezra nodded as if this was the answer they were waiting for. "When people lose the one thing they're afraid of losing, it can…" They searched for a word. "It can unmoor them. Something like that makes a person reckless. They stop being careful."

"I'm being careful," Grace said, her spine straight.

"You are." Ezra's feet hit the floor. "But people have been killed for less."

GRACE WAS ADJUSTING the sunbrella against her shoulder when her calorie watch beeped.

"We need to eat," Heron said. "You have this horrible habit of working through lunch, but it gives me headaches and makes me grumpy. We're quite close to Sindu Serves. Don't you love that place?"

"I do. Do you?"

"I love Indian." He came up onto the balls of his feet. "Who doesn't love a nice warm, garlicky naan?"

Grace's lenscape mapped the two-block walk toward the restaurant. As they walked, she reviewed the classified warrants that Ezra had issued her before they left their office. The warrants would allow Grace to prove that she was lawfully entering Tristan's apartment and accessing his medical records, should someone try to say otherwise.

They arrived at the restaurant to find Sindu Serves was bright, with several empty tables along one wall. Grace checked the time and saw they were about an hour early for the lunch rush.

"Commander!" a man chirped. He came around the

counter with his black eyes alight. "I am so happy to see you."

The younger Vihani was one of two owners for Sindu Serves. He was taking it over from his uncle, who was close to ninety years old. His smile was quick and his tone light. "We were very worried that we wouldn't see you again."

Grace forced a gracious grin. "It's nice to be back."

Heron was giving Vihani a hungry look.

"This is Inspector Heron Jane," Grace said, and Heron was quick to extend his hand toward the other man.

"So nice to meet you," Heron said, in full flirtatious mode. He winked.

<<Don't you think one boyfriend is enough,>> Grace pinged.

<<You need to have the semblance of a dating life before you can comment on the adequate number of boyfriends,>> Heron pinged back, never faltering in his small talk with Vihani.

Helped along by Vihani's friendly, enthusiastic attention, they were ushered to their seats, where they ordered chana masala and butter chicken, sag aloo, biryani, and two portions of garlic naan, all of it to be shared family style between them.

"I hope you intend to eat most of this," Grace said as Vihani hurried away with their order. "I won't be able to eat even half of that."

Heron lifted his chai to his lips. "I couldn't say no to him. He was adorable and helpful. Usually at restaurants it's only the table that talks to you. I can't remember the last time I was actually served by a real-life human."

Grace wanted to point out that usually the table *was* the only one who spoke to her when she came here, but given the fact that this was her first visit since the accident, she supposed Vihani wanted to add a more personal touch.

"I've been researching the brother." Heron stretched one arm along the back of the booth. "The sister wasn't lying about his views on cyber living."

"Show me."

<<Accept scapeshare with heronjane1?>>

Grace was bombarded by a flood of documents. Bold titles stood out on each page as she sifted the work.

…these algorithms are a centuries-old method to train humans like dogs, transforming them into mindless consumers who salivate on command, while the power-hungry vampires of our "elite" can continue to prey on this gluttonous cycle.

By privatizing our resources and inalienable rights, they increase their wealth exponentially, convincing the masses to want what they don't have, buy what they don't need, and pay heavily for what should be free to everyone. Food, water, air, our own minds…

She scanned each one, taking in the highlights.

…the use of filters and lenscapes has already altered present reality to such an extent that humans are detached from their normalcy. We no longer see the world for what it is, but rather as how we wish it were. If we were proactive dreamers pursing pure potentiality, this wouldn't be a problem. We could indeed build the perfect world.

Have we not suffered from this disconnection enough? Are we really so blind and ignorant of the damage we cause when we try to live separate from rather than integrated with the natural world? Isn't it this disconnection that caused us to first disrupt the harmony of our ecosystems, the catalyst for our decline? Why do we run away from the one chance we have at salvation?

"It seems very unlikely that a person with these views would become a CyTown resident, doesn't it?" she asked Heron.

"It does," he replied. "What do you think? Maybe he's not even in CyTown? Maybe they killed him and threw his body on the Midnight Train and the CyTown residency story is a cover-up."

Grace reviewed Tristan's public profile again. He'd been working as an adjunct history professor. He also sometimes taught night classes in introductory ethics at the local community center. He wasn't a wealthy or influential person and seemed to have no real-world ties other than his sister.

"These publications are mostly in small presses with limited readerships." Grace rubbed her chin. "It seems unlikely that someone with power would even read them, let alone be upset enough by them that they would come to his home at night, kidnap him, and force him into CyTown residency. It doesn't make sense. It's possible we're making the wrong connection."

Heron twirled his fork between his fingers, casting glances at the closed kitchen door. "So why target him?"

Grace's pulse jumped in her throat. "You don't think that someone is capturing people at random, do you? Someone who wants to increase CyTown's population might be scouting for Zone 2 residents with little to no connections, perhaps no interzone family?"

"Tristan has the sister."

"And views," Grace admitted. "But that might've been a mistake. Maybe they've already gotten all the low-hanging fruit and have moved up a tier to those with only a few connections."

Heron cocked his head. "A decent theory. How can we look into it? The zone has over twenty million residents. You've already proven by finding the erased workers Viscosity dispatched that thousands of people can disappear almost overnight."

Grace clasped the back of her neck and massaged the sore muscles there. "We would need to look at all the names of CyTown residents, maybe check their records to see when they changed residencies."

He shook his head. "Data like that can be forged. We can't be sure how long they've been snatching people—"

"*If* they're snatching people," Grace said. She didn't want her theory to be made fact prematurely. The truth mattered to her more than not being right.

Heron bit his lip. "Truth is, we don't have a good system to figure out who has been moved from Zone 2 to CyTown, especially if there is no one like the sister to vouch for them. Our first goal will have to be how to identify those taken. What criteria might suggest that they've been forced in?"

"Cognitive decline," Grace said. "Tristan was listed as having cognitive decline. If that's untrue, and simply keeps anyone from interviewing or visiting the resident, maybe there are others. Can you get me a list of every CyTown resident who is listed as 'declining'? You'll have to scan their records, which we don't have a permit for, but I can circle back and get one from Ezra if the evidence starts to add up."

A slow, mischievous smile spread across Heron's face. "I knew it."

She sat back. "What?"

"I knew there would come a day when you would deliberately ask me to do something illegal." He pretended to wipe joyful tears from the corners of his eyes. "I didn't know it'd be so soon."

She scowled at him.

"Right. I will have you that list as soon as possible. But look. Cake."

His eyes were fixed on some point over her left shoulder. Grace turned in the booth to see Vihani leading a caravan. Vihani, his two younger brothers, his twin, his mother and father, his three uncles and four aunts, and a smattering of other faces that Grace didn't quite recognize. But they were a set, all right. All thick black hair and glistening black eyes. Their smiles were bright as they came to stop at Grace's table, most of the family remaining about a foot back, unfurling a long sign with the words *Thank you, Commander Grace!*

Vihani put the cake on the table in front of her as the cousins piled their dishes of food on the table, their little silver bowls spinning in place.

One of the little girls threw confetti into the air above Grace's head, and it rained down on her hair and shoulders.

"Ah, not in the food!" her mother shouted.

Grace tried to maintain a smile despite her mounting confusion. "What's happening?"

"We were there that night," Vihani explained. "Mia and Marli were in the winter parade for their school."

The winter parade.

It had been a blur of red and green streamers that night as the light danced around them. Davion's arm had been heavy across her shoulder. She'd run her hand through Kaiden's soft curls as he leaned against her leg.

Vendors sold roasted nuts soaked in oil and cinnamon, which they ate with slick fingers. The dancers had twirled by, the marching band had pranced, and the music lingered long after the holographic circus had arrived. Kaiden had lit up at the sight of the sparkling elephants coming up the wide boulevard.

She'd been deliriously happy that night, more than contented, sandwiched between her loves.

Until she'd turned toward the precinct and found the red X tapping out its warning. And everything changed.

Had she seen Mia and Marli that night? She couldn't

be sure. She remembered a swarm of elfin children, glitter sparkling on their cheeks. But she couldn't match those gleeful faces to the shy smiles she was getting now.

"If you hadn't evacuated the area, we would be dead," Vihani was explaining, tears in the corners of his eyes. "You saved us. You saved every single one of us."

"Not me," a little boy said. "I was at Nanoo's house."

An uncle slapped the boy on the back of the head. But Grace's smile only deepened.

"You made all this?" she asked, gesturing at the sign and cake with its lit sparkler and all the cheerful, happy faces.

"We made you the sign while you were in the hospital, but we weren't allowed to deliver it. We've been saving it for the next time you came in."

Heron pinged, <<That cake looks amazing. I hope you plan to share it.>>

Grace looked down at the cake. At the red and green flecks of confetti on her shoulders, hands, the table, to the white cake and the vanilla ice cream melting on it.

Something in her chest tightened. She flicked her gaze up to meet Heron's.

<<You told them I like vanilla,>> she wrote. <<You helped them with all of this?>>

Heron put his chin in his hand. <<I might have had something to do with it.>>

SIX

"THAT WAS NICE." Heron patted his stomach. "What a tough act to follow! It will be hard for me to top confetti at dinner tonight."

"It was nice," Grace admitted.

"Then why do you look like mites are nibbling on your liver."

Grace glanced up the street, looking for the auto. "I hope I thanked them enough."

"You said it six times."

"I wasn't sure what I was saying. They surprised me. I don't like surprises."

He considered this. "Understandable. But you saved their lives and you love their food. They just wanted to show you some gratitude. Why are you looking at me like that?"

She glanced back at the restaurant, small now in the distance. "I thought you were flirting with Vihani, but you were coordinating with him, weren't you?"

"You think I flirt with everyone."

"You *do* flirt with everyone."

He shrugged. "To answer your question, yes. He came by the precinct and asked for my help a few days ago. They were probably getting tired of holding on to the sign. I've been looking for a chance ever since. The timing had to be natural, or you'd suspect something was up."

Grace only distantly noted this information. Her brain remained on the same track. "But now I have to consider the possibility that you're not always flirting. Sometimes you're also scheming."

"You already knew I was a schemer."

"Yes, but I thought I could tell the difference between the two."

His smile deepened. "Isn't flirting a *kind* of scheming?"

The auto rolled up to the curb and they climbed inside. Grace thought of the takeout containers that must be sitting in her garage by now. Vihani had offered to use their delivery belt to send them directly to her house so that she didn't have to carry her leftover cake and food around the city. They'd finished the ice cream, but everything else had been packed up.

She accessed her home camera, selecting the garage camera.

Sure enough, the white bamboo boxes sat on the metal delivery platform.

She gave her house instructions to move the items from the platform to her refrigerator, and watched as the platform lifted until it was level with a slot on the side of the garage wall. Then the slot opened and the takeout boxes disappeared inside, taking the same route as all the other groceries and cool storage items that entered her home.

<<How should we label this item, Grace?>> the house asked.

<<Sindu Takeout,>> Grace replied.

<<Sindu Takeout,>> the house confirmed, and Grace returned her attention to Heron.

"I can see you're struggling with this idea," he was saying, clearly amused. "That I can be *both* a flirt and functional. A functional flirt."

The auto was already slowing. Grace lowered the transparency and looked out.

An apartment building loomed on her right, its rose-gold exterior dotted with black windows. Grace opened her lenscape and reviewed the warrants approved by Constable Ezra, paying particular attention to the apartment number.

"His apartment is on the sixteenth floor," Grace said as the auto rolled to a stop and their seatbelts unfastened. When the doors opened, Heron let her go first.

The apartment building's lobby was dark, quiet. An AI sat behind the desk, immobile until it registered their movement. Upon seeing them, it straightened its back and smiled.

"Good afternoon, welcome to Green Meadows. How can I assist you today?"

"No, thank you," Grace said, pushing the buttons on the elevator and holding it until Heron stepped inside.

This refusal didn't bother the AI in the least. "Have a wonderful day."

The elevator opened on a long hallway with bright red carpet and endless doors on each side. Between the doors, a single bulb burned.

"What if you lived at the end of the hall," Heron said. "Imagine coming home at the end of a long day. You're tired, you just want to fall into bed, but you're confronted with this monstrosity of a hallway."

Grace counted the doors until she arrived at the one labeled 1655. She used the override access code to open it. The handle turned freely.

There was something about entering someone's home that had always bothered her.

Grace hesitated in the doorway. "Mr. Range?"

She took a tentative step over the threshold.

"Mr. Range? Are you home?" Still no answer.

Heron closed the door behind him.

"It's too quiet, isn't it?" Heron looked around, seeming to note the dark brown, lumpy sofa along one wall of the living room. A decent-sized television was pinned to the opposite wall.

On the left was a tiny kitchen. There was no Chef-Mate, no windows. Only a fridge and counters.

There was a pot on the stove. Grace crossed and looked inside it, noting the sauce dried and stuck to the bottom of the pan.

"Either he's a slob or he definitely hasn't been home in a while."

There was very little in the apartment itself. A few essentials for cooking in the little kitchen nook. Nothing but the rug and screen in the living room. Down a short hall there were three more doors. One opened into a bedroom, the bed still ruffled, covers thrown back and pillows crumpled as if punched. On the floor by the bed Grace spotted a white string sticking to the gray carpet.

The other door opened to a bathroom, also very small with only a shower stall, toilet, suspended sink, and glass shelf holding a ToothBlast. Given the shape of the Blast, Grace could tell Tristan Range had very crooked teeth. Surprising in an age where dental modification was almost a rite of passage.

In the bedroom there was a small closet with neutral-colored clothes, and the books Lenorie had mentioned were piled on the nightstand.

It was the third room that had the most to absorb.

Originally, it was likely meant to have been the master bedroom. It was nearly twice the size of the little room that Range had shoved his bed into. In contrast, this room had two large desks stretched against catty-corner walls, creating one large L shape. On it were more papers and documents than Grace could've actively gone through in a week.

Books were piled on top of each other, likely in an order that only the compiler comprehended. Grace used her lenscape to catalogue everything. Their positions, the titles, the organization of the room. She turned their spines and took snapshots. She'd find copies later, if needed.

She stepped over precarious stacks on the floor, careful not to disturb anything. "He wrote a lot of things by hand. There's a lot of paper."

She couldn't remember the last time she'd seen so much paper. There was a small fortune in this room alone.

Heron's fingers trailed the spine of a book. "Before the invention of the Internet in the twentieth century, all knowledge was contained in books like this. Hard ones." He knocked on the cover.

Grace shook her head. "It's been a while since you've spouted historical facts at me."

"I know you find it tiresome. I'm trying to do it only when I think something is *really* interesting."

"That must be hard for you. Don't you think most things are interesting?"

He tilted his head. "I do."

She sifted through the pages, her eyes snagging on phrases here and there.

She lifted a page, turning it. "He seems to be arguing that living in a virtual reality isn't living at all."

"I'm not sure I agree." Heron stood beside her, looking over her shoulder.

Grace could smell the soft scent of his soap or shampoo.

"What is living except a bombardment of sensory input? If you fully immerse yourself into a virtual reality like CyTown, isn't that living? I'm not sure, technically, inner experience is much different than our outer circumstances."

Grace turned the page. "He seems to be arguing that direct sensory perception matters. 'That living in a perfect utopia is dishonest to the human experience. Real life is suffering, and it's suffering that will set you free.'"

Grace frowned and read that again.

"You have your unhappy face on." Heron mimicked her scowl. "You don't agree?"

"It doesn't make sense."

"Which part? The—"

"No, it doesn't make sense that someone might hurt him for this. They're only ideas. Little more than musings."

"Ideas are dangerous," Heron countered. "When in the wrong hands."

"True, but I can't imagine that someone would come to his house in the dead of night and kidnap him because he thinks people should live their lives in real-time. We have to be missing something. It's possible he wasn't kidnapped."

Heron's grin turned devilish. "Let's find out, shall we?"

"What do you mean?" She turned on him, putting the papers back on the desk.

"I've been working on a prototype. Let's field test it."

She sighed inwardly. "You're about to show me something illegal, aren't you? It triggers my anxiety when you do that."

"It's not illegal!" he scoffed. "It doesn't even exist yet. There aren't laws for things that don't exist."

She only stared at him.

"Shall I go on or…"

"Please," she said, feeling the heat rise in her face.

He rubbed his hands together. "Okay, we'll need to share because I haven't figured out how to export the software without corrupting some of the code yet."

<<Accept scapeshare with heronjane1?>>

Grace accepted. "Are we on your private server for this?"

"You're thinking like a criminal now. I love it."

She could argue that she was always thinking like a criminal. That's what made her good at her job. But she let him go on.

"And yes, the only one who can follow this is us. Watch what you say aloud if you're so worried."

She was worried. Always.

"Let's start by the front door."

They retraced their steps across the gray carpet back to the front door.

"Come stand by me," he said. "It'll eliminate some of the doubling."

Grace pressed her shoulder to his.

"Okay, here we go."

At first nothing happened. The living room and kitchen remained as they were.

"We're rewinding in time," he explained. "Here we are."

Two bodies—or the shapes of bodies—exited the office, walked backward into the bedroom, then from the bedroom backward into the bathroom.

<<It's only giving us heat signatures?>> she asked.

<<No, not heat. I added that bit of color because it was hard to get any detail without it.>>

When it was clear she didn't understand, he added, <<I've tapped into the home AI. The home software. I'm

using its motion-sensory function to track movements throughout the space.>>

She thought of her home's software and how it tracked her from room to room, adjusting the lighting, temperature, and other pre-programmed preferences.

<<But that wouldn't distinguish between an AI like Henry and a human,>> she wrote.

<<No,>> he agreed. <<I would think that animals would be distinguishable. A dog, for example, could be mistaken for another canine but not for a human. However, AIs are humanoid. The only way to know I'm seeing a human and not an AI is the biometrics. AIs have none.>>

Their previous selves—now red and purple—backed out of the apartment. For a long while, nothing happened again.

<<Because it's been empty,>> he explained. <<But time is passing. You can see the clock in the upper-right corner.>>

Grace glanced up and saw the numbers spinning in reverse.

Then a red shape with an orange fringe stepped into the room, hesitantly at first. It turned toward the stove, inspecting the pot as Grace had, then knocked on the bedroom door.

Then she opened it, inspected the room, and moved to the bedroom. Then, for several minutes, stood in the hallway looking into the large office as if unsure of what to do.

<<This is his sister,>> Heron pinged. <<It's Tuesday morning by the timestamp, though she's here a bit later than she said.>>

<<If the house has stored bio-signatures, you can use those to identify people,>> she pinged.

The whole scene froze.

<<At my house I store everyone's readings so that the house can greet them properly when they arrive, offer them their favorite drinks, mind their temperature and light preferences, etc.>>

What she didn't say was that it was necessary for the salvation of her marriage. Davion had liked a horribly warm house, and Grace preferred hers cold. She liked soothing, dim lights and he bright ones. Having a house that adjusted to whoever was present had quelled many an argument, especially given the fact that he deferred to her settings when she was around.

Her heart kicked.

<<I used colors to sort the different signatures, but I can't possibly know who is who unless I compare them grid-wide. I can label ours, and the sister's. Even Tristan's. But the others will take time.>>

Four shapes, one green, one blue, one red, and one yellow, stepped into view, moving through Grace's and Heron's bodies as if they were ghosts. Between them hung a fifth shape now labeled *Tristan*.

The four shapes carried Tristan backward from the front door to the bedroom.

"Oh, let's see what's happening!" he said, trotting toward the bedroom.

Grace and Heron crowded into the small space at the foot of the bed and watched as the four shapes seemingly tucked Tristan's sleeping form back into the bed.

Heron played it forward for a moment, confirming they were really seeing it correctly. And yes, they were. The figures surrounded the bed and grabbed his limbs. When Tristan began to thrash and fight almost instantly, it didn't last. The limbs softened, grew still.

<<A sedative, maybe,>> Heron wrote.

<<He was taken,>> Grace pinged, noting the time-stamp. It was nearly three in the morning. <<But did he really end up in CyTown Towers, and if so, does that mean CyTown took him? Or someone else?>>

They watched as Tristan was carried out of the apartment again, this time moving forward through the hours.

Grace was about to end the scapeshare, thinking they were done, when the yellow form reappeared. It walked down the hall straight into the large office. It circled the space for five or six minutes, then left, closing the door behind it.

SEVEN

"IT COULD'VE BEEN ANYTHING," Grace argued as the auto rolled to a stop at the curb outside her house.

Heron was as animated as she was. "It could've been an anti-VR manifesto or it could've been a hard copy of his last will and testament, hiding what his end-of-life plans really were."

"Or confirming them," she said, unwilling to completely table the idea that Tristan wouldn't change his mind about VR if given a terminal diagnosis.

One could argue that no one knew him better than his sister, his own flesh and blood, but Grace's faith in outward appearances had been shattered when she'd discovered her dead husband's truth.

He'd kept part of himself well hidden from her. That part was a total stranger who saw her every day and slept beside her every night.

On the outside, he'd been a top security analyst at one of the zone's premier cybersecurity companies, Charlotte's Web. His position meant that he was bound to protect and serve the cyber security of the zone.

Yet the other Davion, his second self, had violated all those promises. He'd lied, stolen, forged. In the name of a good cause, sure. She understood that, but it didn't change the fact that no matter what Tristan's outer face might have been, there was always the possibility of a second self hiding just behind it.

Heron looked up at her from beneath long lashes as she slipped out of the belt and stepped onto the sidewalk. "We can both agree that four people came into his house and took him, and some of his papers, though. Right?"

"Yes," she said. "Agreed."

"And that this is definitely evidence that something bad has happened to him. I mean, if he wanted to go to CyTown, he would've gone during business hours, don't you think?"

"Right. Who makes three o'clock appointments?" She glanced over her shoulder at her waiting house. It was nearly 17:00. "Are you coming in?"

"No. I'm going to head home and get ready for dinner. What time will you be over?"

Her brows lifted in question. "Seven thirty?"

"Works for me," he said, and the auto's door began to close. "See you then."

She watched the white beetle of a machine speed away.

On her front step, the house greeted her. "Good evening, Grace. Welcome home. We're happy to see you."

We, she thought. She should change that program setting. *We* had been the default when she was a *we.* She wasn't a *we* any longer.

"You have no messages," the house told her as she crossed the threshold and it shut the door behind her. "But you did receive a delivery from Sindu Serves."

"Yes, thank you."

Her eyes swept the space. The kitchen connecting to the garage was quiet. The ChefMate's mechanical arms sat suspended above the stove in their resting position as if awaiting instruction. The fridge's surface lit as she passed it, drawn by her movement. She wasn't hungry, but she read the menu anyway.

There was a chocolate bar listed in the second row. Grace selected it, and the fridge clicked to life, mechanical sounds whirring inside.

Then the food slot opened and Grace's chocolate slid out on a tray.

She took it, nibbling at its chilled edges.

She slipped her shoes off at the door and crossed into the living room, her tired feet sinking into the soft carpet.

The walls were at minimal opacity, the eastern wall projecting a beach scene at low tide.

She liked the sound of ocean waves crashing and decided to keep it. The sky-blue ceiling, too. But she maximized the opacity on the other walls to close herself off from the world around her.

She fell onto the sofa with a thud. For a moment, she only lay there, nibbling her chocolate. She was enveloped in her exhaustion and closed her eyes against the raw, overused feeling. They felt like they'd been rolled in sand, scratching against her eyelids as they moved.

As the last of the chocolate melted away on her tongue and the ocean waves crashed around her, she drifted in and out of consciousness.

Her mind tried to work, turning over pieces of the day —of Tristan's case—in its greedy, insatiable hands.

It was best to forget about it if she could. Even if only for a little while. That was when the work would shift to the background, to that secretive inner chamber of her mind where all her real processing was done. In that back room, real connections were made. Minute details pieced together and truths revealed.

Then the revelations would surface, magnificent and full-bodied to her consciousness.

But only if her heavy-handed foremind could bring itself to hand off the task. Unfortunately, that part of her didn't know how to rest.

When she woke, the room was darker. The digital sky and beachfront now showed the first signs of twilight. Grace stretched and her hip cried out in pain. She lifted it, sliding her hand into that pocket.

The golden cylinder fell into her palm.

She brought it up to the light, turning it. In her living room, it wasn't very brilliant. Its shell didn't sparkle in the absence of direct sun. Instead, it seemed darker, condensed.

She turned it over in her hands and considered it.

When Adams had accepted his invitation to the society years before, she'd told the then-alive Davion about it. What had she said?

She searched the metadata and scrolled through the thumbnails until she found the memory she wanted.

"Replay memory five sixty-three," Grace instructed her lenscape.

It searched her memory bank for the recollection and brought it full-bodied to her present.

The living room shifted suddenly to the right, giving Grace a crash of vertigo.

That's right, she thought. *We used to have the sofa against the wall.*

The memory unfurled, so fresh and real that she couldn't separate her present from her past.

On the sofa beside her, Davion said, "I'm not surprised. He's a pretentious fu—"

"*Dave*," Grace snipped—the old Grace, the Grace who still had a husband and son and faith in the zone she served. That Grace flicked her eyes up toward their son's closed bedroom door.

Grace tried to gauge the hour but didn't feel like reviewing the memory's metadata again. For now, she'd let it unravel around her.

Alive Davion lifted his drink and smiled devilishly over its rim. He tipped it back, ice hitting his lips, taking a piece between his teeth before saying, "We had a club like that at my old school. It was a ritzy place. It comes with the territory, I guess. People can't be satisfied with the fact they're already living the best life possible on this planet. They've got to find a way to pull themselves above the others. Reinforce their delusions of superiority."

His disgust had showed as he'd crushed the ice between his teeth.

"I don't know much about it," then-Grace said, playing the role of diplomat.

"It's a good-old-boys club," Davion said, placing his free hand on her foot and squeezing it. "A bunch of rich people who want to make themselves richer by backroom deals."

Grace would give anything to feel those hands on her now. Those lips. She wanted to reach out and cup that jaw, press the ridge of his ear between her fingers.

Then-Grace didn't appreciate how lucky she'd been as Davion began to rub a circle on the ball of her foot, using his thumb to press into the muscle. Even if his fingers were chilled by his frosty glass.

"If I ever get a chance to investigate them, I should," Grace said then, tipping her own glass up. "Think of what I'd uncover."

He was watching her, a sour look on his face. "I don't want you near people like that."

Now-Grace sat very still, begging, pretending inwardly that it was her real face he saw. What would he think of the scars, of this woman who'd been born of his loss?

They weren't the same, were they? The Grace he'd loved and the Grace she was now.

"But yes, you should," he said finally, his lips folding into a smile. "Corruption like that needs to be checked, whenever possible. If you think you could pull it off, you should take your shot."

She saw his lips twitch, grow stiff in the corners.

He'd said what he was supposed to say as the supportive, encouraging husband, emphasizing not his fear but his faith and trust in her abilities.

He also didn't want her to do it. It amused her now to watch him tiptoe the line of encouraging her, pushing her forward toward the hard task, all while waging war against that protective part of himself.

Her stomach knotted at the idea that Davion would disapprove of her next move. That he would resist, if only a little, the idea of her accepting the Egg Island invitation, of stepping willingly into the lion's den.

You did a lot of things I would've asked you not to, Grace thought back, anger bitter in the back of her throat.

Things that had gotten him—*my son*—killed.

"You're not easily manipulated," he said, searching her face as if it would provide evidence for his argument. "I don't think there's an offer they could make you that you couldn't resist."

You don't know that, she thought now, looking at his beautiful, proud face. *If they offered you or Kaiden. If they rolled back the clock and returned you both to me—what I'd give for that.*

Finally, his face broke into a beautiful grin, a real one. "You'd scare the living hell out of them."

The bedroom door opened, and Kaiden stepped into the hallway, rubbing his eyes with his fist.

Grace's heart kicked as if struck.

"Daddy?" he called from the top of the stairs, frowning down at them.

Grace's throat tightened, her stomach revolted. Panic rose in her like a dark wave, splashing over her mind, her reason.

How could she have forgotten?

She'd been careful.

She'd avoided all memories of Kaiden in the four months since his death.

Davion she'd indulged in. Sure, it hurt to see him. The act always filled her guts with longing, but it'd been a manageable pain. A comfort to pretend she had him back with her—if only for minutes at a time—no matter how angry, how furious she was—

But Kaiden—no. *No…no…no…*

With Kaiden standing there, she found she couldn't breathe.

Davion leaned forward and put his drink on the table. "Did we wake you, buddy?"

"Yeah," Kaiden said, his pout pronounced. "Why you up so late?"

Her dead husband and then-Grace shared a laugh.

Grace watched her heart rate monitor appear in the upper right of her lenscape.

142 bmp 154/92

A frantic heart tapping a rhythm. She ignored it, watched then-Grace begin to rise only to have Davion press down on her knee. "I've got this. You've been on your feet all day."

He stooped and gave her cheek a kiss—her ruined cheek that felt nothing.

She felt the tears streaming down the good side of her face as Davion mounted the stairs and lifted her boy into his arms.

"Wait!" Kaiden pleaded. "I want to give Mommy a kiss, too."

"Give Mommy a kiss?" Davion asked, turning back toward her with their baby in her arms. "What do you think, Mommy?"

"Yes, please," she'd said, reaching her arms out to him but dutifully remaining off her feet.

Davion carried him to her, bent, let Kaiden reach toward her, lines on his cheeks and soft light in his eyes.

She reached for him—then and now—and—

Grace's hands and knees hit the floor as she collapsed beside the sofa. The recall ended on impact, as if she'd had to physically wrench herself from the memory, from the perfect life she no longer had.

Her sobs enveloped her.

"Grace, have you fallen?" the house asked.

Run CALM program? her lenscape asked.

All the inanimate objects of her life called out to her, offered to help her, wanted to attend to her distress, but she didn't want them. She wanted Kaiden.

She wanted that soft, unruly hair in her hands. She wanted that kiss—that goodnight kiss.

Grief was strange. She could have several good days in a row, feel almost like herself, her mind clear, her spirit light. Then the smallest trigger could call it back. Sweep into the room like winter air.

She wanted to feel Kaiden's hot breath on her cheek and smell him, touch him, hold him.

Her baby. Her sweet, sweet baby. Gone.

She screamed. She called out his name, curling herself into a tight ball between the sofa and table. She sobbed until sound could no longer escape her throat and only dry air whistled between her lips.

SHE WOKE to her lenscape pinging. But she didn't answer it. She let the soft *ping ping ping* alert go unanswered as she lay raw and broken on the carpet. Her body felt hollowed out, scraped clean like a harvest gourd.

I need water, she thought as her mind sank into the darkness again. She wasn't sure if she made it fully back to that empty place before hands were on her, turning her over, demanding answers.

"Grace! Grace! Are you hurt?"

Her eyes fluttered open. The room was blurry, out of focus. Her face felt hot, swollen.

It was Heron, looking down on her, his face a mask of fear and confusion. His hands were running down her arms, her stomach, as if looking for something.

"Grace! Did someone hurt you?" he demanded.

It took her a moment to remember how she'd gotten on the floor, replaying the steps of her mind until she saw Kaiden open the door to his room and step out onto the landing.

Her heart kicked. Her lips began trembling again.

"Please tell me what's going on," he begged. "Is there someone here? Did you drink poison? Get shot? *What the hell happened?*"

Her lips trembled. "K-Kaiden."

Fresh tears slid down Grace's cheeks.

She sucked in a half-breath. "He-he's gone."

"Oh." Heron's relief was palpable. His face softened with understanding. "Right. Okay."

He slid his arms under her body and lifted her. She wanted to protest. She wanted to demand he put her down. The indignity of it was enough to embarrass her. She never cried in front of anyone, let alone fell apart in their arms.

But she wasn't in control now. She wasn't in control of the ache in her chest or the way her insides were turning to acid and burning her from the inside out. The way her throat had somehow grown tight, too miniscule to draw a full breath.

He placed her on her bed and slid the suit jacket off her shoulders.

He stepped back and turned toward the dresser. "Pajamas in here?"

She shook her head. Davion had been the one who'd used the dresser. Her mother had emptied it while she was away, and it had stayed empty. Like many parts of her life, Grace had found nothing yet to fill it with.

He crossed to the closet. "In here?"

The door lit at his approach, showing him all the items stored in its collection.

He made selections with a few quick taps of his fingers on its digital surface. "It says you've worn this pair about eighty percent more often than the others. I'm going to assume they're your favorite."

The mechanisms inside the closet clicked to life, retrieving the requested items. Then they were fed through the slot in the wall.

Heron laid them on the foot of the bed, his eyes hesitating a moment on the shirt.

"You change into these, and I'll get you something to drink."

He disappeared into her bathroom for several minutes,

her ears pricking to the sounds of cabinets opening. Of metal clinking against ceramic.

Then he reappeared with a tissue box in one hand and a trash can in the other. He must've pulled open the wall compactor to retrieve it.

"In case you need to puke." He placed the trash can beside the bed. He placed the tissue box on the coverlet, within reach. "Be right back. Ping me if you need something."

She looked at the tissues and the pajamas—which were in fact her favorite—then back at him. He was already on the stairs, disappearing down into the living room below.

This left her in the dark of her bedroom, noting the pooling shadows around her. The way her work clothes felt wrong beneath her sheets. She pulled her shirt and bra over her head, dropping them to the carpet beside the bed, and pulled on the soft white hemp shirt.

She thought of the way Heron's eyes had stuttered on the shirt and realized he must have noted its size. *He knows it's Davion's.* Or perhaps he only suspected.

Beneath the covers, she wiggled free of her pants and lay for a moment in only her underwear and dead husband's shirt, regarding the ceiling above. The screen replicated the sky, soft clouds rolling past as the first stars stood out in the early purple of evening.

She pulled her pajama pants under the covers and slid into them, her body fully relaxing against the mattress for the first time. She expected Heron to ping her, to insist that she assure him she was fine. His face had been full of terror when he'd discovered her in a heap on the floor.

But he didn't.

He left her alone with her thoughts and the deep well of sadness within her.

Listening to him move around her kitchen, to the opening and closing of cabinets, the sound of ceramic clanking onto the countertop—it turned her mind toward him.

She liked the sound of it, of him nearby. Her house had been too quiet since her family died.

When they were alive, it seemed like Davion—and especially Kaiden—had filled every corner of this house with noise. With their laughter, their voices.

With living.

It had taken her a long time to get used to the silence. To have it broken now was a comfort.

Affection for Heron built in her chest.

For all his silliness, despite his refusal to take things seriously, he wasn't ridiculous when it mattered. He had good intuition when it came to the feelings and needs of others. She'd seen it countless times in their weeks together.

And while it was clear he thought institutions were fallible, worthy of his disrespect and ridicule, he treated people like they mattered.

Davion was like that, Grace thought, and the ache came again.

Blessedly, it couldn't hold a flame to the pain of Kaiden's sweet face. His shy grin breaking open as he extended his arms toward her.

She began to observe her sadness at a distance. She could see herself, understand that she was upset, and yet not be consumed by it. *It's like my mind has split in two*, she thought. *I'm broken.*

The possibility didn't frighten her.

She fell back against the pillows and covered her forehead with her hands. Tears rolled from the corners of her eyes onto her pillow, blurring out the evening above.

Time stilled, stretched into one unpunctuated moment of pain, deadened at the edges by her own fatigue. It amazed her really, that even as deep as her grief was, she couldn't sustain it. Her body, her mind, couldn't bear its brute force for long.

The bedroom door creaked as it was pushed wider.

Heron appeared with a wooden tea tray balanced in his hands. He slid it onto the bed beside her.

"I put together a little something." He pointed at each item in term. "Soup, crackers, water with lemon, and tea, also with lemon. Lots of lemon here to clear this up."

He gestured at his face.

"It'll help with the congestion."

She sat up, pressing her back against the headboard. It occurred to her to check the time. It was nearing 19:00. She'd thought he'd come over because she'd missed dinner. Not showing up would've caused red flags, certainly, but they hadn't yet reached their agreed-upon time.

"Why did you come over?"

Heron sat on the foot of her bed, crossing his legs under him. His toes wiggled in his dark gray socks. "Your house told me to."

"My house told you I wasn't okay?"

He held up his hands in surrender as if already expecting a protest. "The house is wired to alert me if anything happens to you when you're home."

"She spies on me," Grace said flatly. "For you."

"*No.* But if you fall or your BP spikes or if someone unregistered comes over—anything like that. After they killed Davion, I was worried someone might attack you. It would be easy for them to make it look like an accident if you were home alone."

"It was Davion they wanted. Not me."

"Not if they thought you knew something. They could show up, hurt you, and make it look like a suicide. Then you'd be all over the bulletin as the tragic commander who killed herself months after losing her husband and son. And who would investigate that? Who would question it? Apart from me."

She lifted the tea and took a sip. The scent of lemon was bright, cheerful. "You programmed my house to call you?"

He laughed. "All of that and that's what you got?"

"My head hurts."

He held up a finger. "Ah, right. I have something for that."

He patted his pockets until something crinkled. Then he pulled out a small film of white powder.

"What is that?" Her brows arched. "Heron, I'm not taking drugs."

"Relax."

"Exactly what a dealer would say."

"It's only medicinal."

"More dealer talk."

He opened the little film and passed it to her. "Medicinal for your *headache*. And the feelings. It will also help your feelings." When she didn't take it, he added, "It's not illegal."

She sniffed it and it didn't smell like narcotics. In fact, it had a faint herbal scent, like wet earth and long grasses.

"It's all natural," he insisted. "My mother Nora makes it for herself. She has...episodes."

"What kind of episodes?"

"Melancholic ones. This stuff is distilled from plants in her greenhouse. It's the only thing that helps her."

Grace tried to remember what Heron had said about his mother. Not the scientist, Victoria Jane, but the other one. Nora Avignon was the one responsible for filling Heron's head with history and facts, and she was also prone to depression or a mood disorder.

"I suppose you have experience with emotional people," Grace said, reaching for the water.

Heron handed the glass to her. "There's nothing wrong with emotions, Gray."

She threw the powder back and chased it with several gulps of water. It tasted like it smelled, earthy, coating her tongue and leaving a slightly floral aftertaste.

She finished the water and then handed him the glass. He refilled it, placing it on the tray.

"Will it make me sleepy?" she asked.

"It shouldn't. But it should help your body relax. All the cortisol and stress hormones accumulating in your system should stabilize. And it'll raise your serotonin. If you have another spike, it should be harder for the stress to stay in your body."

"Sounds wonderful."

He gave her a sad smile. "It only lasts about twelve hours. But I have more at my place if you need it."

"Is it habit-forming?" This was something she should've asked *before* taking it.

"No. It's really only crushed plants."

"Isn't cocaine also a crushed plant?"

"We do quite a bit to cocaine before it's consumed. It's pretty removed from *planthood* at that point." He pouted. "Do you really think I'd give you something that would hurt you?"

"No." That's why she'd agreed to take it.

The knots in her neck and shoulders began to loosen, sliding down from her ears. The ropes of muscle in her back also began to uncoil. "That was fast."

"Yes, it's one of the reasons Nora likes it. Her panic attacks can come on rather quickly."

Grace softened against the pillows.

The emotions remained, lying like thick clouds across

her mind, but her body was letting go. The revving coils of its engine softened to a purr.

But Heron hadn't taken the drug, and he was relaxing too.

Because I'd scared him, she marveled again. *I really scared him.*

She reached out and put her hand on his. She squeezed. "Thank you for coming."

Color rose in his cheeks. "You're welcome."

"I'm sorry about dinner."

He sighed dramatically.

"I had wanted to date you before Adams had the chance, but I'll settle for ending up in your bed first." He stretched himself long at the foot of her bed.

"I didn't realize you were competing with Adams."

"Your mother is right about him wanting you. I've been watching him watching you."

Grace grimaced.

"I'm delighted to see you're disgusted by the prospect."

"Here come the jokes," she said. "You couldn't hold back for long."

"Then you know me well." He put his chin in his hand. Grace looked at those Tahitian-blue eyes, made dark by the room's shadows.

If the darkness bothered him, he didn't say so.

Grace used her lenscape to turn on the small lamp in her bedroom, keeping it at its lowest setting.

"Your eyes are pretty in the lamplight," he said.

She was certain that her eyes were puffy, red, and over-wrought.

"Stop flirting." Grace adjusted herself against the pillow. It was harder now with the deadness of her body. It was slow, sluggish, unwilling to cooperate. "I can't take you seriously."

Heron scoffed. "Why not?"

"You have a boyfriend."

He seemed to consider this. "Hmm."

"And look at me," she said, gesturing toward her ruined face. "I'm never dating again."

It felt like a betrayal, to joke about this while Davion lay in the Soul Grove next to her son. But so much of her marriage had felt like a betrayal since she'd learned the truth about him, about his ambitions, and how he'd lied to her—and what those lies had cost them both.

Heron's mouth pursed. It was a minute before he managed, "Grace, you're beautiful."

She pinched her eyes closed. "Don't humor me."

"I'm not. What reason do I have to flatter you? You know everything about me. There's no way to cast myself in a better light."

She snorted. "I've known you for six weeks. That's not long enough to know anyone. A whole marriage isn't long enough to know someone."

And she would never make the mistake of believing she knew another person again.

He squeezed her hand. It was cool and smooth against hers. "You knew him."

"It doesn't feel that way."

Heron squeezed harder. "The way he felt about you and Kaiden. The life you shared. None of that was a lie."

She desperately wanted to believe him. But there was the whisper of doubt now. There would always be that whisper. And nothing she could do, or discover, would take it back. Where there'd been one lie, surely there'd been more.

Heron let the silence stretch between them, his hand still holding hers. His thumb began to trace small circles over her knuckles.

"I understand why people move to CyTown," she said finally, her eyes on the stars above. It was dark enough to see them.

More lies. There were stars, but she could never see them if she stepped out into the street and stared at the sky above. The haze would prevent such clarity. How like her marriage this was. The stars were real, but not the ones she could see. And the haze—all those lies—was what obscured her view.

"You mean it has merits besides anti-aging? That's what I hear most people like it for. Residents never have to see themselves with wrinkles or saggy bellies if they're only looking at digital projections of themselves. It's more convincing than filters, apparently."

"If someone like me went in," she heard herself say, "I could have my life back."

Heron pulled his hand away.

"Kaiden would be there. It would be like none of this had happened."

She searched his face but found it unreadable.

"They can use a person's memory bank and reconstruct the life they want from all that stored data. My memory bank is extensive," she confessed. "And their sensors could trick my body into feeling. I could feel Davion again."

And Kaiden's arms around my neck.

"Would you really be happy with that?" Heron asked. "Even if it was a lie? Is that how you'll make it better? Repair lies with more lies?"

She thought she heard a hint of accusation in that voice.

"And what about the people here?" His eyes fell to the covers. "What about everyone in this zone who needs you? What about those thousands of people we saved from deletion? There are more people like that—*countless* more."

His fingers tugged at a thread she couldn't see.

"Could you walk away from—?" He swallowed whatever word he was about to say next. After a breath, he offered, "Away from your work?"

"I'm tired. I'm tired of pretending I'm okay every day when I'm not. I'm *not*."

"Then don't be okay! Be a mess! But don't give up."

She thought he was being unfair. He was asking a lot of her. More than she thought she could give.

His eyes shimmered. It seemed like an infinity before he said, "I miss him too, you know."

When she saw the tears pooled in the corners of his eyes, a wave of shame washed over her.

She was whining.

She was indulging in pity and weakness, and it was blinding her to the pain of others.

Heron had lost Davion too. Heron had known him longer, and arguably better, in many ways. She wasn't the only one who was heartbroken.

She had to pull herself together.

"At least solve this case before you give up." His mouth was tight. "Find out what happened to Tristan and then— then you can do whatever you want with your life."

He gave up on the blanket's imaginary thread.

"Are you mad at me?" she asked.

He began to flash one of his bright, dazzling smiles.

"Don't." Her own anger rose. She refused to have another man in her life hiding things from her. "You just saw me fall apart."

She thought he was going to ignore her. Maybe get up, walk out of the room without saying another word.

Instead he lifted his head and met her eyes. And his

anger was laid bare.

"Yes, I'm angry." His jaw worked, the whites of his eyes shone.

"Why?"

"Because it's bullshit."

Her heart skipped a beat, but she didn't back down. "Which part?"

"That you would give up like that. That you'd crawl into some digital hidey hole and try to forget everything that's happened, everything that needs to be done. You're better than that."

Her stomach clenched.

"You're *stronger* than that," he continued. The anger softened and Grace saw something behind it. A flash, almost too quick to recognize. Fear? Grief? "Your work is important. Living is important."

"Is it?" She wiped at the corners of her eyes. "Anyone could do what I do. The zone is held in place by generations of infrastructure. None of that depends on what I do."

Heron ran a hand through his hair. "No one is willing to pull back the curtain and look into the dark. How can we make things better when no one wants to look the monster in the eye?"

"You overestimate me."

"I don't!" he hissed through gritted teeth. He took a breath. "You underestimate yourself."

She searched his face.

She hadn't seen him clearly before. Was that because he was still hiding the most important parts of himself behind jokes and flirtation? Could it be possible that he didn't trust her as much as she thought?

If so, it was no one's fault but her own.

After Davion, she trusted no one. Not even herself.

EIGHT

WHEN GRACE WOKE, it was almost eight in the morning. She sat up in bed and found herself alone. Her heart sank.

If not for the tissue box and the strange, disembodied trash can on the floor beside her piled clothes, she would've thought Heron a figment of her imagination. A mere projection of her grief-ridden mind.

But the evidence was there, even if the man himself was gone.

She rose, slipped from the bed, and stepped out onto the landing at the top of her stairs. She stretched and contemplated if a shower or koffee should come first. She'd decided on the shower and had half turned toward the door when something caught her eye.

A dark mess of hair poked out from one end of her sofa.

She leaned over the railing for a better view. One of the sofa's pillows was tucked under Heron's head and a blanket thrown over his body. Soft snoring rolled through the room.

She crept down the stairs and stopped in front of the sofa. She traced his serene face with her gaze, something inside her cracking open.

"Do you often watch people sleep?" he grumbled, his eyes still closed.

She nudged him with a knee. "Get up."

He opened one eye. "Why? Has something happened?"

"No," she said. "But we'll be late for work if you don't."

He stretched under the blanket, arching his back like a cat. "I'll make koffee then."

Grace closed the bathroom door behind her, unable to explain the sudden relief in her chest and limbs.

From the glass shelf, she grabbed her ToothBlast, fitting its mold over her teeth. She opened and closed her mouth until the device was snug over her teeth and compressed the button to activate it. The blue light flashed in her mouth, and the warm tingle spread along her gums.

A second later it beeped, notifying her that the cleaning was complete. She replaced it on the glass shelf and stepped into the shower.

The head above activated at her presence. This morning, instead of disabling the auto wash, she let it run its mechanical brushes through her hair as the wall jets pummeled her body. She watched its progress on the embedded screen, moving her limbs in the positions it requested for each wash and rinse cycle.

She was in the final rinse for her hair when she received a lenscape notification that her conditioner was running low, and used her household account to approve the purchase of more.

It would travel under the city today, be delivered to the

platform in the garage and then carried through the wall dispensary to the bathroom upstairs.

Once, while riding in an auto, Heron had quipped, *Not too long ago, people had to go to the store and buy their supplies and restock them themselves. Who has time for that?*

She'd argued that she liked going into stores, looking at things, selecting things. That shopping could be a major stress reliever.

Yes, but who wants to carry it around or put it away?

She'd conceded that point.

<<You have one unplayed Informed Citizen report,>> her lenscape announced. <<Beginning now.>>

She wiped the water from her eyes.

Tropical Storm Rytta overtook the coast late Saturday night, causing storm surges to assail the lower west zones. Damage includes eight destroyed solar grids. Restoration teams have been working through the night to repair the grids. Efforts have been slowed by the approach of Tropical Storm Senica. Expect rolling power disruptions in Zones 198–252 until replacement is complete. Water shortages have worsened in Zones 100, 103, 141, and 306 due to temporary closure of two contaminated desalination plants. Citizens from water-rich zones are encouraged to revert or donate their water allotments to affected areas. An outbreak of C. auris has spread through Zones 122, 123, and 125, causing border closures until the outbreak is deemed controlled.

<<Would you like to donate your water allotment to help the affected zones?>> her lenscape prompted. Grace selected <<yes>> and gave seven percent of her monthly allotment. Maybe she could give more once she'd had time to sit down and run the household numbers.

When Grace stepped out of the bathroom, her body wrapped only in a towel, she found Heron standing in the living room below, a cup of koffee in his hand.

The extra blanket and pillow had been returned to

their closet, and the living room looked untouched. His hair was still mussed.

He took a sip and smacked his lips. "Koffee is ready. And I asked your ChefMate to make breakfast. Eggs, bacon, and toast."

"Thank you." She used a second towel to squeeze the excess water out of the ends of her hair.

He was staring at her again with that unreadable look in his eyes. She'd begun to worry he could see up her towel from his angle.

But his eyes weren't on her legs. They were pinned to her shoulder as he mounted the stairs slowly, careful not to slosh the second koffee over the rim of the mug.

"What?" she asked, the hair on her arms prickling. "Do you need to use the bathroom?"

He stopped on the landing, half a meter between them.

She followed his gaze to her shoulder and realized it must be the scars.

"How far down does it go?" he asked, his voice tight.

Grace cupped her breast with the towel, keeping it covered, and opened the side, peeling back the bamboo fabric enough to expose herself from throat to hip.

The crushed velvet of her skin, warped and ruined, trailed over the hip bone to the top of her thigh. There the skin evened out and grew smooth again.

Grace thought he was going to reach out and touch her, if not for the koffee in each hand.

But he didn't.

His cheeks were full of color when he met her gaze again. His eyes looked bluer.

"I didn't realize they ran this deep."

"They do." She watched his face, searching it for judgment. But she found none.

"Did you lose sensation, too?"

"I did."

He licked his lips. "I remember you saying you'd refused to have the scars removed. But I don't remember why."

It was true that the hospital offered to remove the scarred tissue and replace it completely. Such procedures were routine and easily done in the medical facilities they had available in Zone 2. But cosmetic surgery of any kind was elective. They couldn't make her do it, unlike the arm replacement, which had been ruled essential in order for her to keep her job.

What could she tell him?

That it had been a decision made of bitterness? Out of anger born of her loss? That she hadn't wanted to give the people around her the chance to forget what had happened, the chance to look at her and imagine a world where sons and husbands weren't ripped out of your life?

That she wanted a physical, tangible reminder for herself, too. Part of her was dead, lost, irretrievable. And there was no forgetting it.

He searched her eyes, waiting.

She answered honestly. "I didn't want to. It felt like something to do for other people, to make them more comfortable. It wouldn't have restored sensation either way."

And it would've done nothing for her own peace of mind, her own happiness.

The ChefMate beeped. "Mr. Jane, your breakfast is ready."

Heron stepped back as if the spell had been broken. "Here."

He offered her the extra cup of koffee, holding it long enough for her to put her towel back in place.

"Thank you."

"I'll set up the table. Then use the bathroom, if that's okay with you."

"Absolutely."

Ten minutes later, they were both at the breakfast table, their hair wet and bellies grumbling.

She noted his crisp, unwrinkled clothes. "You changed."

"Arjun brought me some things while you were asleep." He flicked his eyes up to hers as he added more creamer to his koffee. "He didn't stay."

She snorted. "Why do you say it like that?"

"In case you're upset about someone coming over to your house without permission."

Grace brought the warm koffee to her lips. "He's your partner. You don't need my permission to see him."

He looked at his plate for a moment as if considering what to say. Then the brightness returned, that lightness she'd come to expect from him. Was it only her imagination that his lips looked tight?

He gestured to her plate with his fork. "If you don't eat that, I will."

The smell of bacon made her stomach gurgle in anticipation. She laid her cloth napkin in her lap and picked up her utensils.

She was about five bites in when he asked, "Are we going straight to the office or do you have another destination in mind? There's nothing on the agenda until eleven twenty-five, when you're meeting with the junior inspectors."

She lifted the koffee and took a sip. "That depends."

"On?"

"Whether or not you can do something. Illegal."

Heron sat up straighter, his interest piqued. "Careful, Gray. The dark side is addictive."

She pressed on. "Can you create a back door to CyTown?"

"What do you mean by 'back door'?"

"I'm thinking of the way we spoke to Lix Richards after he was in custody. His lenscape had been deactivated, but we were still able to reach him."

Heron considered this, sipping his koffee, his gaze distant and contemplative. "CyTown isn't connected to any field terminals that I'm aware of. It'll be a matter of accessing their network directly."

He slid another slice of bacon into his mouth, his gaze tilted up as his mind worked through the problem.

"Actually, I can. I can't mimic the full sensory experience like you'd get if you were in one of their body units, but if we find a way to hack someone's reality, we can get in and have a look around, sure. There's only one problem."

Grace scooped the egg onto her toast and placed the bacon on top. "Only one?"

"Like Rise pointed out, CyTown isn't a shared reality. It's made up of whatever was created for you. The people you meet or love inside are essentially part of the program. No one is real."

Grace didn't miss the emphasis on *or love*. He was still mad about what she'd said last night.

She kept her face blank, not wanting to reengage the issue. "Okay. And?"

"*And* I don't think you want us to wander around a bunch of useless programming. We need to have an objective."

"My objective is to interview Tristan and see if his mind is actually deteriorating."

"Right," he said. "So we need to target *his* CyTown, and that's harder, because we won't be part of the actual programming. If I don't do it right, we'll seem like ghosts or goblins. Something weird. Not a good guise for interviewing."

"You need to make us solid enough that he mistakes us for part of the programming, you mean?"

He spread butter across his toast. "Exactly. *That's* what will take some time. I have to figure out how to create CyTown-compatible avatars that will fully integrate with *his* CyTown. Then we'll use those avatars to navigate his reality and speak to him. And all of this programming will have to be clean enough that it doesn't set off CyTown's security."

Grace reached for the H-nee and a knife. She spread it along her toast. "While you're working on our CyTown back door, I'll take a look at his history and see if we can uncover some suspects and motive. It would be helpful to find out which of his ideas might have gotten him killed."

<<Accept cache from heronjane1?>>

She cocked her head. "You did it already?"

"My mind is a busy place." He crossed to the counter to refill his koffee. "I like to run programs in the background."

Grace accepted the data cache and opened several files onto her lenscape. The blue light of her eyes reflected off the white ceramic plate, giving their breakfast an eerie glow.

"May I?" <<Accept scapeshare with heronjane1?>>

Grace accepted his second request, and their scapes merged.

He began to sort and drop files, explaining as he went.

"These are his publications. I found quite a few in e-zines and broadcasting sites. Most of it is fringe-ranting, screaming into the void, as it were, but a few pieces broke into the mainstream. I stuck to the mainstream pieces since those would've had the most attention, but included a few fringe pieces that give a good overview of his positions. This file here contains the audio segments. He has over two thousand hours."

Grace ripped the toast with her teeth. <<*Why?*>>

<<He has a MyCast that airs twice a week. The show runs ninety minutes on average, but sometimes he goes as long as three hours.>>

<<Who can listen to him for three hours?>>

"He has a nice voice," Heron said aloud. He returned his koffee to its saucer. "And when he gets really passionate, he's engaging."

With her mouth empty again, she switched to verbal speech. "Don't tell me you've already listened to all of this?"

Grace wouldn't have been surprised, given the technology at Heron's disposal.

Heron snorted. "No, only some of it. You'll need a keyword or search strategy to comb it all, is my point."

"If there's any variety at all, it'll be impossible to know what he was targeted for with this level of content."

"Difficult, but not impossible. Most of it is quite similar."

"Can you get a list of the people who listen to this show? Maybe we can figure out who might have heard something they didn't like."

"Over two million tune in to his audio show."

"Two *million?*" Grace marveled. "How have I never heard of this guy?"

"Minor celebrities are a dime a dozen these days. But here." He moved a file into the center of her lenscape, relabeling it before her eyes to *The Good Stuff.*

"Here are the articles and audio clips most relevant to

our search. They'll give you a good idea of what his core argument is."

"We can start here, but we're looking for someone who needs to discredit him."

Heron brought the koffee to the table and refilled her mug. "That would explain the forced admittance to CyTown. It would make him look like a hypocrite."

"Exactly." She stared at the koffee, something in her stomach twisting. Her throat was a hint tighter when she flicked her eyes up to meet his. "Thank you."

He winked. "You're welcome."

"We should keep our ears tuned to any mention of his move. The person who leaks his whereabouts might be the one wanting to discredit him."

"Noted."

She checked her time stamp. "We need to get going. Or we'll miss her."

"Who?"

"Lenorie."

"On it." Heron scooped up the plates and moved them to the wash area so that the kitchen could take care of the mess.

<<We're on our way over to interview Lenorie,>> she pinged her mother. <<I hope you don't mind.>>

This was the most diplomatic way of inquiring whether or not her mother would be dressed and Henry properly stowed upon her arrival.

A hint of a smile tugged at Heron's lips.

Grace caught it. "What?"

"Did you just ping your mother to tell her we're on our way?"

"Yes, why?"

The smile deepened. "Because you always get this look when you're talking to her. You look *pained*."

"It's not her."

He arched a brow. "What is it then?"

The scent of him filled the auto. The fact that it was his scent mixing with her soap gave her a strange tingling sensation on the back of her neck. Or perhaps it was the newfound heaviness in her limbs.

"It's Henry."

"Ah, you have automatonophobia." He seemed disappointed by this news.

Grace could argue that she wasn't *completely* horrified by the Bois, Grrls, and Duos found all over the city as personal companions and domestic servants. She encountered them every day in her job and was fully functional in their presence.

"Have you told your mom?" he asked.

"No."

"Don't want to hurt her feelings?"

"It's none of my business if—" She found she couldn't bring herself to finish the sentence. "I just don't understand why she wants to…with a bot."

Heron cocked his head, his lips tugging into a smirk. "They're learning AI. They figure out what you like pretty quickly. They're designed to anticipate what you want, when you want it, how much you want, and they absolutely do *not* tire prematurely."

Grace felt the color rising in her face.

"Also, they can tell when you want to change it up, so it doesn't get repetitious or—"

Grace held up a hand.

Heron snorted. "Personally, I prefer the unpredictability of human sex. People surprise me. Maybe I don't even *know* what I want. Besides, I'm a giver. It's impossible to give pleasure to a bot."

Grace refused to ask him if he'd ever had sex with a bot before.

"Why do you still have the Boi in your closet if you hate it?" He scraped something from beneath his nails.

"I can't get rid of it. I've tried." She told him the harrowing tale of trying to return the Boi with no success. "They won't take it if it doesn't have a receipt."

He seemed to consider this while the auto stopped in front of Caroline's living unit.

Heron moved to get out of the auto, but Grace put a hand on his arm.

He froze. "What is it?"

"My mother never responded to my ping, and she didn't come out to meet us."

He looked at the door and back to her. His face pinched in concentration.

"It's only her, Henry, and Lenorie in there."

Grace activated her own police-issued scanner. It penetrated the walls of her mother's condo, and she noted the two forms in the living room, a third upstairs. But it wasn't clear who was who.

She released her hold on his arm. "How do you know it's Lenorie?"

He climbed out before reaching back to help her. "I log everyone's biometrics when I meet them."

Still, Grace pushed against the door tentatively. "Mom? Mom, is everything okay?"

Lenorie sat on the sofa, her head tilted back. Her mother crouched in front of her with a towel.

A black eye was forming over Lenorie's right socket, the swelling along her cheekbone pronounced and deeply red.

Heron gasped. "What happened?"

"Someone attacked me outside my apartment. He *hit* me."

"Did you report it to the police?" Grace asked.

"Yes! I went to the precinct to talk to you, but you weren't there. The guy at the desk took my name and information though."

Grace pinged Lore. <<Can I get Lenorie Range's testimony when you have time?>>

He pinged back. <<Are you psychic? I was two minutes from contacting you. We're on our way to her apartment now.>>

The report arrived seconds later, and Grace read it as Lenorie ran through the details for Caroline and Heron.

Heron was in the kitchen extracting ice from the refrigerator. "Kitty, where are your towels?"

"Under the ceramic ballerina, darling."

Lenorie touched her swollen eye and hissed. "I realized I'd forgotten my sunbrella, and I went back inside to get it. When I turn around, this guy is in the doorway of my apartment, blocking my exit. He's looking around my place like a complete *creeper*. I tell him to buzz off, but he won't move. I shove him because I'm trying to get out of my apartment before he gets the bright idea to come in or something, and he hits me. Hauls back and *hits* me in the face! Can you believe it?"

"Barbaric." Heron adjusted some ice in a cloth towel before holding it up to her eye.

Lenorie frowned. "So I'm in the doorway, cradling my eye, *bleeding*, and he starts tearing my apartment apart. I turn on my lens capture and start recording the whole thing, but he doesn't even care. He goes through my cabinets, my bedroom, my bathroom. At this point, I realize he's an absolute crazy person and get out of there. What the hell was he looking for?"

<<Two units have arrived at her building,>> Lore pinged Grace. <<We'll report to you once our initial assessment is complete.>>

She thanked him.

<<Sure thing, Commander.>>

"We have officers at your apartment now," Grace told Lenorie. "If he's still there, we'll take him into custody. Did you give the video feed to Inspector Duchovny?"

Lenorie hissed, scowling at Heron. "Yeah, I gave them the recording."

<<Not to bring up bots again so soon, but they're going to realize that's an Arnold 2000,>> Heron pinged. His attention remained on the ice bag in his hands and Lenorie's wound.

"I have something for your cheek," Caroline said, rising. Her knees popped as she stood. "One second."

Grace took a seat on the sofa, a cushion between her and Lenorie. To Heron she said, <<Why would a bot go to her apartment?>>

"The guy was a complete lunatic. He was on drugs or something."

<<They're mostly retrieval units. Someone must've programmed him to find something. Search and destroy, maybe.>>

"Did you keep any of your brother's work at your apartment?" Grace asked.

"No, I don't have any of his stuff there. Do you think they were searching for Tristan's work?"

"It's possible," Grace confirmed.

Heron offered her the wrapped bag of ice. Clearly, he was tired of holding it up to her face. She shook her head and pushed Heron's hand away. "You *do* think he was taken against his will."

Grace wasn't ready to tell her about the residual imaging—of seeing him hauled out in the dead of night.

"We're still gathering evidence, but in light of your attack, you need to assume the worst. Someone might want to hurt you both."

"Ow!" She slapped Heron's wrist. "That *hurts*."

<<Drama queen,>> Heron pinged. <<I wasn't even touching her.>>

<<You mean someone besides you loves attention?>>

He glanced at her. <<Ouch.>>

"Lenorie, we went to CyTown to speak to Tristan, and we were denied access to him. They say it's because he has a deteriorating brain condition."

"That's bullshit!" Lenorie cried. "There was nothing wrong with his brain. Except that he was too damn smart for his own good."

"Is it possible that his doctor diagnosed him with a condition, and he simply didn't tell you?"

"No, why would he do that? I'm a home care nurse! And his sister. I'd be the first person he'd tell if something like that was true. Who better to take care of him than someone with my experience?"

<<She has a point.>> Heron stepped back to make room for Caroline, who'd returned with a bottle in one fist.

"He had high blood pressure and ate too much sodium, and had some gout in his feet, which he *refused* to get lasered, but otherwise he was in perfect health!"

Caroline squeezed a little bit of cream onto the tip of her finger. "Okay, this might sting a little, but it will pull all that swelling and redness right out. I promise to be gentle."

Lenorie cut her eyes at Heron. "You can't be worse than this one."

<<I love it when someone gives you a hard time.>>

He glared at Grace. <<You delight in my misery?>>

<<No,>> she pinged. <<But I enjoy it when you can't charm someone.>>

<<It's always a surprise to me, too.>> He placed a hand on his hip, watching Caroline work.

"Tristan's physician is listed as Dr. Ezekiel Tove. That's who gave him the evaluation for his CyTown residency. Had he ever mentioned Tove before the evaluation?" Grace asked.

"Our family physician is Winnie Ute. Why would he go see a separate physician?"

Heron cut his eyes to Grace. <<Maybe he didn't. At least not willingly.>>

"We aren't sure, but we'll interview Tove and Ute both."

To Heron she pinged, <<Find openings in their appointment books, please.>>

<<Commander,>> Lore pinged. <<We have a situation here at the Range apartment.>>

<<Show me.>>

<<Accept scapeshare with LDuchovny34?>> Grace accepted.

The scene at Lenorie's apartment was jarring compared to the little gathering in her mother's living unit. The clean, comfortable domestic scene was replaced by people shouting, screaming, running. Sirens blared around her as officers pushed to organize the chaos.

<<Can you see it?>> Lore asked.

<<Yes,>> Grace replied. The apartment was in flames.

NINE

GRACE AND HERON climbed from the white auto onto the congested sidewalk. Residents stood in clusters, shielding their eyes as they regarded the black smoke billowing above. Officials ran in and out of the building, securing the area as best they could, while the firefighters applied a liberal dose of foam to the fire, extinguishing the last of its flames.

Heron's eyes shone as he spoke beside her. "Ute is on vacation for the next three weeks. She has a tourist visa for EU Zone 6 until the fourth."

"Convenient," Grace said, shielding her eyes as she searched the windows for any sign of movement.

"I reviewed her appointment book for the last eighteen months, and there's no mention of Tristan except for a physical from last year. In the physical's notes, there's the gout the sister mentioned and also the high blood pressure, but that's it. Nothing about his brain. Not even a mention about a referral."

She didn't bother to point out the confidential nature of medical records or that they'd need the constable's approval to have even accessed them legally. Heron was going to do whatever Heron wanted to do. She was getting used to this fact. Sometimes she even liked it.

She spotted Lore shouldering his way through the crowd, trying to reach them. "And Tove?"

"He's got an opening at twelve forty-five. I've added us to his schedule. I've also moved the meeting with the junior officers to sixteen hundred. We'll have plenty of time."

"Good work," she said as his blue light clicked off.

"My pleasure, Commander." He rocked onto his heels, beaming.

"Commander! Thank you for coming." Lore stopped a foot short of her. His breath had not yet caught up to him, but he squeezed out a nod to Heron. "Inspector Jane."

It was Grace's job to appear on the scene for all crimes that endangered human life, including arson. "We know it was an Arnold that assaulted Range and entered her apartment, but did it also start the fire?"

"That's unclear." He used a bamboo cloth to dab at his damp brow. "We've requested a warrant from the constable for the Arnold. We have the serial number of the bot and are trying to figure out who it's registered to, but there's been no luck yet."

"Can I get that number?" Heron asked.

Lore ran a hand through his dark hair. "Sure."

Smoke rolled from one of the broken windows. "I'm assuming that's her unit."

"The flames are out," he assured her, hooking his thumbs into the waistband of his pants. "The fire is completely under control."

"Smoldering is normal," she said, hoping to ease him. "As long as you evacuated the floor until the cleanup crew comes, it should be fine."

"We did. We did."

Heron touched her arm to get her attention. "The bot is registered to a rental shop in Low Town. Body Electric. They lease by the hour. Let's call them and ask if they're missing an Arnold and who might've taken it out."

"Inspector Duchovny can do that." She nodded to Lore. "We need to keep our twelve forty-five appointment."

Heron looked wounded, a slight pout to his lower lip. "Right. Of course."

<<This is part of the job,>> she pinged him. <<We have to delegate, prioritize. We can't chase every rabbit in the grass.>>

<<But I like the chase part.>>

<<We need to remain indifferent or they might get the idea that this is a case we're already working.>>

His eyes finally lit with recognition. To Lore, he said, "But you'll let us know what the shop says and if any information surfaces as to why the bot might have targeted Range?"

"If it's a bot shop, it'll be insured out the ass." Lore wiped his brow again. "They'll claim no liability for whatever we find, I'm sure."

"We won't let that stop us." Grace pulled her sunbrella from her pocket and opened it. The ruthless sun threw her shadow across the sidewalk.

<<Incoming,>> Heron pinged.

Grace looked up in time to see Adams shouldering his way through the crowd. He tossed encouraging words to the inspectors he passed, but his eyes were on her.

<<God, look at him. It's like he hasn't eaten for weeks. Absolutely ravenous.>>

Grace ignored this. It was hard enough to manage her emotions around Adams without Heron in her ear.

<<Did he just rake your body with his eyes? Does he have *no* shame?>>

<<Be quiet or I'll mute you,>> she warned. To Adams she said, "Good afternoon, Commander."

"Grace," he said, a smile spreading on his lips. He barely cut his eyes to Heron and Lore beside her. "Inspector Duchovny. Inspector Jane."

<<Why are we inspectors and you're *Grace*? Disrespectful, I say.>>

Grace didn't bother explaining that for Adams it would be the reverse. The lack of formality was the compliment. An attempt at intimacy.

Adams searched her face. "What time?"

"We moved the junior inspector meeting to sixteen hundred. I thought we could—"

"No, what time for tonight? I'm still taking you to the induction. We need to be there by twenty hundred."

Someone called Lore's name, and he excused himself. Heron remained on the walkway, his hands in his pockets.

When Grace looked at him instead of Adams, Heron arched his brow. <<Yes? Do you need me for something?>>

She looked away. "I can be ready by seven."

"I don't mind waiting. I'll come earlier if you want me to."

<<Gag,>> Heron pinged.

Grace fought to keep her face neutral. "I'll meet you at the precinct at seven fifteen."

Adams looked like he wanted to say more. *Do* more.

<<If he kisses your hand or something, I'm going to vomit.>>

But Adams was backing away, a smile on his face. "Seven fifteen it is. See you then."

Heron's shoulder grazed hers under her sunbrella as

Adams disappeared into the crowd again. "His grin worries me."

"Does it?" Grace asked, a headache forming behind her eyes. She did the math, counting the hours since her last koffee.

"It's what my mother called a *scheming* smile. Whatever he's up to, it can't be good."

"Which mother?"

"Victoria. What's wrong? You're squinting."

"I'm getting a headache. I need a koffee. And we need an auto."

Heron bowed dramatically, his blue eyes lighting again. "As you wish."

HER NEW KOFFEE was nearly emptied by the time the City-Ride auto rolled to a stop. Dr. Tove's practice was located on the eighth floor of Westside General, the largest health-care facility in the zone. By pairing with the building's onboarding system, they were able to navigate the maze of hallways and patients to the doctor's suite.

Outside his office door, Grace tossed her cup into the recycling compactor.

A human receptionist looked up as she entered, Heron closing the door behind them.

He was young, bubbly, with bright anime eyes.

"We have an appointment to see Dr. Tove."

The receptionist's gaze slid from Grace to Heron. "I must say, you'd make beautiful children."

This stopped Grace's mind. "Excuse me?"

Heron leaned into the counter, his swagger dialed to its max. "I mean, he's not wrong."

"Has Dr. Tove seen you before?" the receptionist asked,

pushing black curls away from his face. Grace recognized the filter for what it was.

"No, but—"

"Dr. Tove asks that all new patients fill out his questionnaire before he commences with the examination." His filter gave his face a shiny appearance, glitter sparking in the corners of his eyes. Grace nulled the filter, seeing his face for what it really was, and found a middle-aged man with a soft belly and slumped shoulders.

<<Accept welcome cache from ToveOffice4?>>

Even the voice had been altered. Now, a new, gravelly voice matched its exterior. "Be sure to specify who will be carrying the child or if you plan to rent a womb for the duration of your—"

"No." Grace pinched her eyes together. "We aren't a couple. We're not here for a fertility consultation. I'm Commander Buteo, and this is Inspector Heron Jane. We need to speak to Dr. Tove regarding an investigation."

The lenscape prompt disappeared.

"Oh," the man said, straightening. "I'll tell Dr. Tove you're here then. Take a seat, please."

Once they were alone in the waiting room, Heron said, "I think you disappointed him. Think of the beautiful children. And he's cute. I hate disappointing cute people. They take everything *so* personally."

"Walter Judge is married, and not cute at all."

She sent the citizen file that filled her lenscape.

Heron snorted. "Not what I pictured under those doe eyes and all that glitter, but good for him."

A side door opened, and Judge appeared holding it ajar. "This way, please."

Tove's office was cramped, with books lining every visible wall space and crowding the surface of his desk.

Piles had spilled out onto the floor, rising as high as Grace's chest in some places, others stopping at her knees.

Behind the desk was an old man. Grace suspected he was seventy at least, perhaps older. She searched for a filter but found none. That meant the wrinkles, the thinning hair, and the small black eyes sitting behind glasses were all his own.

It was interesting—the fact that he wore glasses. No one wore glasses when vision modification was cheap and quick. She wondered why he relied on such an archaic form of eye correction.

It was also an anomaly that she'd kept her scars. Who was she to judge?

"Dr. Tove." Grace began by extending her hand, offering her embedded profile chip. "Thank you for seeing us."

His hand barely brushed her skin. "Sure. How can I help you?"

Grace noted the sweat on his brow and the dampness at his collar, despite the chilliness of the office.

She waited for Heron to finish introducing himself before saying, "We have some questions about a patient of yours. Tristan Range."

"Okay." He shifted in his seat, lacing and unlacing his fingers. "I'm happy to help."

<<He doesn't look happy to help,>> Heron pinged, following her lead and taking the chair beside hers. <<He looks like he's going to puke.>>

Grace adjusted herself in the chair. "Tristan was recently admitted to CyTown Towers, the cyber community. I'm sure you've heard of it?"

Tove's tongue darted out to swipe at dry, chapped lips. "Of course."

"We needed to interview him but were denied because

he is listed as a deteriorating patient. His file says he has a brain condition that renders him unstable. Can you confirm that this was your diagnosis?"

Dr. Tove reached up and pulled the glasses off the end of his nose. His eyes lit blue, his lenscape activated, reviewing information that they couldn't see.

"Tristan Range?"

"Yes. Male. Thirty-eight."

<<His hands are shaking,>> Heron pinged.

<<I see them.>>

<<He looks familiar to me for some reason. Has he been in the news or something?>>

<<Not that I'm aware,>> she replied.

"Ah, yes. I see." The blue light faded, and the doctor slid the glasses onto his nose. "Tristan Range was diagnosed with Lewy Body Disease."

"Isn't thirty-eight very young for that?"

"It's rare but not unheard of."

"It's my understanding that all CyTown residents must receive an examination before entering into full residency."

"That's correct." He shifted in his seat again.

<<There must be tacks on his cushion,>> Heron pinged. <<He looks uncomfortable. Do you think it's me or you? We both showered this morning.>>

<<Nervousness doesn't denote guilt. Some people simply don't like the police.>>

Aloud she asked, "Can you confirm that you completed Range's exam and signed off on his admittance to CyTown?"

Dr. Tove licked his lips. "I did. Yes."

"Was Range complicit in this arrangement? Do you have verbal or written consent of his agreement to admittance?"

"I do, yes. One moment."

<<Accept informational cache from ToveT3?>>

"Thank you." Grace reviewed the document, letting Heron share her screen.

<<This is little more than a note. Anyone could've composed this. Even if this signature is his, it could've been forged.>>

Grace added the document to her file and ended the scapeshare.

"How many of these pre-residency evaluations would you say you complete in a month, Dr. Tove?"

"Eight to ten." He pushed his glasses up on the bridge of his nose.

"And of those examinations, what percentage would you say have debilitating brain conditions?"

He only looked at her. "I'm not sure. I don't think I've kept track of that."

"An educated guess is fine."

Grace turned on her lie-detection program.

"Twenty or thirty percent."

Lie.

"And would you say that percentage is high for a population of our size?"

"What do you mean?"

"Do you think seeing thirty percent of patients with brain damage is a high number considering Zone 2's population?"

"No."

Lie.

The office door opened, and the receptionist poked his head in. "Dr. Tove, your next appointment is here. Should I reschedule?"

Grace rose, motioning for Heron to do the same. "That's not necessary. I only have two more questions.

"Do you think that Mr. Range's move to CyTown was the best possible option for him in his condition?"

"Yes, I do."

Lie.

"And do you believe that Tristan wanted to be a CyTown resident?"

"Yes. That is what he told me."

Lie.

<<He's lying,>> Heron pinged.

<<Everyone lies.>> The real question was why.

TEN

GRACE CLOSED her office door and sank into her desk chair. She had the harried feeling that often overcame her when she spent the day traveling across the city, making multiple stops. It pressed against the mind, adding a weight that even her second bullet of koffee seemed unable to completely abate.

But the junior inspector meeting had gone well. Grace was pleased with the quality of the trainees who'd been promoted to the position. And seeing a great deal of earnestness and enthusiasm always gave her hope.

And it was hard not to be amused as they hung on to her every word. She detailed only the mundane aspects of their position and the progression they should expect from junior inspector to assistant inspector to full inspector—should they remain diligent in their efforts.

Still, their questions had been endearing, if exhausting.

Her eyes swept the empty office. Her bare desk held the picture of her and Davion from their honeymoon and a picture that Kaiden had drawn of the Earth telling the moon a joke, in a child's uneven scrawl.

Her heart clenched but didn't collapse. She breathed.

Her calorie watch beeped, notifying her that she was past due for a meal, offering selections that would satisfy her caloric needs.

<<I saw that,>> Heron pinged. <<I'll pick up lunch on my way back. You want falafel?>>

<<You're still syncing your calorie watch to mine? What if you're starving?>>

<<Gray, I've never missed a meal in my life. And I assume that's a yes to the falafel. I'll get it after the tour.>>

<<Thank you.>>

Grace turned her lenscape to away mode, seeing the green light on her ear reflected across the patina of her bare desk.

Heron had volunteered to help Lore give the junior inspectors a tour of the facility—likely because Heron himself was not as familiar with the building as he should be—leaving Grace to herself.

The silence of the office pressed in on her from all sides. She closed her eyes, feeling the cool air from the ventilation system flutter over her delicate skin. From outside her door came the muffled sounds of the precinct hard at work.

I'm going to fall asleep like this, she thought.

Reluctantly, she peeled her eyes open and activated her lenscape, the green reflection on the desk switching to blue.

Accessing her files, she found Heron's *The Good Stuff* folder and opened it. Conveniently, he'd labeled one of the essays, *The Price of More*, as *start here*.

"If you're sure," she murmured to herself.

Tristan's article expanded in her vision, and she began to read.

. . .

Given our current difficulties in resource management, it can be argued that VR living is a necessity. After all, it offers advantages to a civilization wrestling with deficiencies such as ours. Physical bodies can be maintained minimally in VR. Any sufficient body rig will do. Therefore, it is cheaper and more efficient to keep a percentage—perhaps a large percentage—of our population sustained through virtual reality—thereby lessening the strain on the few remaining resources we have.

However, this argument is easier to sell to some than others.

For those in the outer zones, a hyper-realistic VR life would be preferable to one of starvation and lack. The lives they could experience (if we can call VR reality experience or a life) would be far more comfortable and extravagant than any could have in real-time.

But if you are an elitist, you can be convinced to buy real-time itself—at a premium.

If only the desperate must rely on VR to indulge their programmed whims—an excellent steak dinner, a ski vacation in the Swiss Alps, one night in the bed of Molly Devalore—then the rich will pay a premium for that authentic, real-time experience. To *breathe the actual air of our golden cities.*

A golden city.

That's what Davion had called Zone 2. It had always fascinated her, to listen to his earliest experiences in the zone, what it had been like for him to see it for the first time. Since Grace had spent nearly all her life in the zone, she couldn't imagine what it looked like to someone for the first time. She had asked if it was the rose-gold solar panels covering most of the buildings that earned the zone its name.

No, he'd said. *It's more than that.*

He'd tried to describe the enormity of it. The way the tops of buildings seemed to disappear into the sky above. How everything shimmered and glowed. How many people there were, on the streets, in buildings. How he could walk for miles and not see an open expanse of land.

From his descriptions, she'd gathered that the outer zones were very rural compared to her urban experience. Perhaps houses were far and few between, the population scarce.

He said even the use of a lenscape, something he hadn't purchased until he was nearly thirty, took some getting used to.

The idea that people lived without lenscapes baffled her. *How do you pay for things? How do you know the temperatures and sun rating? How do you find your way around or look up information?*

He'd only smiled at her questions.

Grace skimmed down the page.

I would've believed that reality was a given. The very initiation of birth, breathing, seems to entitle one to a present, real-time reality.

Yet those brilliant marketing schemes now convince us that we must consider the quality *of our reality.*

That spending one's hours as a vegetable, milked by a machine, is not what anyone could call a quality *life—no matter how extravagant the programming.*

Grace closed this essay and opened a second one at random, not even noting its title.

All is recorded, analyzed. My shopping habits, my biometrics, how I speak to a lover. Every piece of information I search for, all my interests and curiosities.

They offer me more of the same and less of what might surprise me, delight me, challenge me, allow my mind and spirit to expand and grow. How small my world becomes.

And how easy I am to manipulate now…

Am I still myself, or does every selection make me more what they want me to be?

At what point do we stop functioning as autonomous beings and become part of the endless programming?

The office door opened, and Heron stepped inside with a falafel in one hand and a water in the other.

Grace checked the time and sat up, alarmed.

"It's already five thirty," she said, accepting the offered food while also slipping her feet back into her shoes. "I'm going to be late."

"Oh no," Heron said flatly.

"Heron," she warned.

"I'm tempted to give you some juicy tidbit of information that will consume your mind for the next six hours, but I suppose agenda-keeping is part of my job description. You'd better go."

"Do you have some juicy tidbit?"

He pressed his lips together and shrugged. "I don't know. *Do* I?"

"Ruthless." Grace took the falafel and squeezed his hand. "Thank you. I'll see you later."

"Don't mind me. I'll be here. Trying to solve this case of the creepy body snatchers." Looking as sullen as a kicked puppy, he sank into her chair.

Grace spent the ride home eating her falafel and reading Tristan's work. This article was titled *Capital Punishment.*

It had one of the highest read rates.

The very fact that we shackle zone offenders to the Midnight Train and exile them to the stormlands suggests that we view real-time reality as an inalienable right. If even capital offenses such as murder cannot deprive a person of their right to life and reality, then the idea others can be subjugated into forced virtuality is depraved.

At home, she changed into a sensible dress and ankle boots, while his words swirled in her head. She turned them over and over like a puzzle box in her mind, seeing how the tone and content of his writing might enter a person's head and stay there, burrowing like a worm into recesses long overlooked.

Based on the content alone, it was impossible to compose a list of suspects, even a short one. No offender or nemesis was called out by name in Range's articles or on his MyCasts. He wasn't ranting against a particular corporate entity or employer.

The only one connected to him who'd been suspicious thus far was Dr. Tove, with his fidgeting and profuse sweating and lies about forced entry into CyTown.

And now Grace was sure that he'd been taken by force and submitted to the Towers.

However, belief meant nothing in the course of law. She needed proof.

Even if her suspect list was a total of one, there was no clear reason why Dr. Tove would target Range. No motive. Nothing Range had said would have hurt Tove in any possible way.

From what Grace could see, Range had been born and raised here in Zone 2, supported financially from patrons of his MyCast. He was a free agent, with a free mouth.

But she hadn't read or heard anything so inflammatory that a man need be abducted over it.

Except he'd mentioned the abduction outright, hadn't he?

The idea others can be subjugated into forced virtuality is depraved.

What was this "forced virtuality" that he was referring to? Who had begun circulating the idea? It seemed part of a larger, ongoing argument. She applied the search term to all the articles Heron had gathered and found that five articles and MyCast entries returned matches.

She moved these items to a separate file, noting that the date of each fell within the last two months.

A recent passion then.

She did her best to get ready and change without opening another of Tristan's files, but the work was fascinating. She was nearly ready when Heron pinged her.

<<Adams is pacing. I have half a mind to tell him you've cancelled. It would be satisfying to see his face.>>

She checked the time. It was after 19:00. She was going to be late even if she left right now.

<<Don't torture him,>> Grace said. <<We might need his help someday.>>

<<I'd rather chew off my beautiful, sumptuous arm than accept assistance from this vainglorious prig.>>

<<Wow.>> Grace commanded the house to lock behind her as she hurried to the waiting auto. <<Such depth of feeling. How do you contain it all inside you?>>

She could practically hear his dramatic sigh through her lenscape. <<It's a mystery.>>

ELEVEN

WHEN GRACE WALKED into the precinct, she saw Lore first. He was sitting on the edge of his desk, gesticulating as he shared a story with his rapt audience. Heron was standing beside him, serving as the rapt audience. At the right moment, Heron burst into laughter.

Then Lore's laughter died as he saw her. He straightened, rolling back his shoulders. "Commander."

"At ease, Duchovny." She smiled. "We're all off the clock here."

The man's shoulders remained stiff.

To Heron she said, "Where's Adams?"

Heron didn't answer. Instead, his eyes were pinned to her red dress. It cut low, exposing her collarbones, throat, and more scars than either of them had probably seen on her before.

"Commander Adams is in the bathroom," Lore offered, already cutting his gaze away. When Heron remained speechless, Lore nudged him.

Focus returned to his eyes. Heron cleared his throat as

if he'd been trying to speak this whole time. "You look great."

Why did he sound angry saying it?

"Yes, you look very nice, Commander. I like your earrings." Lore offered her a shy smile.

"Thank you, Inspector." Grace touched the teardrop garnets Davion had given her for Christmas one year.

Strange silence stretched between them again. This time Heron's attention was on Lore. Lore looked frozen on the verge of speech.

What is wrong with these two? Grace thought.

When Lore still didn't speak, Heron elbowed him in the side.

Grace arched a brow. To Heron, she pinged, <<What's going on?>>

<<He wants to say something to you.>>

<<Leave and maybe he'll speak up.>>

Heron's lips twitched. <<I would, but one, I already know what he wants to say—I encouraged him to say it— and two, my luck, Adams will appear and whisk you away while I'm gone.>>

"Commander, I…" Lore began.

Heron pinged her again. <<It would help him if you didn't look like an imperial guard.>>

Grace cut him an annoyed look, but relaxed her shoulders, her stance. Gently she prompted, "Yes?"

Lore licked his lips and ran a hand through his hair. "Commander, I want to thank you, properly, for what you've done for me over the years."

"There's no—" *need*, she was about to say. But Heron was already there, shushing her.

<<Don't interrupt! He's been practicing this for a week.>>

<<How do you know?>>

<<I work very hard to be the de facto confidante in this precinct, Commander. Why do you think I have all the best gossip?>>

"You're too humble," Lore managed. "That's how you are with everyone, but for me…I don't think you realize what you've done for me."

"It's my responsibility as your senior officer to train you, support you, and see that you—"

"You saved my life," he barked out. "You saved my wife and daughters. I don't think I need to tell you how much they mean to me."

Grace's heart clenched, folded in on itself. *No, you don't.*

"I…I lost my first wife and daughter in the C. auris pandemic of 2594."

My father died in that, she thought. In truth Zone 2 had lost many people in that epidemic. Instead of pointing this out, she said, "I'm sorry for your loss."

"Yes, it was terrible." He took a deep breath, seeming to steady himself. "I feel like…I feel like you gave up your family, so that I didn't have to feel that pain again. We were close to the IED. *Very close,* and if you hadn't stopped it—if you hadn't left your family to go defuse it, I…I—"

He pressed his fingers into his temples as if to staunch the thought.

Finally, he met her eyes again. "I can never repay you for that, but I wanted you to know that I understand, *truly* understand, what you've done for me, and I'm indebted to you. Always. You're not alone."

She placed a hand on his shoulder and squeezed. "You don't need to repay me. Just keep doing your best, and that will be enough."

It will have to be.

His lip quivered and he broke the gaze, looking down at his lap. Then he nodded.

"Thank you." He dabbed at the corners of his eyes. "You'll never be able to replace them, your husband and son, but you can be happy again. I daresay, more happy. Because the second time around, everything will feel precious."

Irritation nipped her ears, but it didn't drive away the sadness. "I guess you would know."

"What's wrong?" Adams looked from Lore to Grace to Heron as if trying to make sense of the somber faces and tears.

<<Only you, ruining everything,>> Heron pinged.

Grace pasted on a smile. "Are you ready?"

He checked the time. "We're late. I've got my auto out front."

<<Oh, *his* auto,>> Heron pinged. <<I have an auto.>>

<<Are you going to be like this all night? A little voice in my ear?>>

Heron looked hurt. <<I thought you liked me as a little voice in your ear.>>

<<I do, but I'll need to concentrate while I'm at the event.>>

And this was true. Grace didn't intend to squander even a moment while inside. She wanted to record every face, every whisper, anything at all that might help her uncover who was responsible for the IED. For Davion's and Kaiden's murders.

"It's almost seven thirty," Adams pressed again, running his hands down the front of his suit.

"Beauty is worth waiting for," Heron said, his eyes meeting hers.

Adams's gaze raked up her body. He motioned toward the exit. "Yes, it is. Shall we?"

Grace looked away from Heron's sour expression and

gave Lore's shoulder one more squeeze. "I'll see you both later."

THE DOOR to Adams's black sedan opened as Grace approached. There was a moment of hesitation in her guts as she took in the dark windows and gleaming trim.

She'd had a precinct-issued auto exactly like this. Before it exploded.

Adams's hand pressed into her back, pushing her forward, clearly unaware of the glimmer of alarm ricocheting through her mind.

She took a breath and slid into the dark interior. He slid in behind her, the door sealing them inside.

They faced each other, inches between their bent knees.

"This is infinitely better than a CityRide," Adams said, running a hand down the front of his suit again before touching the leather seats. "I don't know why you don't order another auto."

I should think it was obvious. She didn't care to explain to him why she felt safer in the CityRides. Public transport they may be, but they were anonymous, random, and private enough for her tastes. And the chance of her blowing up in one was much lower than in a personal auto.

"I suppose you enjoy the profile it's added to your reputation," he said.

"What do you mean?"

He grinned, clearly pleased that he knew something she did not. "You haven't heard. My dear, Grace, forever the workaholic. Do you ever come up for air?"

She waited. She didn't bother to point out that *he* was the one talking about work, not her.

"Your poll numbers are astronomical. Before…the

accident…you already had a high rating. Sixty-eight percent to my measly forty-four percent. After, it climbed to eighty-two percent. It's been climbing ever since. People see you do the smallest thing, like take a CityRide auto, and begin to praise your humbleness."

"I'm not humble," she said. *I'm afraid.*

He shrugged. "People will always believe what they like about us. That comes with the position."

He reached forward, and for a terrible moment, Grace thought he was going to put his hand on her exposed knee. But instead, he reached for the compartment running along the side of the auto.

"Can I offer you a drink?"

"No, thank you."

He frowned, pulling a glass free. "Oh, come on. We're celebrating. This is your big night."

"About that." She adjusted her dress across her lap. "Do I have to go up on stage or—"

"No, no. It's not as formal as all that. They will simply call out your name, publicly acknowledging your admittance to the club. Mostly this is a chance for people to see you and welcome you. We'll chat, eat, drink. That's it. Think of it more as a meet and greet."

Her face must've conveyed her doubt.

He laughed. "It's a party, Grace. Do you remember what a party is?"

Her scarred face tried to force a smile and resisted. "I haven't had much to celebrate."

Grace's nose twinged at the sharp sting of liquor. He rolled his eyes up to her in a pantomime of sympathy. "This is true. Your losses have been great. I can't imagine the pain of losing a son."

"And my husband."

Adams's hand hesitated above his glass. "Do you want

to talk about it?"

"Not really."

He replaced the caps on the bottles and put them back into the compartment. "I suppose you have *him* for that."

Grace stopped smoothing her dress and looked up. "Who?"

"It looked like I'd interrupted a scene earlier. I didn't realize you two were so close."

He must mean the tears, she thought. But Grace wasn't one to share secrets that weren't hers. "Duchovny was simply offering condolences for my loss."

"No, I meant the other one. *Inspector Jane.*" He drew the name out. "I saw the way he was looking at you."

Was it the same way you're looking at me? Because this was the fourth time his eyes had trailed down her throat to her chest.

What could Grace say to that? Make a quip about Heron's flirtatious nature? Insist that he would charm a doorknob if turned the right way?

Or perhaps she could point out that Heron had a partner, and while she didn't understand the particulars of their dynamic, she had no interest in poaching someone else's partner.

And frankly, none of this was Adams's business.

"I'm not sure what you're implying, but Jane and I are friends," she said, feeling her face harden.

He snorted. "Friends."

"Yes, friendship, comradery. You may have heard of it."

He forced a smile. "You think I'm overstepping again."

She always thought Adams was overstepping. His manner was heavy-handed and carried with it a tone of disapproval. As if Grace's methods needed refinement or micromanagement. The very idea made the back of her neck burn.

"Aren't you? I didn't realize my relationships were your concern."

His face softened into earnestness. "I didn't want the night to be like this, with us bickering. I want to have a good time with you."

It took effort not to arch a brow, but Grace managed to keep her face impassive.

"I'm serious," he said, leaning toward her again. "Can you ignore whatever I've said that upset you?"

The intimacy of the auto pressed in on her. With him bent forward, his eyes looking up into hers, she felt his desire like a fly on her skin. Light, irritating.

If he puts his hand on my leg—

But the auto rolled to a stop, and the door opened. A sultry female voice said, "We've arrived at the Trinity Music Hall, Commander. Enjoy your evening."

Adams threw back the rest of his drink and stepped out of the auto. Bending down, he offered his hand. "Shall we?"

She let him pull her from the dark backseat into the soft lamplight lining the boulevard. Before her, the Trinity Music Hall rose opulent in the night. The hall was modeled after the Taj Mahal, without its four pillars and less grand in scale.

The sight was still breathtaking, serving as a centerpiece for Whitman Park, the wealthiest section of Zone 2. Whitman Park held not only the music hall but also three large galleries, blocks of artisan shops, and high-scale restaurants Grace could never afford.

Two women, barefoot on the patio outside of Sushi Bites, laughed, champagne glasses in hand.

Adams followed her gaze. "See how happy they are? It's because they've had a drink."

He smiled expectantly, waiting for her to appreciate his joke.

She pitied him with a forced smile.

"Tough crowd. Okay, come on. They'll have started serving already."

By the time Grace reached the top of the stairs, her calves ached from the climb. They weren't used to the arch created by her dress boots.

The air slid along her arms, her throat. She tried to remember the last time she'd worn something that showed this much skin and suddenly grew self-conscious, the unease expanding as the doors to the music hall rose in her view.

Adams, who'd returned his hand to the small of her back, must've felt her hesitation.

He bent and whispered into her ear, "Don't worry. You look amazing."

As if her looks were what troubled her.

They passed beneath the arches into the open hallway. Two grand staircases rose, one on each side. People lingered on the steps, talking, laughing.

More bodies crowded the center of the space.

Women wore dresses that sparkled like the night. Their ears and fingers were clad with gold.

Filters were abundant.

One woman had gossamer wings, fairylike and flittering, extending from between her slender shoulders, glitter shimmering above her eyes and across her cheeks.

Another woman had a tiger—obviously a digital projection— curled at her feet. Its large green eyes tracked Grace as she crossed the room. A pink tongue slid over its white jaws as she passed by.

Adams kept his hand on her back as he guided her through the throng of bodies. Grace balked at how many filters were on. She could neutralize them, but she was too fascinated by the elaborate details. The filters themselves must've cost a fortune, and many were customized in ways that Grace had never seen before.

Men and women with alligator eyes and rough patches of skin. Feathers of every possible color and texture, mimicking birds that surely Heron would know the names of. Plumage sprouted from the tops of their heads or trailed over bare shoulders and down straight backs.

Tails, wings, claws, and pointed teeth.

Sometimes the people didn't alter their own appearances but rather depicted themselves in the companionship of creatures, the animals realistic and fantastical in equal measure.

One man had a large black bird on each shoulder. A woman had chipmunks nestled in the crook of her neck, scurrying back and forth across her shoulders. Unicorns, mermaids, basilisks, and centaurs.

Above her, whales, dolphins, and seals swam lazily in the air, cooing their throaty songs.

All of this filtering on top of the usual age alterations.

"I should've told you that the theme for tonight's gathering is menagerie," he said, bending to speak into her ear. "You can use a filter to embellish your outfit, if you'd like to blend in more. Like this."

She turned to find Adams had added a wolf tail and ears to his own ensemble.

"How do I look?" He grinned, the smile exaggerating his newfound wolfish traits.

Ridiculous, she thought. "Nice."

"Here she is. The woman of the hour."

Grace turned and found a man with cropped white hair and thick eyebrows. It was the man with the two black birds, one on each shoulder.

"Crows?" she guessed.

"Close. Ravens. I see that you wear nothing but your own charms." He took her hand, kissed it and smirked. "That's a bold statement. Much like this."

He drew an index finger across the right side of his face, to indicate her scars.

"Few of us are brave enough to appear exactly as we are. Unmasked."

"I'm Commander Grace Buteo."

"I know." He straightened but didn't release her hand. "I'm Orrin Khan."

Adams straightened beside her. His pout had returned. "Mr. Khan is the founder and ranking board member of Trinity Trust."

Grace started as if slapped. She'd known his name through her research into Trinity Trust, but not his face.

Davion's confession returned to her.

I took only from the wealthiest corporations. When I pulled money from Trinity Trust, I realized I'd made a mistake.

And here was the man her husband had stolen from.

Khan ran a thumb over Grace's hand. "When Adams suggested that we invite you into our little fold, I was certain you wouldn't accept. You must have your reasons for being here tonight."

A chill crept up her spine.

"Grace is deeply honored by the invitation," Adams said.

Khan arched a brow. "Is she?"

"She will be a wonderful asset to the Island."

"Do you think the accident rendered Commander Buteo mute? Or do you always speak for the women around you?" Khan asked. There was acid in his tone, but his face was curious.

The sharp rebuke made Adams flush.

Grace couldn't suppress her smile. "I *am* flattered by the invitation. Did you issue it yourself?"

Are you a spider drawing me into your web?

Khan's eyes sparked. "It wasn't my decision alone, but I supported it, yes. In truth, Adams here advocated hard on your behalf and has for years. In the last few months, he's been particularly ruthless."

Grace was one to give credit where it was due. To Adams, she said, "Thank you."

She wanted to say more, press Khan in particular for details of her induction. But then her stomach rumbled *loudly*.

"Excuse me," she said through tight lips.

"You're not taking good care of your date, Adams. I'm ashamed on your behalf." He turned, his eyes sweeping the room. "There's Vatore with the mini crepes and champagne. Fetch him."

Adams squeezed her free hand. "I'll be right back."

The wolf began to nudge his way through the crowd of laughing bodies.

Khan turned his full attention on her, his sharp blue eyes assessing her. "Now. Would you like to wait for those crepes or escape your overbearing partner and get a real look at this place? The choice is yours."

His voice dripped with mischief as he offered her his arm.

The idea of escaping Adams for even a few minutes was tempting, but what she wanted most was to learn more about this man, this possible suspect and his involvement, if any, in her husband's and Kaiden's deaths—and what it might mean that Khan had approached her first.

Had he been looking for her? Waiting for her?

She took the offered arm. "Escape."

TWELVE

KHAN LED her to the staircase. "Let's take the high ground, shall we?"

Grace was pulled through the leopards and antelopes, pandas and elephants. A capuchin monkey ran up the bannister ahead of them. "Do you give everyone a tour of your music hall on their first visit?"

He gave her a sheepish smile. "No. But I do greet all new inductees on their first night with us. Because you were late, I had the pleasure of welcoming the others before you arrived. That means you have me all to yourself."

Fortunate for me, she thought.

"Unlike Adams, however, I can see when a woman is not interested in my attention. Was I wrong in sensing that you wanted to talk more?"

Grace had hoped that she wasn't so transparent. She pasted together a story. "I'm very curious about Egg Island and its members. You seem knowledgeable about both."

"I should be. I founded it with my brother. What do you want to know?"

Did you kill my husband?

"What is its purpose? Does it have a mission statement or goal? Or is it simply full of the power-hungry celebrating their eliteness?"

She worried she'd gone too far. But his smile was companionable, non-threatened. "It is absolutely true that some people in this organization did not merit their invitation. Money speaks as loudly today as it did a thousand years ago. If I am completely honest—and you seem like a woman who values honesty…"

It seemed like a question, so she answered it. "I do."

"I thought so. Then the truth is that Egg Island isn't what it was thirty years ago when my brother and I created it. It's not even what it was ten years ago. But that's what happens with our creations, isn't it? Often, they become something else entirely once they're out of our hands. We can no more control their trajectory than we can the stars in the sky."

A red Chinese dragon dove over her shoulder, circling the air above their head before passing through the crystal chandelier. "Tell me what you wanted it to be."

"I imagined a group of concerned individuals with means, committed to solving the worst problems of our time."

Too good to be true, she thought. *Why would he want to position himself as a benevolent benefactor? To gain my trust? To hide his true intentions?*

She hoped her face betrayed none of this suspicion. "And what is it now?"

"There are still those of us who want change, absolutely. But there are also a great many who think only of themselves. They see EI as an opportunity to further their own ambitions. The idea that they should use their blessings in service of others is unthinkable. I'd hoped by securing your invitation we could begin to shift that power balance. But I won't lie, Grace. Not everyone is happy you're here. Not even half."

The ravens on his shoulder threw back their heads and cackled.

"Is that so?" Her eyes swept the crowd congregated below. More than a few stole glances her way.

"Some see you as a toy to manipulate. Others as a threat in need of elimination."

She watched his face as he spoke, matching his steady gaze.

"I can see you are trying to decide whether or not to trust me."

She pulled back, disliking that he could read her easily.

"That's good. Be cautious."

He considered her, his eyes searching her face, pausing considerably on the burn scars. "Perhaps my business dealings, wealth, or reputation bothers you. Or perhaps…"

He took a step toward her, bending close to her ear.

"You have a more personal reason to distrust me. A reason much closer to *home*."

Her heart took off like a shot, the blood rushing loudly in her ears. She was sure he could hear it, as close as she was.

He knows about Davion. He knows, he knows, he knows…

Her mouth was impossibly dry, and it took her several breaths to find her voice.

"What are you saying, Mr. Khan?"

"Only that you *could* have refused us. You could've turned down the invitation to join this society—and I half expected you to. But you didn't. You're here, and I can only assume that you have your reasons. Perhaps even your own plan." He took her hand and kissed the back of it again. "I want to be your ally, Commander, not your enemy. Remember that when the time comes."

"There you are!" Adams appeared with his yellow eyes and wolf ears flicking. He lifted a plate of mini crepes higher. "I lost you."

"I thought she would enjoy a better view." Khan released her hand and swept his gaze over the crowd below. "But it's almost time to begin. I'll leave you both."

Grace accepted the plate of bite-sized morsels Adams pushed into her hands, watching Khan go.

He slipped into the crowd like a shark who'd traveled these waters often.

"A talkative bastard, isn't he?" Adams laughed companionably. "He didn't burn your ears off with his views, did he?"

Grace lifted a crepe from the plate. She didn't want to eat it. But hunger dulled the mind, and she wanted to be sharp tonight. Khan's clear and accurate assessment of her had been unsettling. She hadn't expected him—or anyone else—to see through her from the start.

I was naïve, she thought. *These people play games and politics as a lifestyle. Step up, Gray, or they'll outmaneuver you like a child.*

"What views?" She took a bite of the crepe.

"Oh, he has many. Resource management. Utopian living. The roles of the rich and the poor in society. Get him going on water rights and he won't shut up. Did he mention water?"

Khan stopped to speak to the woman with the tiger. She seemed delighted to receive his attention, sliding a golden arm over the back of his shoulders, sending his black birds into agitated flight.

"No," she said. "He didn't."

"I wanted to tell you how beautiful you look tonight." The tone in his voice made Grace look away from Khan and meet his yellow wolf eyes. Those eyes caused ripples of unease down her back.

"You already mentioned it. I suppose you've never seen me in a dress." She couldn't remember the last time she'd worn one.

She froze, her eyes snagging on two men. One was covered in elaborate iridescent plumage, his face hidden by a flattering hawk mask. He spoke to a pack of leopards who threw back their heads and cackled at his words. The man beside him, just past his shoulder, was a mouse—or nearly one. His face was covered in gray whiskers and small velvety ears protruded from the top of his head.

And he looked as uncomfortable in the group as a real mouse might be, his eyes searching the room for an exit.

Mouse ears and twitchy nose aside, there was no mistaking him. Dr. Ezekiel Tove. *What is he doing here?*

"Do you know what I mean?" Adams asked.

"About what?"

Adams sighed. "Were you listening to me? I was trying to tell you that—"

"Who is that?" Grace pointed, not at Dr. Tove but at the man he seemed to be trailing like a pet.

Adams leaned over the bannister, following her finger.

"Arden Pendam," he said.

"As in the Pendam district?"

"Yes, his family has been here for a long time."

Grace wasn't interested in a history lesson. She only found them interesting when delivered with Heron's boyish charm and enthusiasm.

Heron.

His company was far superior to Adams's on nearly every level: intellectually, emotionally, physically.

She found herself wondering where he was now, and what he was doing.

If he were here with her, she might actually be enjoying herself with his humorous quips. She wondered what costume he would've chosen.

Focus, Grace chided. "What's Pendam's business?"

Adams scratched his wolf chin. "Right now, I believe he's the board director for CyTown Towers. And he holds a position in acquisitions. It's hard to keep track since his family owns most of the real estate in that part of the zone. They float around, taking positions in different companies as it suits them."

Grace captured the scene with her lenscape and sent the image to Heron. She didn't expect him to answer. He was probably with Arjun, or if Arjun was unavailable, likely at a bar, flirting the pants off some beautiful person.

"Dr. Tove *is* connected to CyTown," she muttered. "Why am I not surprised?"

"Who?" Adams lowered the plate, following her gaze. "What's this about CyTown?"

Heron's ping flashed across the bottom of her scape. <<What am I looking at? Some sort of animalistic sex party? Gray, I'm surprised.>>

<<Dr. Tove is the mouse. He's here with the director for CyTown Towers, Arden Pendam, the gold hawk(?) in front of him.>>

"You don't have any active investigations for CyTown listed," Adams said, his lenscape lit blue. "Why are you asking about CyTown?"

<<Naughty,>> Heron pinged. <<What are the chances they're only good buddies and not running an underground kidnapping ring together? And actually that's a golden eagle.>>

Adams grabbed her elbow and half turned her. "Grace, talk to me."

She put her hand over his, prepared if necessary to wrench it off. "Take your hand off me."

He looked ready to resist, perhaps pry or question her more. But then he softened and let go. "I'm sorry. I only want to know what's going on. Is there something you need to tell me? I can help you—"

"No, you can't," she said flatly.

He looked ready to argue more, his mouth opening in protest when a loud voice boomed across the room.

"Welcome, everyone, welcome. It's wonderful that we could all gather together again tonight, in honor of a most auspicious occasion. I feel particularly hopeful about the potential of our newest recruits and welcome them whole-heartedly into our ranks."

A smattering of applause circled the room.

"I'd like to introduce you to our three new members tonight…"

"You're right," Adams went on, his voice low but desperate. "You don't have to tell me anything. But I would greatly appreciate it if you did. How am I supposed to keep you safe if you keep—"

"Keep me safe," Grace hissed. "Keep *me* safe?"

A couple to their right turned, and with forced smiles, escaped into the crowd as if standing too close to the pair arguing might prove infectious.

"What do you mean you've been keeping me safe? Safe from *what*?"

Adams's eyes slid around the room. "Not here. Okay. We can't talk about this here."

"Talk about what? What do we need to talk about?"

"It can wait. Please. Wait until we get outside and—"

"I don't want to wait. I want you to tell me what you meant when you said—"

"Grace, shhh. *Shhh.*"

"If you don't tell me what the hell you're saying—"

"*Stop.* Everyone is looking at us."

Grace turned and saw that everyone *was* looking at her. More than that, Khan was saying her name, seemingly not for the first time.

"Yes, there she is. Commander Grace Buteo."

Heat flooded her face. She was about to apologize, ask him to repeat the question, if there was one, but Khan pressed on.

"Her valor cannot be understated. She has sacrificed much for our safety and the security of the zone. She deserves to be welcomed with open arms into our fold. Hopefully, in time, we can repay her."

Spontaneous applause circled the room. Several revelers cheered and called her name.

But not all, Grace noticed. Many remained stoic, their eyes fixed upon her in a silent challenge.

"This is your moment. Smile," Adams said, pressing a hand into her back.

She didn't smile.

Khan's eyes bored into hers. "Some of us have made mistakes, and it cost us dearly. But let us find a way to forgive each other. Let us find a way to move forward, for the good of all."

Her heart pounded, her mind repeating, *He knows, he knows, he knows…*

"*Flectere si nequeo superos, Acheronta movebo.*" Khan still hadn't turned away, those eyes begging. "If we cannot sway heaven, let us move hell."

THIRTEEN

GRACE KNEW she should control her temper. If she'd taken a deep breath and focused on what needed to be done rather than let Adams's words get under her skin, she could've stayed at the party. Asked questions. Maybe even cornered Pendam and interviewed him about Tristan Range or his work with Dr. Tove.

But she couldn't. It was all too much. The way Khan had seen right through her. Adams, too, with not only his secrets but the blatant desire so suffocating she might as well be trying to breathe underwater.

To escape the weight of it all—the eyes, Adams, Khan—she'd fled the music hall with Khan's words in her ears and Adams calling after her.

He didn't catch up to her until she was nearly to the auto stop across from Sushi Bites.

"Grace, wait, please!"

She ordered an auto and was informed that it would arrive in four minutes.

On the dark sidewalk, she turned on him. All the confusion and anger building inside her found a target.

"You said you can't *protect* me. What did you mean by that? What exactly have you been protecting me from?"

He stopped two feet short of her and ran a hand over his head. "I don't want to fight. I'm on your side."

On my side, on my side. Why is everyone trying to convince me they're on my side?

"On my side against *what*? Who ordered the IED? Who wanted to blow up my auto?"

"Lix—"

"Bullshit," she said. "Lix Richards was in the wrong place at the wrong time. He didn't have the means to plan a multi-device attack. He was framed to protect someone else. Someone with more power. And I think you know who."

He looked to the sky then pinched his eyes closed. "Grace, please."

"Who really ordered that attack? Tell me."

"I can't."

"Why?" When he didn't answer, she scoffed. "How can you look the other way? How can you—"

"Because your life depends on it! If I want you alive, I have to look the other way!" he yelled, then pressed his fingers against the bridge of his nose as if to stem the flow of his words. When he spoke again, his voice was lower, more controlled. "Why am I the villain here? What about Davion? Did it ever occur to you that *Davion* might be to blame for what happened?"

Grace stopped pacing. Her eyes and throat stung. Her stomach clenched. The idea that everyone might have known who her husband really was except for her hurt. It *hurt*.

"Shit." He looked toward the sky and swore. "When did you find out?"

"After." She didn't see a point in lying about this. "At first, I thought I was the target."

It had been easier when she'd been the one to blame for their deaths.

"When did you find out?" she asked.

"A couple of months before the attack, I'd heard that someone was forging visas and smuggling in outzoners." He rubbed the back of his head, seemed to compose himself. "Seven weeks later, I heard Davion might be involved."

"A rumor from who?"

"It doesn't matter."

"The hell it doesn't!" She stepped back as if slapped. "And you let Lix take the fall. *Why?* How could you?"

"You don't understand."

"Because you won't tell me what's going on or who's killing people or—"

"Keep your voice down." He spoke to her but his eyes were on the luminescent music hall.

"Or what?" She took a step toward him. "Are you threatening me?"

"Everything I've done has been to keep you out of harm's way. You weren't wrong about them wanting to kill you, too. That was the original plan, but I fought against that." He took a step toward her, tentatively, as if she were an animal that might flee at any hint of danger. "I fought for you."

I fought for you. Not for Davion. Not for Kaiden. Her.

He reached out for her. She backed away. "You let them kill my son?"

He shook his head. "No. Kaiden was a mistake. I wish that hadn't happened."

"It *did* happen. And you're stopping me from finding

the person responsible. *You*, so-called commander. You're impeding justice."

"It's not that simple. There are things in play here you don't understand. Can't begin to——"

"Because I'm too stupid to——"

"No. That's not what I'm saying." He pressed his fingers into his temples. "Ask me why I work so hard to protect you. Why I do everything I can to make sure you're safe."

She didn't want to ask why.

"I love you, Grace."

"Don't——" she began.

He ignored this. "I've loved you since the moment I saw you in the precinct. Day one as a junior trainee. I tried to talk to you then, but you were too focused on the job, on getting ahead."

"Stop."

His words had a bizarre, rehearsed quality to them, as if he'd memorized them only to deliver them now, heart-lessly. It made the situation feel more surreal.

"Then you met Davion, and life carried you away from me. I know his loss still hurts you."

You don't know the first thing about how I feel.

"Don't throw away this second chance. *Please.* We finally——"

"It's never going to happen." She suddenly felt hollowed out, raw and tired. She wanted her bed. She wanted Davion's arms around her. She wanted to kiss her son goodnight.

He must've misinterpreted her tiredness for resignation, because he took a step toward her. "You don't have to hold on to him anymore. You don't have to stay loyal to a man who betrayed you. He got your son killed. Surely you see that."

She didn't like hearing her own judgments repeated back to her. It was one thing for her to blame Davion. It was another to hear the accusations from someone like Adams, someone who was using her heartbreak as a means to get what he wanted.

"I can give you everything you want, Grace. That's all I want to do. You want a faithful, honest husband? Done. You want more kids? Let's have a brood. You want to leave this zone and start over? Whatever it is, I'll give it to you. Everything and more. I'd never be so selfish as to put you or our children in danger for my own—"

When his hands brushed her arms, she wrenched herself free.

"I don't need you to give me anything," she hissed. Heart pounding in her temples, she said, "You're a *thousand* times worse than Davion. He broke the law for the right reasons. To *protect* people. To *help* people. You only do it for yourself."

Adams's jaw clenched, his hands falling to his sides. "Is that what you think? Is that what you *really* think? Wow. He did a real number on you, didn't he? You're smarter than that. You can't possibly believe all the bullshit he fed you."

Davion hadn't fed her bullshit. But he also hadn't told her the truth until it was too late.

Adams's calm façade cracked, his anger breaking through. "I've done *everything* for you. Just so you could stand there and look at me like that. You can believe me or not, but I'm the *only* one in this whole city who is fighting for you to—"

"Is everything okay here?" a man asked.

Grace recognized the voice even before she turned.

Arjun stood on the sidewalk at the edge of the building's shadows. A well-tailored suit with a red dress shirt clung to his body. It highlighted the bulk of him.

His sandstone skin shone in the moonlight as his hands rested casually in his pockets, his long black hair smoothed back from his face.

Adams turned, his speech faltering. "We're fine. Move along, buddy."

"She doesn't look fine." Arjun met her gaze. "Are you okay, Grace?"

"I want to go home." She was tired. Her feet ached. Her heart ached. She was shivering, and she couldn't tell if it was from the cold or her adrenaline.

Adams looked between them. "Do you know this guy?"

"My auto is a couple blocks from here." Arjun gestured up the street.

Her auto was still two minutes away. She couldn't wait.

"He's a friend. And I'm leaving." Grace fell into step beside Arjun.

Adams threw his hands up in the air. "Grace, please! At least let me take you home. We can finish this conversation."

"Finish it with yourself if you have so much to say."

"Grace!" he called after her.

She walked in silence, aware of her throbbing feet and the damp sweat building on the back of her neck. Her hair, which she'd fixed for the first time in ages, was curling around her face rebelliously, assaulted by the thick, humid air.

She smelled food and alcohol wafting from the open restaurants they passed. Laughter and conversations trailed out into the night.

She searched the wide, shadowed boulevard and lit patios. "Is he following us?"

"No, he headed back to the music hall," Arjun said. "Heron is asking where I am. Do you mind if I tell him?"

A touch of tenderness ran through her. That he would

bother to check with her before bringing Heron into the drama, into her exhaustion and embarrassment. And it was embarrassment that she felt now.

First Khan. Then Adams. She even replayed the earlier conversation with Constable Ezra, and found that it, too, was suspicious. Maybe they all knew who Davion really was, what he'd done. The whole damn city. Everyone except poor, blind, *stupid* Grace.

She should've known Davion better than everyone. She hadn't.

"It's fine," she said. They were a block up the street when she finally added, "Thank you for stepping in back there."

Arjun flashed a nervous smile. "Don't thank me yet."

Her steps faltered. "Why?"

"I don't actually have an auto. I just thought you'd welcome any excuse to walk away."

"You're right." She laughed despite herself. There was no humor. Her voice was too high, a gloss of panic painted over her words.

"There's another auto stop about half a kilometer up. I'll walk you there and wait until it comes, if you want."

"That would be great. Thank you."

A heartbeat later, Heron's ping appeared at the bottom of her lenscape. <<What's going on? Are you okay?>>

<<I'm fine.>>

<<A says that Adams was being a prick and he's walking you to an auto stop. What did the bastard do? Did he hurt you?>>

<<No, I just wanted to leave. Adams wanted to keep talking.>>

A gross oversimplification.

<<About what?>>

She could practically see his Tahitian-blue eyes

gawking at her. It made a small smile tug at her lips. <<All I'll say is that my mother was right.>>

<<Oh, you hate that.>>

<<Yes, it was uncomfortable. I could have done without the confession.>>

<<No, I meant you hate that your mother was right. That'll be under your skin for ages.>>

Against her will, she smiled. <<Yes. That too.>>

A sleek dark shape whizzed down the deserted street, far above the speed limit.

Grace hesitated on the sidewalk. "Is that—"

"Yeah," Arjun said. "He sent the auto."

A water-blue ride slid up to the curb beside them, and the doors opened like swan wings unfurling. Grace expected Heron to climb out, maybe chastise her for going to the induction without him in the first place.

But the interior was empty.

"He's at home," Arjun said, understanding her hesitation.

She pinged Heron. <<You sent your unregistered auto? Your *illegal* auto?>>

<<Yes.>>

<<How fast was it traveling? What if you'd hurt someone or…>> She wasn't sure how to finish the ping. She looked at the deserted streets. What exactly did she think would happen?

<<Get in and you'll be home in two minutes. It'll take you three minutes to get to the auto stop and another six to catch a ride.>>

<<Fine.>> She ducked beneath the door frame and slid onto the far seat. Relief washed over her pitiful feet.

Arjun took the catty-corner position, giving her room to stretch out her legs.

While they'd had some space between them on the

street, in the auto it was impossible to overlook Arjun. Not just because of his imposing build, but his scent soaked the interior. Something between wood and water saturated the air.

She relaxed, her shoulder blades softening against the seat.

<<Do you want to come here?>> Heron pinged. When she didn't respond right away, he added, <<You're probably tired and want to go to bed, but I thought I'd offer.>>

She considered her empty house. Its accusing silence. How absolutely alone she would be inside its walls after a night like this.

When she'd had trying public engagements in the past, she could always count on Davion to be home, waiting. He'd take her into his arms, rub her shoulders and feet, put a drink in her hand. If she wanted to talk, they'd talk. If she wanted silence, he'd hold her.

But he wasn't waiting for her now. Nothing was waiting for her.

Tears stung her eyes.

<<Gray? Where should I send the auto?>>

<<I don't want to intrude.>> *And I don't want to be alone.*

<<You won't,>> was his instant reply. <<I want you here.>>

Grace wasn't so sure Arjun felt the same way. She measured his strong jaw and profile as his eyes remained on the street outside the window. What did he think of her? Of all this crying?

"I'm sorry for interrupting your evening," she said.

"You didn't." He tugged on his cuffs.

"It's clear you have plans." She shifted in her seat. "You look very nice."

Another one of his brilliant smiles. "I was working."

"Oh. Right." She felt heat rise in her face.

His smile filled with amusement.

When it was clear she could find nothing to add, he said, "We'll be at Heron's in a couple of minutes. Do you need anything from your house? I can take the auto to your place and retrieve it for you, if you want."

"Oh, I'm not staying the night." Her blush deepened. "I just wanted"—*not to be alone*—"to talk." *About anything except how I'm feeling.* "About work."

"Okay."

Grace wondered if this open, neutral face was natural or if he'd developed it through practice.

When the door opened outside Heron's unit, Arjun helped her out of the auto but didn't follow her up the walkway leading to the lit door.

She stopped. "Aren't you coming?"

He shook his head. "No. Have a good night, Grace."

Then the swan doors were closing, and the auto sped away. She watched it go, trying to understand the sensation in her arms and chest.

The door opened and Heron appeared. His wet hair was hanging down in his eyes, grazing the tops of his cheeks.

"Gray?"

"It's just me." As if she might need to apologize for his boyfriend disappearing.

"I know." He waved her forward. "Get in here."

Before she fully understood what was happening, he was helping her out of her shoes, ushering her onto his couch, and covering her with a blanket.

"Do you want a shower? A strong drink? Maybe another dose of Nora's cure-all?"

"Yes. Yes. No. Or maybe. If the drink doesn't work, I'll try the powder again."

"You prefer red wine, right?" he asked, moving around his kitchen. "That's what you had when we were at the bar. I have a spiced Shiraz in here."

"That's perfect." She was touched that he'd remembered.

He opened a cabinet and pulled down a large wine glass and the bottle of red.

"You don't have a ChefMate."

He shook his head. "No. I prefer to cook for myself."

"Did your mothers teach you?"

"No, they were too busy for a hobby like cooking, though Nora is quite the bartender. It was Evita who taught me how to cook. She was our kitchen manager, the person in charge of our meals."

The fact that Heron's childhood home had a kitchen *manager* spoke volumes. She couldn't imagine wealth like that.

"Does she still work for your family?"

"She passed a few years ago," he said with a sad smile. He put the glass of wine in her hand.

"I'm very sorry."

"Don't be. She died peacefully in her bed surrounded by the people who loved her. She was a hundred and thirty years old. I dare say she had a good life."

"Oh. I was imagining a young woman."

"No, she'd been working with Nora's family since Nora's father was a boy. She'd been with us a long time."

"Nora's family sounds fascinating." Grace couldn't imagine growing up in a manor house, complete with staff. Heirlooms and wealth passing down through the ages. It sounded like a romantic novel where everyone died tragically in the end or two distant cousins fell in love.

"It is. They have a long, detailed history. And they were the type to keep track of it all."

"What about Victoria?"

"She cut ties with her family when she was young, and she didn't like to talk about them. I don't know much about that side of things."

Grace drank her wine, snug under the heavy blanket, and let her mind wander.

Over the rim of his glass, Heron asked, "Do you want to talk about what happened tonight?"

"There's a lot to process."

"From Adams?"

"Adams. Khan. Tove and Pendam." She waved a hand as if to say, *Take your pick.*

Heron's brows raised. "Orrin or Alabaster Khan?"

"Orrin. As in Trinity Trust." *The last corporation my husband stole from.* "He approached me almost as soon as I arrived. He knows about Davion."

Heron's brows rose. "He said that to you?"

"No, but he alluded to it." She took another deep drink. "So did Adams. I guess everyone in Zone 2 knew what he was doing but me."

Heron cocked his head. "You'd better start from the beginning."

She did. She glossed over Adams's *I love you* but suspected Heron wasn't fooled. His jaw had begun working furiously and hadn't stopped.

When she finished talking, his face was nearly as red as her wine. Unable to read him, she asked, "What are you thinking?"

"I think he's a bastard, and I'm going to kill him." When Grace didn't speak into the silence, he went on. "What a piece of human garbage. Don't you see what he tried to do?"

She replayed parts of Adams's conversation. "Do you mean the love confession—"

"No, when he said, 'Did it ever occur to you that *Davion* might be to blame'. It's clear that when he said this, he thought that you didn't know about Davion. He was prepared to drop that on you, *devastate* you, all to make Davion look like shit. What a piece of human trash."

"But you'd already told me."

Heron held up a finger. "*No.* I delivered the message that Davion recorded. It was his story to tell. It would've never been my place to tell you that. Any idiot with half a heart could see that the truth would hurt you."

"He thinks he loves me." Grace took another deep drink, feeling the wine cling to her lips. "He's trying to get what he wants."

"Gross." Heron cringed.

"Gee, thanks." Grace laughed despite herself.

"Don't be ridiculous. I was imagining him getting what he wants." He shuddered again. "It's not a pretty picture."

When she drained the first glass of wine, he refilled it. "How do you feel now?"

She looked into the red patina, noting her puffy face and dark eyes. "Tired. Stupid."

He frowned. "Tired I understand. Why stupid?"

"I should've seen what Davion was doing. I should've stopped him."

"He wouldn't have stopped," he said, his face a mask of certainty.

He was right.

"I know, but at least I could've protected Kaiden. I could've sent him to live with my mother or…"

Or what? She wasn't sure what options she would've had, but she would've found one. She would've moved heaven and earth for Kaiden.

"Davion loved your son, and you. But he was an

idealist for thinking this wouldn't touch you. You can't challenge power and come away without losses."

Grace met his gaze over the rim of his wine glass. "Would you have risked it?"

"With a child? No. With someone who understood what we stood to gain—and lose—absolutely. But that's just it. It has to be a decision made by capable adults. You can't gamble a child's life like that."

Grace's stomach turned.

"I think it's why Davion didn't tell you even though he wanted to. He understood you'd side with Kaiden."

"He should've sided with Kaiden," she said, her stomach hollow. *With me.*

She recalled the memory she'd played a hundred times since learning who her husband really was. Davion coming up behind her and slipping his arms around her waist. That tightening smile.

We're lucky, aren't we? When I think about the kids out there, the ones without water or shelter or anyone to look after them. When I think of them—It shouldn't only be our child who has what he needs. We have to do more. Grace, I can't live with myself if I don't.

He'd been trying to broach the subject with her for months.

"I know." He turned his own drink in the light. It sparked off the glass. "And he knew it, too."

"Sometimes I wish he was alive so that we could redo that conversation."

"What would've changed?" Heron watched her, his gaze encouraging her to go on.

"He'd tell me what he was doing. We'd fight about the recklessness of it, and I'd leave, taking Kaiden with me. Kaiden would be safe. And maybe Davion would stop before it was too late."

Heron said nothing. He didn't need to. Grace understood this was a dream, a fantasy. She didn't need Heron to point out the impossibility that Davion would've stopped doing what he'd believed was right. And even if he had, if he'd chosen them and reunited their family, for how long?

How long before he started up again, lying to her about what he was doing in between those programming jobs?

She wondered—and not for the first time—if it would've been better that Kaiden had never been born. If erasing him would erase all this pain inside her.

Or getting him back, another voice whispered—thinking of the millions of souls dreaming their lives away in CyTown Towers. They'd erased the pain, hadn't they? They'd found ways to remove the devastation from their lives.

"Children do complicate things," Heron said.

She rolled the wine around in her glass. "Is that why you don't have any?"

Because Heron loved to challenge power. He was probably as rich, or richer, than the wealthiest citizens of Zone 2, yet he didn't care. It was clear to Grace that for him, his wealth was a means to an end. A way to meet those around him resource for resource. To have what they had—but also no fear of losing it all.

"One of many reasons." He leaned into the cushions and smiled. "I love kids. But I wouldn't be a good parent."

She thought of him putting the trash can by the bed. Of fetching her clothes from the closet. For making her breakfast and koffee. All of this after he carried her to bed while she sobbed. "I think you're wrong about that. You're very good at taking care of people."

"As equals, maybe. But when you treat children as equals, they turn into horrible, insufferable know-it-alls. *Completely* spoiled brats. Ask my poor mothers."

He winked, and a weak smile twinged across her lips.

But his humor didn't stick. He was regarding her with that soft expression again. His voice was low when he said, "You have to stop blaming yourself for seeing the best in Davion. That's requirement number one in a good marriage."

She exhaled, her cheeks puffed. After several beats of silence, she said, "Am I correct in guessing you asked Arjun to hang around the music hall? Otherwise, it's a hell of a coincidence."

"I *may* have asked him to keep an eye on the situation. He's good with things like that."

"He said he was working."

"Yes, but don't let him fool you. He loves it when I pay him to dress up and look handsome."

Grace started, the wine glass stalling halfway to her mouth. "What do you mean, 'pay' him?"

Heron snorted. "Pay. To give someone money to do the things you ask them to do."

"You paid him to hang around the music hall?" Grace recalled the conversation in the Low Town bar when Heron mentioned giving Arjun a percentage of his income. "Why would you have to pay your boyfriend for that?"

"You're the only one who calls him my boyfriend. No, sorry. Your mother also."

"I assumed the money was for..." She couldn't finish the sentence. Already her face was turning red.

His eyebrows shot up. "Are you telling me that you really think I'm giving him thirty percent of my monthly income for sex?"

Her face was on fire.

"Heavens, Gray. I'm not desperate. I'm a beautiful,

charming man, if you hadn't noticed. I can sleep with nearly anyone and not pay for it."

Her lips twitched.

I had *noticed that you're a beautiful, charming man,* she thought, but refused to say it.

Heron put his wine glass on the table. "Listen. You've probably had your fill of intense conversations for the evening, but we should do this now. Rip the bandage off. It's obvious you have questions."

"Okay." Grace took another deep drink of wine.

He gestured at her. "Please ask your questions."

"Does it bother your boyfriend that—" Grace began.

"Never mind." Heron shook his head. "You're bad at this. I can see that you won't ask your *real* questions. I'll do it."

"What—"

"Is Arjun really a sex worker?" he asked. Then, twisting his body as if now he were a second person answering the first, he said, "He has been trained in the sexual arts, yes."

"I didn't want to know if—" she began, but Heron continued as if she hadn't spoken.

"Are you and Arjun having sex?" He turned again to his imaginary second half. "Why yes, we are. Whenever the mood strikes me and he's feeling it too, we do have sex. But only if it goes both ways. Consent is important even with sex workers."

"I know that, Heron, I don't—"

"Are you and Arjun in a relationship?" The head turn. "No, not in the way you're thinking. He is first and foremost my bodyguard. We've been together a long time, but it's mostly been a working relationship."

Here he met Grace's face and gave her time to speak.

Her confusion scrunched her features. "You hired him and then, what? Fell in love?"

Heron's smile turned devious. "I didn't hire him. My mother did. A long time ago. I told you, I was a very *naughty* boy growing up. It was his job to keep me out of trouble."

Grace took this in. Arjun had known Heron since he was a boy. That meant Arjun might've known Davion, too. She filed this away for later processing. It had never occurred to her that she could ask Arjun about her husband.

She also wondered when they'd begun sleeping together—Arjun and his charge—and who had initiated it. Not that any of it was her business, but she imagined their backstory had been a complicated one.

Heron watched Grace puzzle all of this out, sipping his wine and saying nothing.

"The truth is that Arjun has been my bodyguard since I was ten years old. I love him. I trust him. He's my best friend. But as much as I love and trust him, it really is more of a working alliance than what you're imagining."

What I'm imagining. With her face on fire and thoughts softened by two large glasses of wine, she couldn't be sure *what* she was imagining.

Heron shrugged. "Mostly, I capitalize on the fact that he's devoted his life to mine, and he is *very* beautiful."

Arjun was beautiful. Grace had eyes.

"Does it bother you when he sleeps with other people?" she asked. Because surely, if he was a sex worker, he slept with other people.

"It might if we were in some sort of monogamous relationship, but we're not."

"But you love him."

"You can love someone and not want to own them. He doesn't have to be mine for me to love and want him."

Grace could argue that Arjun was definitely his. They might not be exclusive, but Grace saw the way Arjun looked at him.

With devotion.

Now that she knew about their long history, and the fact that Arjun had known him as a child and what he'd been hired to do, it made more sense why Arjun constantly assessed and measured Heron's needs. Perhaps that was their pattern.

But he measures your needs too, she thought, seeing him again on the dark sidewalk, stealing glances at his profile in Heron's auto. *Perhaps Arjun just takes care of people.*

"I don't know if I could sleep with someone I'd known as a child," she said finally.

Heron snorted. "It took a lot of begging. I think I harassed him for a solid three years before he caved."

"Three years would be a long time to resist Heron Jane's charms."

A light blush spread across his cheeks. Something lit in his eyes that Grace couldn't quite place.

He licked his lips and looked away. "You're making fun of me."

She let her head fall against the pillows. "I'm too tired to make fun of you. I should head out before I fall asleep on your couch."

Heron's eyes were full of soft light. "You can stay. I'll let you have my bed."

"I can't take your bed. Where would you sleep?"

One of his brows arched as he considered the wine glass for a long time. "I'll probably end up on the couch..."

Though her face was still warm and her mind spinning

with thought, Grace didn't want to leave. She was cozy. "What if I just sleep here? Like this."

She closed her eyes.

There was a tug on the blanket as Heron stretched his legs long beside hers. And there they were, side by side on the enormous sofa.

"Shall I tell you stories until you fall asleep?" he asked.

She pulled the blanket up to her chin, hyper-aware of every inch of her right side that was touching his. "This should be interesting. What kind of stories?"

He seemed to consider this. "I could tell you about my progress on breaking into CyTown."

"All right." She closed her eyes again, the last resistance in her body giving up the ghost. "Tell me."

"I'm in."

FOURTEEN

GRACE WOKE FIRST. The first sensation she grappled with was the horrible crick in her neck. She sat up, groaning. She stretched the muscles on one side, rolled her neck, then did the other. Her cervical vertebrae cracked, easing some of the tension.

She quickly realized why she woke up feeling cramped.

Heron was still on the sofa, turned toward the cushion, his cheek pressed to the overstuffed pillow beneath his head.

She leaned forward, watching the pulse in his neck, slow and steady. His chest rising and falling.

She remembered the remnants of his story—a dramatic, highly technical tale about what it took to copy and infiltrate Tristan's version of CyTown. Something about neuroreceptors. No, that wasn't it. Neuronreceptors? Neural?

She checked the time in her lenscape and found they'd been asleep like this for nearly six hours. No wonder her neck hurt like hell.

Watching the curve of Heron's jaw, she thought, *I'd like to kiss him there. Bite him right on the bone.*

And was absolutely shocked that this was what had occurred to her.

Kiss him. How in the world would I kiss him?

With your lips, her mind chastised.

"You do love to watch me sleep, don't you?" he asked.

Her face filled with heat, but fortunately irritation flooded out her desire, effectively suppressing it. "How do you see with your eyes closed?"

He pulled the blanket up to his chin. "Were my eyes closed?"

"They're closed now."

"Hmm. If you want them to open you should make koffee. It's your turn."

She looked at the gleaming kitchen counters and standing fridge. "I would but you don't have a ChefMate."

"So?"

"So, what do I make koffee with?" At home, it was a matter of pressing a few buttons on her wall unit. Even the cafeteria at work had a dispensary.

He sat up and sighed. "Right. I'll make it this time, but that means the next *two* times are on you."

"Done." She pulled the blanket off of him.

He sat up and rubbed his eyes, rolling his neck from one side to another. As he moved into the kitchen, Grace watched him go. She replayed last night in her mind. The way he'd looked with a glass of wine in his hand. How low his voice had been as they'd talked. How heavy and consistent his eye contact.

His refusal to leave her even though he had a perfectly acceptable bed upstairs.

Not to mention the fact that Arjun hadn't come back.

Had Heron sent him away? Kept him away? Why? Or

was the other man simply busy with his own work or Heron's?

"I can do your usual bullet and half," Heron called from the kitchen. "But my koffee is stronger. Do you want me to tone it down or let you try it as is?"

"As is," she said. Given the fuzziness of her head, she couldn't imagine that a stronger koffee would be a problem.

He whistled from the kitchen, a tune Grace thought she might recognize but couldn't place. The sound of it tugged a smile from her lips.

She used this moment to activate her lenscape and check the precinct's work log. She saw two unread messages from Commander Adams but pushed them to the end of the pile.

She gave her attention to the junior investigator files. She'd flipped through the progress reports for nearly thirty active cases by the time Heron slipped a warm mug into her hand.

"Let me finish this," she asked, knowing he would see the blue light reflected in her eyes. "Once I'm done, we can talk about CyTown."

"Croissants and bacon then," he said, and disappeared into the kitchen again. "Maybe cheese. How do you feel about smoked gouda?"

"Sounds delicious."

Once she'd left her replies for the junior inspectors, she moved up the ranks. It took her only about fifteen minutes of concentrated effort to make sure everyone in the precinct had been checked on and the work was progressing as needed.

That left her only with Duchovny's follow-up on the bot shop and Adams's two emails. Duchovny's last note in the log read, *Shop closed when I arrived though it was business hours. Tracking down the owner now. She has a place in Low Town not far from her shop.*

That was at nine p.m. last night.

With nothing but Adams's messages awaiting her, and Heron placing plates and cutlery on his two-person table, she decided not to delay the inevitable.

She took a breath and opened the first message.

We need to talk. There's still a lot I need to tell you. Please call me. That was timestamped at 23:58.

The second was sent almost forty minutes later.

You don't believe me but what I said is true. I'm your ally in this. And you need me.

In this. What, she wondered again, was *this*?

It was clear that Khan, Adams, and perhaps even Constable Ezra saw a greater game afoot here. And for whatever reason, she had not been invited to play. She'd been kept from knowing the rules and the objective from the start.

If it went on like this, she would get hurt, undoubtedly. Someone could only stumble around in the dark for so long before they slammed their knee into a table or fell down the stairs.

But did she believe that Adams would be forthright with her? Tell her the truth about what was going on in the zone?

No. Clearly he didn't trust her not to expose whoever was involved. He would continue to "protect" her from whatever he thought the threat might be, but while also protecting his own interests. In truth, Grace thought it was more likely that he was protecting the other party, too. It was *they* who stood to lose.

I have nothing to lose.

She thought of Ezra. *Everything crosses my desk. And I do*

mean everything. Do they think I can't put together the connections or see the patterns?

She could speak to the constable, ask them to share their insights. If Ezra had reason to hold back or hide something, they'd at least tell Grace. Or at least she thought so.

There was also Khan. He seemed to have a sense of what was happening around them. But his willingness to help Grace, to pull her into the fold—it gave her pause. If he was the man who killed her husband and son, he wasn't to be trusted—for any reason.

"Do you want butter for your croissant?" Heron asked, forcing her to look up from her musings.

"No, the cheese is fine."

"Very well then." He pulled out a seat and pointed to it. "If you please."

She joined him at the table. He offered her a bamboo napkin and a glass of goberry juice. It sparkled pink and shimmery in its glass.

He pulled the plate of bacon toward him. "You have that look on your face."

"What look?"

"I call it unhappy thinker."

She snorted. "Is there a happy thinker?"

"No, but there's a curious thinker and a serious thinker. Dare I ask what the subject is?"

"Khan and if he can be trusted."

"Trusted to…?" He waved his knife.

"Tell the truth. Help us find Davion's killer."

Heron fed a second strip of bacon into his mouth. "He might be the killer."

"Both Adams and Khan keep hinting that something else is going on in the zone, and I want to know what it is."

She tore the croissant in half. "These are good. Did you make them?"

He laughed. "You really aren't a cook, are you? Croissants take hours to make. Sometimes a whole day with all the butter and folding and—" He saw the look on her face. "Short answer, no. I bought these yesterday. I did fry the bacon though."

"Impressive."

His lips twitched. "If you say so."

She sipped her koffee and whistled. "Whew. You weren't kidding. That's *dark*."

"Do you want some sugar or cream to cut it?"

"No, I like it. But I feel my eyes dilating."

He leaned toward her, leveling her with his gaze. As she moved to meet him, giving him a clear view of her eyes, her stomach hitched.

"They look fine to me." His eyes slid to her mouth.

It seemed to take considerable effort for him to return his attention to his plate.

After a long silence he said, "I wouldn't worry about Khan yet. He'll reveal his cards soon."

"How do you know?"

"I have a feeling."

"Investigators don't deal in feelings," she reminded him.

"Let's wager then."

"They also don't wager."

"As you've kindly pointed out many times, I'm not a real investigator."

Had she pointed it out? His lack of training? The charade of his assistant inspector position? If that was true, she'd make a note to stop. He might not have her training or experience, but he did good work. He'd fulfilled the role of assistant inspector better than she could've hoped for.

And she valued his efforts and support too much to deride him for unconventionality.

"If I *did* have a gut feeling and I *did* bet, I'd say that Khan is serious about befriending you."

"Why?" she asked

"Based on what you told me last night, he has a clear disdain for Adams. And you said that Adams was snide, too."

"He mentioned Khan had views."

"Right. He wouldn't have sided with you against him without reason. Why and for what purpose? I don't know."

"It doesn't mean he didn't kill my son."

"No," Heron agreed, opening his croissant. "People like that see puzzle pieces. Pawns."

She arched a brow. "You think I'm a pawn?"

"Oh no." He slipped a piece of bacon between two flaky bits of pastry. "I think you're the *queen*. Or a knight at least."

She let this go. Davion was the one who'd loved to play chess. She barely remembered what all the pieces were called.

"All I'm saying is that it's very possible that he's our murderer—*and* he wants your help. They can be very compartmentalized like that."

"*They?*"

"The rich and powerful."

"Heron, do I have to keep reminding you that *you're* rich and powerful?"

He drew back, pretending to be insulted. "Excuse me? I don't think I heard you correctly. Are my diamond ear implants acting up? Can you say that again?"

She rolled her eyes and slid the last of her breakfast into her mouth. It had been very delicious.

"Please. I have more." He rose from the table and went

to the kitchen. He reappeared with two more warm croissants in his hand. He placed one on each of their plates.

She ate this one more slowly, savoring it with the dark koffee.

They fell into an easy silence. She marveled at the fact that despite how chatty Heron naturally was, he could also be quiet. Sometimes.

So she ate her croissant and looked around his unit.

"What is it?" he asked finally. "You look confused."

"You once told me you had a cat. A miniature tiger. But I've never seen it."

"Duchess?" He took a sip of koffee. "She's shy."

"Her name is *Duchess*." Grace felt ready to burst into laughter.

Heron sat up straight. "What's silly about that?"

"Nothing."

He sniffed. "No wonder she isn't ready to meet you."

"Do you really have a cat?"

"Yes." He laughed. "I do. But she won't come out until she trusts you."

"Trusts me?"

He shrugged. "I don't make the rules."

It stung to be rejected by a cat she hadn't even met.

<<Accept cache from heronjane1?>> Grace opened the cache and found hundreds—no, thousands—of photos inside. A golden-striped cat with piercing amber eyes stared back at her in most of them. In others, she lay curled in a fluffy ball, the white fur of her belly hiding all but the black-tufted tips of her ears.

Grace recognized the living room and Heron's bedroom in the shots.

"These are fake."

He laughed. "I would tell you to stop being paranoid, but I like that about you. You'll have to trust me. I really do have a cat. And her name is Duchess. Okay, that's a lie."

"Which part?"

"I call her Duchess, but her actual name is Penelope."

She closed the photo cache and filed it away. "*If* she's real, Duchess Penelope is beautiful."

"Thank you. I've put in a good word for you, but these things really can't be rushed."

"I understand." What else could Grace do, really? "Let me clear these dishes."

She gathered their empty plates and took them into the kitchen.

"Put them in the cleaning tray," he said.

The mechanical arm was extended from the wall, wiping the counter where flakes of pastry had fallen. Another was lifting the butter and leftover bacon from the counter and moving it to the fridge.

At least Heron still used machines for cleaning. He was somewhat civilized then.

He came up behind her, reaching past her to grab the carafe of koffee. "Now," he said, refilling both their mugs, "shall we go to CyTown?"

"Do you think we can find Tristan without being caught?"

"Unlikely. Let's do it anyway."

"Your confidence is…alarming." She joined him on the couch, steam rising from her mug, the heat pressing into her palms. The blanket they'd shared the night before was thrown over the back of the sofa.

"Here's my honest assessment. I think we'll get pretty far before we're noticed. How far depends on how closely he is being monitored. If no one is checking his data, then we won't be seen, but if someone is mining his mind—"

"Mining his mind?"

"If someone took him for his views, it's possible they're trying to find the ideas within his mind, to eradicate or pollute them."

"Why?"

"In case he's ever released from CyTown," he said to the tone of *obviously*.

She let this slide.

"He didn't create this reality, which means he doesn't control it. I assume they mimic reality close enough so that his mind doesn't reject it. But there's always the possibility some sick bastard forced him into a hellscape to torment him."

"Is it dangerous to link up our software with this CyTown? Especially if we don't know why or how it was created?"

"Oh, absolutely." He scoffed. "You have to be careful what you put in your head. That's why I want to install about three levels of anti-malware before we go in there. I don't want us to end up like vegetables. Who will feed Duchess Penelope—I love this compression of her name, by the way. I don't think I'll be able to call her anything else."

She threw back her koffee. "Let's go then."

Heron extended his hand toward her, palm up. "If you please."

She arched a brow.

"For the software," he said. "I told you. I'm not taking you in until I install the anti-malware."

She slid her hand into his and found it cool, soft. A chill ran up her arm, coiling at the base of her neck before tightening the muscles in her core.

His hand tightened on hers. <<Accept cache from MrBlue?>>

Yes. "Should I be concerned that you're using your alias?"

"Covering our tracks. I gave you one too. Look."

She pulled up the data details of her current profile and saw Commander Grace Buteo had been replaced with <<Asturina>>.

"It's a gray hawk," Heron said. "Did you notice?"

"Notice what?" She was trying to quell the rising dizziness. Whatever Heron was implanting into her mind was massive amounts of data. She could tell by how she felt, the off-centered swell of its onslaught.

"We're both named after birds."

She'd known that Buteo was a type of hawk, or a family of hawks. No, it had buzzards, too. Maybe. But she hadn't put two and two together.

"Birds have short lives," she said.

"Morbid." He snorted. "We need to work on your outlook, Gray. Optimism goes a long way."

The spinning stopped, and she found opening her eyes helped. She wasn't even sure when she'd closed them.

"Sorry, that was a lot." He was running a thumb over her knuckles. It was in that moment she realized he was supporting a lot more of her weight than she'd thought. "But I needed to upgrade some things if I was going to take you into the programming I built."

"Is there more?" she asked.

"Nope, I got it all in one go. You can take a lot." His brows flicked.

She squeezed his hand hard. "Stop being a pervert."

"Sorry." He pulled back, laughing. "You make it too easy."

He was rubbing his hand, but he smiled. "The rig I built is upstairs in my office."

"You built a rig? With what time?"

"I was trying to keep myself busy while you were out last night. An idle mind isn't good for me. If I hadn't I might've done something crazy. Like crash the party."

"Way to show restraint."

"I have my moments."

He opened the door at the top of the stairs to reveal a small room with only a single centerpiece. The white-and-black rig didn't have quite the finesse of the rigs advertised in media, or the ones they'd seen in their CyTown tour, but it looked complete enough.

"Is this safe?" she asked.

"Perfectly."

"But there's only one."

"Yes, I'm going to enter and bring you along as a scapeshare. You'll basically be a ghost program in my mind."

"Then why did you have to send me that enormous cache?"

"That was the minimum for sharing with me," he said, eyebrows up. "Just to piggyback into Tristan's CyTown, I had to bring you up to speed for that interface. To make you compatible with this rig—god." He puffed his cheeks. "You'd probably need six more caches at least."

"Are you telling me that my lenscape is subpar?"

"No…" He paused in rolling up his sleeves and pointed at the red recliner in the corner. "I brought that chair up for you. You can recline in it and close your eyes. I think that'll help. Don't want you to get dizzy and fall down."

She did as he instructed, trying to make herself as comfortable as possible. For the first time, she realized she was nervous.

"This is safe, right?" she asked.

"Hopefully."

"Heron."

"I don't aim to die, if that's what you're asking."

"*Heron.*"

"We'll be fine," he said with a noncommittal shrug. "Probably."

Before she could demand he outline the risks and give her a chance to problem-solve the situation, her mind was alight with sensory input. Her back pressed into the chair as if she could get away from the lights whizzing by or escape the flood of color.

"Hold on," he said, and Grace reflexively tightened her hold on the chair's arms. "We're passing through the external firewall now."

Through gritted teeth she said, "Is that what's happening?"

The whirling tunnel of lights was too much. She felt dizzy, sick. Her top and bottom perspectives kept flipping, twisting, agitating her stomach in turn.

Just when she thought she might vomit, when she might tap out and let Heron enter CyTown on his own, the tunnel broke open.

A blue sky erupted overhead. Blessedly, the ground appeared green and stable beneath her feet. She took a deep breath, hoping the nausea would subside.

"Breathe. A hell of an entrance, wasn't it?" Heron's voice was crystal clear in her ear, though it seemed they shared a single pair of eyes. "You okay?"

"I'll be fine," she said. "Tell me what we're looking at."

In their view was a large field. Flowers, hip high, swayed in a light breeze. She could hear the babble of water but couldn't see it for the thick line of trees along one side.

"Where are all the buildings?" she asked.

He pointed at the horizon. "There. Think of this as a back door. An undeveloped part of the program. Plenty of free radical data here. I thought we'd be less detectable if we entered this way."

He's really not expecting us to get far, she realized. Before she could consider what it might mean—for Tristan's mind to be totally controlled—Heron began walking toward the distant digital city. One moment they were in the flowers, the next, concrete pressed hard against her—his—feet.

Passing through a stone arch, she recognized where they were immediately.

Tristan's apartment building loomed above them.

"He's inside." Heron's hand reached out and pulled the handle. It was strange to see Heron's hands in place of her own. Feel the shift of his body, also unlike her own. He seemed to have a higher point of gravity, more of his weight in his chest and solar plexus, as opposed to the hips, where she held hers.

But fortunately the view was steady now. As long as that held, the dizziness abated.

At Tristan's apartment door, he reached for the handle.

"Wait!" she said. "Knock first."

His hand hesitated. "Right. We know this is a dream, but he doesn't. I don't think he'd appreciate a stranger storming into his apartment."

"Assuming he's in there," she added.

"He is. I'm tracking his signal, and it's coming from here."

Heron rapped on the door and waited. Grace's heart fluttered. At least, she thought it was her heart. Or was Heron feeling nervous?

"Who is it?" a man called.

"We are with the Zone 2 precinct," Heron called out, his voice reverberating off the door. "We would like a moment of your time, Mr. Range, if you'd be so kind."

"Polite," Grace said.

"Thank you."

The door opened. Tristan Range stood there with a drink in one hand, the other on the door frame. He didn't quite look like his photos on record. This Range had long blond hair and brown eyes. His bushy brows were pulled together, a carpet of concern. His lips pursed in question.

"What's going on here? Did you say you're with the police?"

"Mr. Range! Good afternoon. Do you have a moment? We—I mean, *I*—need to talk to you. It's very, very important." Heron stepped into the apartment.

"Wait, I didn't say you could come in." His scowl deepened. "You didn't give me a name."

"Inspector Heron Jane. And to be clear, we don't have a lot of time. I'm absolutely sure that we will be interrupted."

"By who?" Range shut the door. "I'm going on the air in six minutes."

"On the air. Your show, you mean? Are you still broadcasting?"

"It's all I ever do these days." He gestured to the back bedroom. This place was an identical replica of the real apartment that Heron and Grace had searched. His office stood open, his projected workstation visible through the cracked door. "It seems like the ideas never stop. As soon as I get one out, another floods in."

"Can I see your transcript for tonight? I'm a huge fan of your work."

Tristan's face colored. He was obviously pleased by the attention. "Sure."

He disappeared down the hall. The rustle of papers echoed back to them.

"Shit, we have company already," Heron whispered. "Look."

He turned toward the door, and in his view, the walls became transparent, the floors fading to mere architectural lines as his vision reached past all opacity. Red dots, six in a row, were running to the elevator on the first floor.

"How many minutes do we have?" Grace asked. "We need to know—"

"Okay, okay." Heron came up onto the balls of his feet.

His nervousness skittered through her mind, a pang of electricity through her limbs.

Tristan returned with his papers in hand. "Here."

Heron shuffled through the papers, capturing the text with his lenscape.

Tristan frowned. "You're not even reading it."

"Oh, I'm a very fast reader," Heron said. "Tell me. How do you feel about CyTown Towers?"

Tristan shuffled in place, clearly restless. "They're raping the people of this zone. They're taking their minds and folding them like clay. Emptying the most susceptible and vulnerable of their agency and using them like—"

"Great," Heron interjected. His eyes kept flicking to the red dots traveling up the floors, moving closer and closer to Range's apartment. "And would you ever become a citizen of CyTown? Willingly?"

"How are we going to get out of here?" Grace asked.

"Never." Tristan took his papers back. "I abhor everything about that community. If you can even call it that. A *community*."

The elevator dinged at the end of the hall. "Heron. We have to go."

"I wouldn't want to ruin the surprise," Heron replied. To Tristan, "Even if you were dying, deathly ill, would you commit to CyTown? Are you deathly ill?"

"No," Tristan said, his face screwed up in irritation.

"Never. Why in the world would I give control of my mind to these vultures? I'm better off dead."

The door began to buck and bulge. "Police!"

"Thank you very much for your time today, Mr. Range. You've been most helpful."

The door splinted, bamboo shards raining into the living room.

Heron moved to the window and yanked it open. "Time to go."

"Hey, what's going on?" Range yelled. "What the hell is happening right now?"

Grace caught sight of the street below. Very *far* below.

The white CityRides scurried between the rose-gold buildings. Ferns and other air-purifiers growing from solar panel cracks swayed in a breeze.

"We can't jump out a window. We can't—" The wind swallowed Grace's words as her body—Heron's body—fell backward from the window.

Fingers grabbed at her clothes—*his* clothes—but the hold weakened, slipped.

The sky rushed away from them, the edges of Heron's suit flapping wildly in the wind.

Through his eyes she saw herself—or rather her double—staring down at them. Her hair covered each side of her face as she leaned out the window, watching them fall.

And in her eyes—nothing. Nothing at all.

FIFTEEN

WHEN GRACE'S back hit the pavement, she sprang up from the recliner, gasping. Strong hands pressed against her chest, compressing her.

"It's okay," Heron said. "Breathe."

She swore. "A window? Was there really no other way?"

Sweat had broken out on her brow.

"Okay, so I didn't build a proper exit."

"Obviously!" She stood on shaking legs, pacing. She needed to release the adrenaline somehow. Even as a spectator, and her body free from a rig, she had underestimated how convincing the landscape would be. The smell of sweat on Tristan's skin. The sound of the wind whipping around her face—Heron's face. The crease between her doppelgänger's eyes as she'd reached out the window to grab them and missed.

Everything had felt as real as the heart beating in her chest now.

Heron's pupils were too large. "I knew that if I killed us, it would eject us from the programming."

"You should've warned me that was the plan." Her pulse was still knocking in her throat.

He pouted. "I feel terrible about that. I guess I was hoping I'd figure something out before they caught up to us."

Grace figured they'd had no more than five, maybe ten minutes inside Tristan's CyTown. "They were quick," she conceded.

"*So* quick," Heron agreed. "I was right about them monitoring his mind."

"Why would they do that?"

"Drink first," Heron said, and Grace realized he was also sweating, his pulse jumping in his throat as high and skittish as her own. "Questions second."

The fact that his body was telegraphing signs of distress soothed her. At least it had been as real for him as it had been for her.

In the kitchen he splashed cold water on his face and dabbed his skin with a bamboo towel. Running wet hands through his hair, he stepped aside. "I have another towel if you need to…" He gestured at the sink. "It was very real."

"Incredibly real." She splashed the water on her face and accepted the clean towel he offered her.

"More black koffee or do you want something stronger?" he asked.

"Koffee is fine."

Once they were on the sofa, faces cool, drinks hot, Heron sent her another invitation to scapeshare.

She accepted, and the documents unfolded on her screen.

She skimmed, her frown deepening as she read. "Have you read this?"

"Quite the about face, isn't it?" He sipped his koffee.

"Did you get that part about zone *fealty*? Fealty! As if we were in a monarchy rather than a democratic republic."

Protection of our zone's resources should be the paramount concern for our citizens. Our freedom is protected by the might of our wealth. The might of our wealth controlled by the security of the resources that provide that wealth. Zone 2 must protect its resources—particularly our water—as if our life and liberty are at risk. Because they are.

She scanned the rest of the document.

Then looking up, Grace searched Heron's face. "He's talking about water as if we don't have much. Why? Zone 2 has plenty of water. I must divert part of my water allotment two or three times a week."

Heron ran his hands through his hair again. "Look."

A comms link appeared in her screen, a blinking *Live* button beside it.

She opened the streaming program and her ears were flooded with Range's voice. They searched each other's faces while the broadcast ran.

"Considerations for ecological security must be made. The sacrifice isn't ideal, not by anyone's standards, and certainly not my own. But in order to ensure that our liberty is protected, that we can live to fight another day, we must relinquish certain freedoms for the good of all."

"What is this?" she asked.

"That's Tristan speaking."

"How can he be speaking? We found him embedded in the CyTown program."

Heron's eyes flicked down in concentration. "Listen to his voice. Let me check something."

His lenscape shifted from blue to a soft, iridescent purple.

"It's really his voice," he concluded. "But it's running slower than usual. It's almost like he's—"

"Talking in his sleep," Grace concluded. "They've got him broadcasting in his sleep."

"Not just broadcasting." Heron's jaw worked. "Broadcasting propaganda. He's arguing that citizens should apply for CyTown residency in order to conserve our resources and protect the zone's wealth."

Range continued, unaware of their dialogue. "Your comfort would be assured, your lives far more luxurious than the one you experience now, and you'd have the additional benefit—no, honor—of knowing that your contribution was ensuring the future of our children, of our children's children. Our resources must be protected."

Grace pinged Constable Ezra. Their response was immediate.

<<How soon can I meet with you?>> she asked.

<<This sounds urgent, Commander,>> was Ezra's reply.

<<It is.>>

Seconds passed before Ezra wrote, <<I can be in the office in thirty.>>

<<Thank you.>> Grace assessed her clothes.

"What?" Heron asked, rising up off the couch. "What is it?"

"Can I borrow a shirt?"

In the CityRide, Grace tugged at Heron's shirt, adjusting the knot at her hip. With his shirt pulled over last night's dress, it gave her a semblance of professionality. It was tight across her chest, but otherwise it passed inspection. She checked the reverse field of her lenscape and examined her complexion. She'd done the best she could in his bathroom, but it wasn't easy without her usual resources.

She let this go and focused instead on what she was going to say to Ezra.

Heron kept chewing his lip.

"Stop that," Grace said. "You'll make it bleed."

"I'm worried they'll know it was us." He exhaled. "I shouldn't have brought you in there. If they suspect you're on to them, they'll retaliate."

"It's you I should worry about. They didn't see me," she said.

"They'll assume that anything I did was on your order. I should've made a face. I should've hidden my identity, but I thought that if I wore my own, then Range could check it against public record and see that I was really who I said I was. I'd hoped gaining his trust would speed up the interview."

"Logical," she agreed.

"*Stupid.*"

"Take a breath." The golden buildings blurred as they passed, their auto maneuvering around the other white CityRides in the wide boulevard. "If this works out with the constable, they'll put the blame on me."

"Is that where we're heading?" Heron asked. "I wondered."

"I didn't tell you?"

He snorted. "No. You said, 'Wash your face and change your shirt.'"

The CityRide rolled up to the High Town administration offices. Before the auto could finish the exit monologue and confirm Grace's final total, they were already mounting the stairs to the building.

Heron made short hellos to the administrators they passed, but Grace barreled on.

The constable was already in—Grace checked the gender profile and found it unchanged. They were sitting on the desk, one leg crossed over the other. Their eyes were lit blue, indicating an active lenscape. Grace refrained from exclaiming her request straight away. Instead, she eased herself into a chair.

Heron mimicked her in the adjacent chair. The constable acknowledged them with a short nod. "One moment, you two."

As soon as the blue light in their eyes clicked off, Grace said, "CyTown Towers is forcibly—"

"Ah!" the constable cut in, holding up a hand. A grid-like light slid along the walls, crossed in the corners, and reversed direction.

"Sealed rooms, Commander. They're essential when discussing delicate matters." They pointed at Grace. "You were saying. What's so important that we are both in the office on a Saturday?"

"I need warrants for Arden Pendam, Dr. Ezekiel Tove, and Abe Rise."

The constable arched their brow. "On what grounds?"

"They're forcing residents into CyTown residency. They're forging medical release forms and statements of will. We have evidence that at least one resident was forced into residency, but there could be countless others. Now they are forcing that resident to use his considerable public platform to recruit others into joining CyTown. He's being forced to broadcast propaganda in his sleep. It's manipulation."

The constable pressed a finger into their temple. "Back up. You'd better start over."

Grace did. She began with Lenorie's visit and finished with the interview.

The constable was frowning. "What's their motive?"

Grace shrugged. "Perhaps they're avoiding ecological taxes like Viscosity, or removing people who might expose their backdoor dealings. I can't be sure until I have more information."

The constable rubbed their brow. "You don't work small, do you? Do you have a list somewhere of the richest, most influential people in the zone on it, and you wake up in the morning and think, 'I'm going to terrorize this one today.'?"

Grace looked at them.

The constable sighed. "These people need to be checked like everyone else, but you are playing with fire here. You will get burned."

Grace gave a wan smile. "I've already been burned."

"Wow, that was dark. I walked right into that, didn't I?" The constable snorted. "Wait. How did you interview him when Rise rejected your first inquiry? Did you return to the Towers then?"

Heron was watching her, waiting to see what she would say.

Grace didn't answer.

The constable's eyebrows rose. "Information obtained illegally cannot be used legally. You know this."

"It was necessary. They're forcing people to—"

"No," the constable said, and shook their head. "I won't give you the warrant."

Grace's heart flopped. "Why?"

"You don't have enough."

"But I—"

"I'm sorry. No."

"You don't believe us."

The constable clucked their tongue. "I believe you, but my belief in your character and good work simply will not suspend the safeholds we have in our legal system. You will need more evidence or this will be dismissed out of hand,

and I for one, refuse to let you destroy your career like that."

"It's a risk I'll take."

"How noble." The constable rolled their eyes. "I'm glad you have such freedom in your life, but the rest of us need you."

When Grace didn't move, the constable's face softened.

"Sometimes I forget how young you are. Money still talks, my dear. Especially in zones like ours." The constable opened and closed their fists. "Pendam will argue that Range entered CyTown of his own volition, and we have nothing *legal* to prove the contrary. The paperwork and testimony support this, and neither Dr. Tove nor Mr. Rise will contradict Pendam. They will be a unified front against you. Publicizing your position will only give them time to cover their tracks."

"What about the broadcast?"

Ezra shook their head. "They'll use the broadcast as proof that his views on CyTown have changed and align with the paperwork they now have. It will be used as proof against you, nothing more. Furthermore, they can argue that it is an old stream, released on a schedule. There will be no way to prove that he is forced to *sleep* broadcast. Unless someone is standing over his rig, watching him do this, they won't believe it."

"But it's wrong!" Grace exclaimed, gripping the chair's armrest. "It's exploitation!"

The constable frowned. "I know. I *really* do know, and I want to help you, but you need more, Commander. A lot more."

GRACE STOOD on the steps outside the administration buildings, unsure of what to do with herself. She didn't want to call a ride. She didn't want to go home. She wanted to go to work, but Adams was likely there. And she was tired. Her adrenaline had crashed, leaving her mind fuzzy and her next move unclear.

"What do you want to do?" Heron asked. All the adrenaline seemed to have left him, too. He stood beside her, his shoulders slumped, the skin under his eyes dark.

She said nothing.

"Lunch?" he ventured.

"I'm not hungry."

"A drink?"

"No."

"We could go into the office and—"

"I need to sleep," she said, her irritation ringing in her ears. "In a bed."

He could've pointed out that he hadn't *made* her sleep on his sofa, that he had in fact offered her his bed, but he didn't. Somehow this irritated her even more.

After a minute of silence, with Grace staring out over the wide boulevard, regarding the rushing weekend traffic, he said, "I've called you a ride."

She noted the *you*, and turned. "What about you?"

"I want to walk."

"Why?" Her cheeks were hot, her arms restless and uncomfortable at her side.

"It's a nice day and I think better when I walk."

There was no animosity in his voice, but she felt his withdrawal like a cool hand pulled from the back of her neck.

Stop, her mind said. *Stop being mad at him because you didn't get what you want. He didn't do that. He's done nothing but help you.*

Whatever Heron must've thought of her irritation, he didn't act on it. He was too well schooled to accept her invitation to an argument. Had that been his mothers' doing? Had he learned that from Nora the historian? Or Victoria the scientist?

She suddenly wanted to say she was sorry, but one of the white, beetle-shaped autos was pulling up to the curb.

"This is yours," he said. "Call me later if you want."

Grace opened her mouth to thank him but he was already halfway down the steps. He was headed in the direction of the High Town strip. It was mostly vertical farms and grocery stores that way. A few restaurants.

What did he want from there? A drink? Food? Company more pleasant than hers?

If he walked far enough, he'd end up in Westside, where Arjun's apartment was. Perhaps even Arjun himself.

She watched him go until the CityRide enveloped her, cutting off her view.

"Good afternoon, Commander Buteo. My name is Harmony and I'll be your driver. Where would you like to go today?"

He hadn't given her address. He hadn't silenced the AI or anything.

Was he mad at her too?

Grace gave the AI her home address and fidgeted with the seatbelt. She lowered the opacity on the auto's walls, but it didn't help in her search. She couldn't catch sight of Heron. There was too much traffic. Too many bodies on the walkways.

He was gone.

"That's a sixteen-minute ride by level-one transport," the AI said, oblivious to the sinking in Grace's chest. "The rate for this transaction is thirty-five dollars. Confirm order?"

"Yes."

A ping resonated through the auto's interior. "Your account has been deducted thirty-five dollars for this transaction. Thank you for choosing CityRide. Safe. Fast. City-Ride. We value your business."

Grace watched the administration buildings grow small behind her as the auto sped away, weaving itself into the flow of traffic.

She thought once that she'd caught sight of unruly black hair and a tapering waist, but when she looked again the sidewalk was empty. Whoever she'd seen was gone.

SHE WOKE after sunset to the house's voice.

"Grace, you have a visitor."

Her eyes pried themselves open. The shadows were long, stretching across the carpet like hands reaching. The fact that she'd fallen straight into bed still wearing Heron's clothes spoke to how exhausted she'd been.

Seeing them crumpled and wrinkled reminded her of the way they'd parted.

Her heart sank.

"Grace, you have a visitor," it said again.

The fact that the house did not identify the person meant it was someone whose metrics hadn't been added to the house's register.

Not Heron, she thought, somewhat disappointed.

Of course not, her mind chided. He didn't do anything wrong. Why should he rush over and apologize?

Grace threw back the covers and stood in the room, groggy and stiff. She would've slept through the night, she realized, had she not been awoken by the mystery guest.

She tried to smooth her hair and shirt as the house announced a visitor for the third time.

"Coming!" she called. "Give me a minute."

Her hand was on the handle when Davion's voice rang through her head. *You don't know who it is, Gray.*

She hesitated, pulled her hand back. "House, show me the guest."

The house obeyed, lowering the opacity on the wall until her walkway, lawn, and the street were as clear as if she were standing outside herself.

The orange rays of sunset rested on Adams's shoulders. His hands wrung a bouquet between his fists, crumpling the paper savagely. Petals were raining onto the stoop beneath him. He seemed unaware of this.

She swore. "Lower the opacity on the front door but don't unlock the house."

"Yes, Grace." The house obeyed. The second layer of opacity was removed, allowing Adams to see her as clearly as she saw him.

"Grace." He breathed her name like a sigh. He thrust the flowers toward her. "Could you let me in please?"

"I'm in no state to have guests," she told him. "I'm exhausted and I've had a rough day."

Adams looked at the flowers as if he wasn't sure what to do with them now that they'd been refused. "We need to talk."

"We can talk later, when I'm feeling well enough to carry on a conversation." Grace wasn't going to justify her needs to this man.

He looked at his parked auto then up the street as if expecting something.

"I..." He seemed to search for the words. "You shouldn't be alone."

"I *want* to be alone, Commander."

He ran a hand over his face. "I want to apologize for last night. I think I..." He looked at the flowers again, squinting as if they might have the appropriate lines tucked into their petals. "I think I came on too strong, too quickly. I didn't mean to frighten you or scare you off."

"You didn't scare me," she said plainly.

Per usual, he didn't seem to hear this. "You don't know how long I've waited to tell you how I feel."

"Do you feel better having told me?" she asked.

This, at least, stopped him.

"No," he said. "I'd hoped you'd reciprocate."

"I don't. I'm not interested in you. How can I be more clear on this?"

He was nodding, but his jaw was working overtime, clenching and unclenching as he looked up and down the street.

"Is it because you've already met someone else?"

"No," she said, even as her mind whispered, *Maybe*. "I've never seen you that way. I don't reciprocate your feelings."

The poor flowers were being tapped against his palm, shaking what was left of the petals off onto the walk.

"Is there any way? Any possibility that with time you could—"

"No," she said.

"Our friendship could—"

"We're not friends." Here the first hot spike of her anger rose through the grogginess of her exhausted mind and lashed out. "My *friend* would tell me who killed my husband. My *friend* would give me the name of the bastard who put a bomb in my auto and blew up my son. My *friend* would help me to understand what the hell is going on and—"

"I told—"

"You told me lies," she said, unwilling to let him gain momentum on that track again. "You know who is responsible. You know what happened. You've chosen to keep that from me in order to protect yourself—"

"To protect you! Not me, *you*!"

"Bullshit."

Adams threw the flowers against the walk. "*Who* suggested you update your IED detection software three days before the attack? *Who* doubled the clock on the IED in the precinct so that you'd have time not only to *find* it but dismantle it? Who's here *now*, checking on you and making sure they haven't come and taken you away like they have the others?"

"What others? Who's been taken away? To where? CyTown?" Her heart hammered. "Do you know something about CyTown?"

"They wanted to kill you and I gave you every chance to survive. You survived because of *me*."

Grace's mind sputtered. "You knew there was an IED in the auto? And the precinct?"

He hung his head. "I suspected the auto was a possibility, and as long as I kept you in the precinct you'd be safe. I—"

Grace saw red. "Unlock the door."

No sooner had the house complied than she was through the door and launching herself at Adams. She struck him once in the neck, again in the stomach. He folded, coughing.

"You knew there was an IED in the auto! You knew they'd blow it up!"

"No." He blocked her third and fourth swings. "I suspected, but I wasn't sure."

"I sent them to the auto because I thought it was safe. If you'd told me...if you'd told me..."

If I'd known there was a bomb. If I'd known, oh god, if I'd known, if I'd known...

Her chest compressed. She suddenly couldn't draw enough air into her lungs. Her legs wobbled. The world spun and she pitched forward.

Adams was on her before her knees hit the walk.

"Don't," she said. "Don't touch me."

"Please, Grace. You have to understand. I wanted to tell you."

"Don't touch me!" she screamed, and swung, but her fists connected only with air.

I can't breathe. I can't breathe.

He was nothing but a hulking shadow bent over her, imposing, unavoidable, and she couldn't breathe.

"Grace. I'm sorry. I'm so—"

She thought he was going to kiss her. She thought he was simply going to force himself on her right there on the sidewalk in front of her house.

Adam's breath was hot on her face. "Grace. Please."

"Get off me."

She jerked her elbow up and connected with his solar plexus. He stiffened, his eyes fluttering closed. Then he was collapsing to his side.

Grace didn't understand what had happened—she hadn't hit him that hard—until behind his slumping body appeared another face.

Dr. Tove wet his lips, looking worried, and out of place against the backdrop of the setting sun.

His finger with the occ-mod glowed, telling Grace that he'd used it to knock Adams unconscious. His expression told her that he now wondered if he'd made a mistake.

"Commander," he said, offering to help her up. "Have I come at a bad time?"

SIXTEEN

IT TOOK the two of them almost five full minutes to push Adams's unconscious body into his auto and command it to return him home.

While they worked, her mind reeled.

He'd known the IED was in the auto.

He'd known and hadn't told me.

If he'd told me I could've sent Davion and Kaiden anywhere else. I could've sent them to an adjacent building.

I could've put them in a CityRide. I could've done anything… anything but tell them to hide in the auto I thought was safe.

She was sweating by the time the auto's doors closed and it sped away. Once it had disappeared into the traffic beyond, Tove said, "Shall we talk inside?"

She didn't think he'd have gone through the trouble of using his occ-mod implant, his right as a medical doctor, to incapacitate a police commander if he wasn't on her side. No doubt he'd be betting on her protection and support to pull off such a feat.

After all, he could face severe consequences for the

misuse of his occ-mod, resulting in the loss of accreditation, the occ-mod itself, or even exile from the zone.

Was he going to use it to incapacitate her as well?

She eyed his hand.

He followed her gaze, twitching the finger.

"I have a solution for that," he said. He reached into his pockets and pulled out two black gloves. He tugged one on up to his wrist. "I can't use the modification if it is covered."

"Okay." She nodded toward the house. "I'm assuming you came to tell me something about the Tristan Range case."

His nod was curt, almost imperceptible. "Inside, if you don't mind. There are a lot of eyes on you these days."

Grace pushed open her front door and held it for the doctor. He entered, wringing his hands as if unsure what to do with them. He regarded her home with a sweeping, uncomfortable gaze.

"You have a lovely home," he said. "Is this as it was when Davion was alive?"

This stopped Grace in her tracks. She'd opened her fridge to pull out the Sindu Serves leftovers. "What?" she stuttered.

The doctor licked his lips, his nervousness palpable. It grated on Grace's own nerves.

"I met him," Dr. Tove said, scratching one of his thick gray brows. "I have quite a bit to tell you, actually. I..." He exhaled. "I'm worried how you will take the news, but Mr. Khan insists that I be honest and so..."

"Khan sent you?" she asked. That was interesting.

"Please," Dr. Tove said, gesturing toward the leftovers in her hands.

She tipped the container toward him. "Do you—"

He waved her off before she even finished. "No, thank you. I've eaten."

Grace fixed her plate and put it in the microwave. It beeped three seconds later and presented her with a hot, steaming dish. She took it to the table with a sparkling water, settling in for Dr. Tove to begin.

He was rubbing his brow again.

"If you're worried about Adams…" she began.

He laughed. "No, no. He didn't see me, did he? It's you I'm worried about. I don't think you will like me when I finish this story."

Her heart clenched. The idea that this man cared what she thought of him touched her.

"I can't promise I won't be upset," she said. "But I'll listen. And I'll try not to judge…prematurely."

He nodded, his eyes roving her home as if searching for something to look at. Finally, he took a deep breath and met her gaze.

"I was smuggled into this zone by your husband. He brought my wife and two boys along also. Joseph and Jacob. Good boys, very good boys."

Grace's lenscape searched the public records as he spoke, pulling up the visa applications of Dr. Tove and his family. She found the boys quickly. They were so close in age they could've passed for twins, but they were thirteen months apart. Their matching thick curls and large black eyes only amplified this twin effect.

"We came from Zone 288. Twenty years ago, I completed medical school in Zone 112, but couldn't find a placement in that zone, or any other. I returned to my home zone. My services were in high demand there, but the wages remained poor. I'd married twice before—both women died in childbirth despite my best efforts. When I met my third wife and she became pregnant, I was terrified. I thought, 'I will bury her, too.'"

Grace pushed her leftovers around on her plate with her fork.

"If not for your husband…" He bit his lower lip. "We'd still be in that hell. Perhaps I would be dead now. What would have happened to my wife, my children?" He shrugged. "If they'd been born at all."

Grace noted the age difference between Dr. Tove and his wife.

"When did he forge your visas?" she asked. "How long ago?"

"Six years ago," he said without hesitation. "Because of him, we were able to travel here, get housing, and birth Joseph safely. Jacob came soon after. He helped us find jobs, gave us funds to start. Commander, your husband was our savior."

Her stomach soured. She thought bitterly, *I lost my son so you could have yours.*

When she said nothing, Dr. Tove pressed on.

"I thought our dreams had come true. Until three months ago."

"What happened three months ago?" She would've been in the hospital still, healing. Undergoing therapy for the integration and use of her bionic arm as well counseling for her loss. Daily offers to regraft the skin of her face and her daily refusals.

"Arden Pendam came to see me. He said he knew my visa was fake. That they intended to reveal my identity to the police and have me exiled on the Midnight Train. Unless I agreed to work for them instead."

"They threatened to have you and your family arrested."

"Yes." He scooted to the edge of his seat. "Commander, you might think I am a coward, and I won't say otherwise, but you don't understand what it's like out there, beyond the inner zones. There's nothing I wouldn't have done. *Nothing* to protect my family from that place. Zone 2 is the only home my children have ever known. I could never take them to the outer zones and expect them to survive, let alone thrive. I would've accepted any offer that Pendam had given me if it meant keeping my children safe. Please understand."

She understood. What would she give today to save Kaiden? To bring him back into her arms?

Anything.

She took a drink of her water. "So my suspicion that Tristan was forced into CyTown is correct."

"Yes." He nodded. "You asked me what percentage of them are classified as brain damaged."

"And you lied."

He sighed. "Yes. I did. I said twenty to thirty percent."

"What's the real number?"

"All of them," he hissed. "One hundred percent. They only send me the ones they want locked away."

One hundred percent. "Why would they do that?"

"The reason varies. But everyone taken is seen as a threat."

"By whom?"

"CyTown's objectives, their mission to integrate nearly all of humanity by 2700."

All of humanity. Impossible. "How many have already been forced in? Your best guess?"

"Thousands," he said. "Maybe ten thousand."

Grace's shoulders fell back against the seat.

She couldn't fathom it. All of humanity living in digital space by the year 2700. "Is this about resource management?"

Dr. Tove laughed. "No. This is about money. The more people enslaved, the more resources that can be hoarded and wasted by the remaining few."

Grace considered this, finally making some progress against the leftovers heaped on her plate. Dr. Tove, to his credit, kept quiet. He let her eat. But his face was dark. His shoulders slumped. Something was weighing heavy on his chest.

"Why would you confess to me?" Grace asked. "I don't believe it's out of guilt."

"As soon as you walked into my office, I knew you'd uncover the truth sooner or later. But I hoped that you would be as forgiving and understanding as your husband."

Grace's heart sputtered in her chest. "Are you blackmailing me? Are you telling me you will expose my husband if I don't help you?"

He shook his head. "No, not at all. I'm begging for your help. If I expose you, not only will I be thrown on the Midnight Train but the others who came here with his help would be found and expelled too. That helps none of us."

Us, she thought.

"I'm begging you," the doctor said, his hands clasped in front of him in prayer. "Please."

"What would you have me do? I can't arrest and charge Pendam or anyone else without proper proof. I'd need your testimony at least, and I can't get that without exposing why you'd help them."

"And you won't walk away from this," Dr. Tove said. It didn't really sound like a question.

"No," Grace said. Her shoulders knotted. "I won't let Pendam get away with kidnapping and enslaving our citizens, let alone all of humanity."

She held back from saying, *Why the hell would I?*

The doctor was nodding, his face resigned. "I can get you the proof you need."

"When?"

"Today. Now."

"Really?" She brought her empty plate to the sink and finished her water.

The doctor was nodding, but his eyes remained on the floor. "I'm afraid I will lose everything."

Grace placed a hand on his shoulder and squeezed. "I'll find a way to protect your family."

And she would. She'd ask Heron to do whatever he needed to do to ensure their visas held. That Davion's efforts were not in vain.

This did little to reassure the man. "Our auto has arrived. Shall we?"

Grace thought of Heron. Thought of calling to give him an update on all that had happened. With Adams, with Tove. Maybe even ask him to join them.

Resistance twisted her insides. He'd seemed like he wanted to be alone. Perhaps he was still upset about her irritation.

I'll give him time and space, she thought. *No point in disturbing him when I don't need anything yet.*

Instead of a video call, she settled on a simple ping.

In the auto she composed her message, explaining all that had happened in his absence. She ended with, <<Dr. Tove is taking me to get the evidence we need now. I'll message you as soon as I have it.>>

Grace had been expecting to go Dr. Tove's office when he made mention of the evidence. But when the white CityRide rolled up to the curb outside CyTown Towers, her stomach twinged.

"Why are we here?" she asked him, turning in her seat.

"What we need is inside," he said, climbing out. "I have a passcode to the system. But we have to go now while everyone is gone. We don't want to be here when they return."

If a victim or informant willingly handed Grace evidence, that would be admissible in court. It wouldn't violate the rules. As long as Dr. Tove willingly handed over the evidence, she could submit it to the constable and it would stand in a trial.

Besides, if Dr. Tove had wanted to hurt her, he could've done it at her house. Or in the auto.

"Let's be quick then." She followed him into the building. It was dark, long shadows from the early evening filling up the lobby. The AI they'd met on the first visit wasn't there. It seemed as if no one was in the building at all.

"Is it always closed on Saturdays?" she asked.

"Yes," he said as the elevator opened, sensing their presence. They entered together.

Heron's ping came a minute later. <<Where are you? >>

A little cold, she thought, but she supposed after her attitude earlier she deserved it.

<<I'm in CyTown Towers. Dr. Tove says he has a passcode for the system and can give us the information we need to move the case forward.>>

<<Davion forged his visa? That doesn't mean you're safe with him.>>

She considered explaining how all he could do was render her unconscious with his physician's occ-mod, but she'd been clear about him keeping his hands gloved. Otherwise, he couldn't overpower her with his frail body. More than that, Grace considered the vacancy of the building and lack of personnel. There was no one here with them.

She wrote, <<There's not much he can do. There's no one here but us. He said that Khan sent him to help.>>

She glanced at Dr. Tove's gloved hands again, noticing him wringing them, his eyes fixed on the numbers mounting on the elevator display above.

<<He isn't lying about the relocation,>> Heron confirmed. <<He did come here six years ago, and I recognize subtle tells that suggest Davion was the creator of his visa.>>

Something in Grace unclenched at that. For a moment, Heron had had her doubting. Was it possible that she was shaken after her encounter with Adams, that her decision to come here had been rash and poorly executed?

<<We need evidence to move forward on the Range case,>> Grace insisted. <<I don't want to turn down an opportunity to get what we need.>>

The elevator doors opened and Dr. Tove stepped into the long hallway first. "This way, please, Commander."

She recognized this hall from the detour that Abe Rise had taken on their first visit. On the right they passed a series of the LiveRite 9000 pods, their interiors lit with soft, pulsing lights.

"Excellent work, Ezekiel," a man said.

Grace jolted at the voice, turning in time to see a man step from the shadowed row into full view.

At first she thought it was Khan. The build was identical even with the absence of the two ravens.

But when he moved into the light, Grace saw her mistake. The coloring and features were the same, but not exact. This man was taller, and his face more sinister in his harsh lines and cold regard.

"Khan?" she asked. *Idiot, I'm such an idiot. I didn't ask.*

"Alabaster Khan," he said.

<<It's a trap,>> Grace wrote, sending the ping across the zone, hoping Heron would receive it in time.

She whirled and found Dr. Tove with tears in his eyes, his hand ungloved. "I'm sorry, Commander. I have no choice. But this is better. This way you will live and you will be together again—you can be a family once more."

"No," she said, taking a step back, but there was nowhere to go.

<<It's not Orrin Khan. It's his brother, Alabaster. I don't know his connection to CyTown or Pendam.>>

<<Grace!>> Heron pinged. <<Where are you exactly?!>>

"I'm sorry," Dr. Tove said, and lifted his hand. The occ-mod in his finger began to glow with its activation. "Forgive me."

<<CyTown Towers near those pods we saw. Tove is about—>>

She didn't finish the ping. She couldn't even be sure that it was sent partially or not at all.

There was only darkness.

SEVENTEEN

"MOMMY!" Kaiden yelled. He bounced once, twice on the bed before colliding with her legs.

She bolted upright, groaning in pain. "Christ."

"Daddy!" the boy continued. "Get up, get up! You said we'd go to the park today!"

Davion moaned into his pillow. "It's only six in the morning."

Grace twisted in her sheets. She stared at the curly-haired boy giggling and bouncing in front of her. Her heart knocked. All the air left her. She reached out and seized him with both hands, crushing his small body against hers.

"Hey!" he squealed. "Ow!"

"Oh my god." Grace didn't let go. She held him close, rocking him. "Oh god."

"Baby?" Davion asked. He was coming up onto his elbows now, watching the tears stream down her face, his eyes widening with alarm. "Gray?"

Grace couldn't stop crying. She kept kissing her boy, squeezing him, touching him to make sure he was real. He had to be. He was warm in her hands. His pulse flicked against her palm as he squirmed.

"Dad, help! I can't breathe!" Kaiden pleaded.

Davion touched her arm lightly. "Gray."

"I'm sorry." She pulled back, forcing herself to relax her hold. "I'm sorry."

"Why don't you go down and have the ChefMate start breakfast, buddy," Davion said. "I'll be down in a minute."

Kaiden, glad to have regained his freedom, bounced off the bed. "Quiche fromage, comin' up!"

He closed the door behind him. When his feet could be heard pounding on the stairs, Davion put his hand on Grace's leg and squeezed. "What just happened?"

She swiped at the tears on her face. "I had this horrible dream that he died." She sniffed. "It was incredibly real. I even remember where you were buried in the Soul Grove."

"Me too?" Davion asked, eyebrows up.

Grace began to cry harder as he wrapped his arms around her.

"It's okay," he cooed, rubbing her back, his hand firm and warm. "No one's dead. We're here. Everybody's safe."

She wrapped her arms around his neck. She took a deep breath, savoring his sent. He smelled like the morning. Of laundered bedsheets and a night's worth of sweat.

She kissed his lips. She kissed them again and again until she could force herself to believe he was here. Real. Safe and sound beside her.

He kissed her temple. He kissed her cheeks. "It was just a dream, baby."

"A dream," she whispered, willing herself to believe it, forcing herself to relax in his arms, enveloped by his heat, his solidness. "Only a dream."

. . .

IT WAS after lunch before they made it to the park. Grace's mood was mostly to blame. Time was inconsistent. First speeding up, then falling behind. It didn't help that she kept finding herself staring in the mirror or any reflective surface. Any polished piece of glass was enough.

Whenever she caught sight of herself, she'd freeze, look harder, examining her skin as if she'd never seen it before.

She seemed to have a particular fixation on the right side of her face. She kept touching it, feeling her finger indent the flesh and frowning. Her arm too, as she opened and closed her right fist.

Had there been something in the dream about her face? Her arm?

She couldn't remember.

Even now she struggled to remember the smallest details. There had been something about an auto. Something about the winter parade? But it was May now. The winter parade was months away. And there was a face, black hair, blue eyes, which she could *almost* see, but not quite.

It wasn't only the strange dream fugue hanging over her, it was also that she felt as if she were forgetting something important. She checked her lenscape appointment book and found it clear. Nothing until Monday morning at oh nine hundred, a co-commander meeting with Adams about the new cases they needed to examine and parcel out to their junior agents.

That was it.

Davion tried to help.

Anytime she'd start to dally, her mind's confusion overtaking itself, he'd gently nudge her back to the present. Urge her to pack their lunches for the day, get their koffee and books together so that they could relax on the benches while Kaiden played.

It wasn't until they'd been in the park for almost twenty minutes that she began to relax. The bench was warm.

Davion sat beside her, his thigh pressing against hers as he turned the page of his book.

Grace took a sip of her koffee and watched the squealing children fight over who would drive the dune machine along the sand.

She was still smiling when she caught the eye of a man on the other side of the park.

Tall, shoulders broad but waist tapering. His hair was black and fell forward into his blue eyes. He was watching her closely, his face unreadable.

He looked familiar.

Grace nudged her husband. "Do we know him?"

"Hmm?" Davion didn't look up from his book.

"Him," Grace said again. "He's staring right at us."

Correction. He was staring at *her*. Staring at her as if she were the only person on this whole playground. The intensity of the gaze made her nervous.

Davion looked up. "Who are you talking about?"

"Him," Grace said, moving to point out the watcher. Only there was no watcher. The place where he had stood was now vacant.

He was gone.

PART TWO

EIGHTEEN

GRACE ENTERED the precinct at 8:42 Monday morning, feeling a rush of productivity that always accompanied the start of the week. As the bio-seal registered her metrics and gave her access to the precinct, she ran through her agenda, noting the eighteen-minute gap between her arrival and her first appointment. She sipped her hot koffee as she prioritized her to-do list in the right side of her lenscape.

She hesitated before sitting, glancing through the transparent walls at Duchovny's desk. She watched agents stroll the halls, chatting with one another, exchanging information or gossip.

There was something off about it.

Had the desks moved?

Were there people missing?

A sense of déjà vu settled in her guts. Had she done this before? This exact day?

That's enough. Pull yourself together, she warned.

She'd found concentrating nearly impossible since the nightmare.

It was essential that she remain focused today, given the limited time she had to accomplish her work. Davion was worried after the strange episode that had stretched from Saturday into Sunday. He thought perhaps she'd had a migraine in her sleep Friday night and that explained her mental fugue. He'd wanted her to go to the doctor. She did not.

As a compromise, she promised that she'd be home at a decent hour.

She'd even thrown in the offer of a mid-week date night, which had seemed to assuage him more than anything else. Her mother agreed to take Kaiden for a couple of nights.

I raised a child once, too, she'd said on the video call this morning. *A marriage has its needs.*

Her mother had implied that it was sexual—these needs—and Grace didn't feel like explaining otherwise.

A rough knock at her office door made her look up before she'd even taken her seat. She turned to find Lore Duchovny hesitating in the doorway.

"Commander," he said with a formal salute.

"Good morning." She placed her hot koffee on the desk. "What can I do for you, Inspector?"

"I heard that you've requested an assistant inspector."

She pulled out her chair. "I did. My workload is unmanageable. Do you have someone in mind?"

His back straightened. "I'd like to nominate myself."

Here she finally noted the red glow in his cheeks and the nervous shift in his stance.

She smiled, hoping that would ease him. She'd always liked Duchovny. He did excellent work and gave wonderful attention to detail.

She noted the timestamp on her lenscape.

"I've fourteen minutes before my next meeting. Do you have time for a quick interview?"

"I have the time." He ran a hand down the front of his suit. *Flexible. Good.*

She gestured to the seat across from her. "Let me start by asking why you want the position."

He perched on the edge of the seat, meeting her gaze but only briefly. No surprise. Many of the junior agents couldn't hold her gaze for more than a second before looking away. Grace had once asked Adams why, and he'd said she was too intimidating.

She'd taken this feedback to heart, trying to smile more and ask encouraging questions. Be aware of her tone.

The truth was that when she was working, she was pure, concentrated effort. The moment she left, she could smile and laugh and relax, but at work, when her mind was most engaged, it was nearly impossible to remain light.

Duchovny squeezed his knees. "The position would be an amazing opportunity to learn from you. A chance to see how you manage and coordinate our teams. You use effective diplomacy strategies between zones and your leadership skills are phenomenal. You're…you're one of the best commanders we've had in decades."

She forced a smile to hide her dislike of flattery. "I fail in my aims often enough."

"Failure is inevitable."

"And how do you know I'm the best commanders in decades? You haven't been with the precinct that long."

He straightened. "By general consensus, Commander."

Her smile flinched. "Is that so?"

This interview wasn't supposed to examine her merits but Duchovny's. She searched for the right question to redirect them.

"What do you want and need in an assistant?" he asked.

Initiative. Another good sign.

Grace took the warm koffee into her hands and leaned back in her chair. "I need someone who is organized, responsive. Intelligent. A second brain. I have a great deal of information sent my way each day and someone will need to understand my priorities and organize that information into digestible briefs. You're organized, responsive, and intelligent, but I'm not sure you'll challenge me when needed. I don't always get it right. And I overlook things when I make snap decisions. Would you be willing to point out an error if I make one?"

He looked down at his hands. "I would find that difficult."

Honest.

"Would you try?"

He paused before answering, giving it sincere consideration, and that was when Grace decided she would take him on.

He nodded. "I would try."

"Good. How soon could you begin?"

"Tomorrow."

She extended her hand across the desk. "Then take today to finish up any outstanding tasks you have and delegate the rest. Report back to me first thing tomorrow."

His smile was radiant. "Thank you, Commander."

Adams had to step aside to let him pass as he arrived at her door. 8:59.

"Why does he look delighted?" Adams asked, closing the door behind him.

"I've promoted Duchovny to assistant inspector. I think he'll do well."

Adams frowned. "I didn't realize you wanted to hire

from within the department. I placed an ad for external candidacy. I had four excellent possibilities in mind for you."

"I appreciate your efforts, but you can remove the ad."

She hated it when Adams pouted like this.

He took the seat Duchovny had just vacated. "I'm here for the oh-nine-hundred appointment."

She *also* hated when he stated the obvious. She sipped her koffee to prevent an unkind reply.

"Several corporations in our zone have been accused of fraud," he said, seemingly unperturbed by her silence.

She arched her brows. "Corporate fraud. Interesting. Which companies?"

"CyTown Towers first and foremost. Trinity Trust, too."

"Have you conducted a preliminary investigation?"

"Yes."

"And your verdict?" she asked.

"No case. There aren't three strings to tie to these companies together. We should dismiss the case out of hand."

And you can't dismiss it without my approval, she thought. "Send me the files?"

<<Accept cache from RTAdams52?>>

She accepted the scapeshare and subsequent cache. Adams's notes were concise, but her eyes snagged on a tag in the file's metadata.

Don't overlook this. Follow Orrin Khan. — H

Her brow hardened. "Who's H?"

Adams, who'd been raving about one of the candidates, sputtered. "Excuse me?"

"There's a note in the case's metadata."

His eyes lit blue with the reactivation of his lenscape. She gave him a moment to review the file.

His frown deepened. "What are you looking at? My metadata is clean."

Orrin Khan. She recognized that name. He was the head of Trinity Trust, wasn't he?

"It must be a glitch in the copy of the file. Some leftover information from a previous case template. Ignore it," Adams said.

Khan. Khan. Khan. Something stirred in the back of her mind.

She wasn't sure she'd ever met him. And yet…her mind conjured a vivid fantasy of standing with him on the balcony of an opulent room. Him in a tailored suit, a digital raven on each shoulder, and her…Adams coming up the staircase toward them and she was angry about—

"Commander?" Adams prompted.

Follow Khan.

Adams's frown deepened. "You're not prone to daydreaming, Commander."

No, I'm not, she thought. Already the image of Orrin Khan was sinking below the dark surface of her thoughts, disintegrating into the shadows.

"I had a migraine over the weekend," she admitted. "My mind is a bit stretched today."

"It's been a while since you've had one of those."

"Yes, it has."

"We can cut this short," he said, adjusting himself in the chair. It was too small for him. "I only need you to sign off on the summary pages at the end. I'll clear the cache on the metadata before submitting it to the constable."

Her cursor hovered above the signature line.

H. H. H. H. H.

"Is there a problem?" Adams asked.

"Actually," she said, "I want to review this myself. Give

me a few days and I'll turn it over to you by the end of the week if I find nothing."

His shoulders tightened, and his eyes darkened. "I assure you I was very thorough in my preliminary—"

"I'm sure," she interjected. "This isn't a matter of checking your work. It's simply a matter of being thorough. Surely you don't object to me being thorough."

"It's only a metadata placeholder that wasn't cleared. It doesn't mean anything."

And yet Orrin Khan and Trinity Trust have a connection.

And when she saw that *H* in her screen, it stopped something inside her. She recognized it, though she couldn't be sure how or why.

"It won't take me more than a couple days to complete the checkup," she insisted. She wouldn't be steamrolled by Adams or any other.

"It's our responsibility to be thorough," he said finally.

"I'll be sure to let you know what I discover." She closed the documents and copied them to her personal server. "Assuming I find anything."

She thought this effort at placation would satisfy him. But his face remained dark, his eyes assessing.

"Yes," he said. "Please do."

TRINITY TRUST WAS LOCATED in Whitman Park, by far the most wealthy neighborhood in Zone 2, from the opulent music hall to the specialized boutiques offering everything from artisan soaps, delicious delicacies, and unique art. There were the restaurants with white table cloths and the crowds clad in the newest fashions.

At the end of the main boulevard was the roundabout circling in front of Whitman Park, with its enormous cherry trees and weeping willows. East of that, Trinity

Trust. A building modeled after the long-lost Jefferson Memorial, which was destroyed centuries ago by a tsunami—or so Grace had learned in school.

She requested that the auto drop her off at the entrance. As it pulled away from the curb, she caught sight of a white-haired man with bushy brows coming toward her.

"Commander," he said, extending a hand. "I was told you were looking for me."

Their skin brushed and she reviewed his public profile embedded in the subdermal chip. *Orrin Khan.*

She'd expected a certain level of red tape to jump through in order to reach him. Most of the people in his position weren't easily accessible to the public. Then again, Grace wasn't someone off the street. But to have him here in the open, ready and willing—*Who told him I was coming?*

She arranged her face to hide her suspicion, hoping she'd been quick enough. "Thank you for meeting with me."

"My pleasure." He pointed at the park across the way. "There's a bench beneath the cherry trees that will afford us privacy as well as a beautiful view."

"A walk would be lovely." Grace checked the sun rating in her lenscape. Green. No need for a sunbrella.

She fell into step beside him, their feet clacking against the stone path leading into the park.

"I'm sure you know why I'm here," she began. There was no point in pretending otherwise. He'd surely heard the allegations as soon as the case was made.

A small smile played on his lips. "Yes, I do. And the allegations aren't without merit. My brother's ambitions have always been unrestrained."

Grace's steps faltered. "Your brother."

"Alabaster. He is one minute older than I am. Not that

it matters when children are removed from synthetic wombs."

"Does your brother work with you at Trinity Trust?"

"He has his hands in most of the companies in the zone. My bank, CyTown Towers, three of the vertical farms, and several of the manufacturing plants in Pendam. Not to mention public works: hospitals, the CityRide grid, and power management."

The path narrowed beneath the hanging cherry trees. A gang of kids pushed past them on hoverskates, whooping and hollering after one another. One clipped his knee on a bench and swore.

Khan gestured at the bench, giving her the chance to sit first. She did.

"Before we begin, you should understand that all of our conversations are recorded for the case records."

Most people hesitated at this point, considering their options before proceeding—or running.

Khan only took the seat opposite hers and smiled. "The benefit of knowing my brother as I do is that I understand his tricks—and his weaknesses—better than anyone. Like now," he said, pointing at the cherry trees around them.

Grace followed his fingers to the swaying blossoms above. The gentle breeze slid over her face and neck, teasing her ears. The rustle of the blossoms was a constant low hum. Beautiful, delicious. But she had no idea what they had to do with anything.

"Now I've interrupted his plans. Despite his efforts, I'm here with you. We're speaking in a way that he can't over-hear us."

Grace nodded companionably. It was to be that sort of interview then. That was fine.

Khan wasn't her first rich, eccentric person. She could

indulge him in order to get the information that she needed.

"I need to be very clear here, Mr. Khan. Trinity Trust is one of the companies accused of fraud. Are you telling me that not only is it guilty but you believe your brother to be the actual perpetuator of the crime?"

"Yes, that is what I'm saying," Khan said. "And despite your current…"

He seemed to search for the word, his eyes roving her body. "Predicament, I hope to be of service to you."

What was that? Flattery?

Was it possible that Khan was also guilty, and to avoid his own persecution he was willing to throw his brother to the wolves?

"The courts may not distinguish between his wrong-doing and yours, especially if your businesses are entwined," Grace said.

He shook his head. "I've no doubt that my lot will be thrown in with his, to one extent or another. The truth is, I'm plenty guilty. God willing, I'll have the chance to confess my crimes soon enough. But the more pressing danger is Alabaster's plans. We have to stop him. If we don't, your sacrifice will be for nothing. I don't expect your forgiveness, but—"

"Forgiveness is irrelevant in the court of law," Grace said. His sentimentality was pulling them off course. She wanted him to focus.

He must've seen it on her face. He laughed. "Right. I'm forgetting myself. Where was I?"

"You were telling me about your brother, Alabaster," she offered.

He straightened, stretching one arm along the back of the bench. "Alabaster is singular in his aims. He wants what he wants, and when he has an objective, he will use any and all means to obtain it. This is no different than the fraud you speak of."

"Has he been forging numbers? Embezzling money?" Grace wanted the details on record.

"He's been falsifying numbers, yes. And stealing."

"From who?"

"The people," Khan said, watching the small group of children attempt tricks on their skates. "He steals their lives. Their hopes, their dreams. Any chance they have of surviving."

Grace's headache spiked behind her eyes. Khan seemed to take no notice.

"I'm going to need you to speak plainly," Grace said. She certainly couldn't take "He steals dreams" to a court of law. "What is he stealing exactly?"

"Water." When Grace didn't seem to understand, he went on. "When a company is given permission to operate within a zone, it is designated a certain percentage of the water rights within that zone. Strict resource management is necessary in our time, after all, but businesses don't have the discipline for it. Even with our measures, they can't abide. Business permits are granted based on that company's abilities to adhere to the strict resource regulation. But *everything* needs water. Absolutely *everything*. Every sector and segment of business is reliant on this resource more than any other. Healthcare, pharmacology, food production, education, manufacturing. Seriously, think of something and I'm sure you'll identify its need for water soon after."

A cherry blossom fell from the tree above and landed on his knee. He looked at it, marveling as if he'd never seen one before. He touched it tenderly with his pinky finger, as if it might come alive at his touch.

"A company's imperative is growth. To double, triple,

quadruple in size until it is the most dominant force in its market. However, growth requires more resources, and in our current setup of tight, inflexible borders and rigid treaties, such growth isn't possible. We've traded our ability to grow exponentially for the security of control."

Grace couldn't find the immediate connection between border security and water, but she didn't want to interrupt him. There was something melodious about his voice.

Something familiar.

"We have closed, inflexible borders for the sake of safety. Or so we tell ourselves." Khan lifted the pink blossom from his pants and held it in the palm of his hand. "But nature doesn't exist within borders. A river knows nothing of a border. Nor does the sky. Nor does the wind. We make our little borders and call land *ours*. But resources move. What happens to that area once the resource is gone? If a zone is depleted and its riches are no more? Then what?"

Grace had no answer for this.

That didn't bother Khan. "In the past, humans moved with the resource tide, as it were. If the bison herds traveled on, the hunters packed up their tents and did the same. If a lake dried, they went in search of a new one. But in our social construction, we've made such movement impossible. We deny the human need for freedom, for movement. We demand that people live in the dirt and make a life from ashes—and it simply cannot be done."

More blossoms were raining down now. They landed on Grace's legs and lap.

Khan spoke faster. "It was easy for us to make this world this way in the beginning, when we believed our own resources wouldn't run out. That all the wealth we had must be protected at all costs. But what happens when we've locked ourselves in and the food is eaten? The water drunk? The air consumed. It's not easy to let ourselves out again."

Grace knocked the blossoms from her arm. "I'm not sure I understand your point, Mr. Khan."

"My point, my dear Commander, is that resources are finite, yet a business's need for them grows as it grows. In this particular case, it's water. Zone 2 is believed to be one of the most water-rich zones in North America. What if I told you that wasn't true? That our water is finite and it's running out fast."

A kick ricocheted through Grace's chest. "What?"

"What if I told you all those bulletins you receive about diverting water rations weren't sent to the outer zones but were in fact stolen by the companies within your district?" He shifted on the bench. "What if I told you that not only were these businesses using up all the extra water in the zone, bankrupting its aquifers, but they're stealing water from zones that don't *know* they have water, or that it's being harvested, stolen, right out from under them."

Grace could barely see him now that the falling blossoms had turned into a near torrent.

"This is my cue," Khan said, rising. "I'm out of time, but please, remember what I've told you. Do what you do best, Commander. You have a gift for finding the truth. I beg you to do so now despite all the odds against you."

"Wait. I still have questions." Grace rose, batting blossoms out of her eyes. She fixed her gaze on the dark shape of Khan walking away from her. Not toward the bank but deeper into the park, deeper into the hurricane of cherry blossoms.

"Sir, wait!" She stumbled forward blindly, but the blossoms didn't abate. They were a deluge, a pink whirlwind through which she saw nothing.

Then it stopped. As quickly as it had begun, it stopped.

The cherry trees were now bare, their branches stark against the blue spring sky. Grace turned in the ankle-deep carpet of blossoms but saw no one. The wide path was empty.

Khan was gone.

NINETEEN

FOR TWO DAYS, her calls and attempts to reach Khan were rebuffed. He had meetings. He was away from the office. She'd even gone to his house only to have his domestic AI send her away, claiming he wasn't home. Grace had expected to start their conversation in this way —with this fight for access. But after the incident in the park…The way he'd seemed to disappear in a rainstorm of blossoms like a figment of her imagination made her skin crawl.

It was true that chasing him around was likely a waste of her time. It wasn't like he'd left her empty-handed.

Water, he'd said. The path to her solving this fraud case was to track the water.

She intended to.

When 17:00 rolled around, Grace remembered her promise to Davion to keep her hours light. As distracted as her mind might have been by the strange Khan interview, she didn't want to let Davion down. She ordered her auto at five past and arrived home to find Kaiden at the table doing his schoolwork.

Or trying not to.

"It's dumb!" he cried, rolling his eyes at her. "No one cares about nematodes!"

Davion was pleading with her silently, his face a perfectly readable mask of desperation. "I'll do dinner?"

"That'd be great." She kissed his cheek. "I'll take over here."

"Bless you," he whispered, placing a kiss at her temple. He rose from his seat, offering it to her. "Nematodes are freaky parasitic worms. Stuff of nightmares."

She accessed Kaiden's lenscape and discovered long worms with bizarre hooked mouths wriggling before her eyes.

Her lips curled. "Thanks for the warning. You usually love gross stuff," she told him. "What's the problem?"

"I have to write two hundred words about them."

Her sympathy bloomed. She'd never enjoyed writing herself. Stringing together a thought on the page had always seemed like a waste of time.

She took his hand and squeezed. "Let's see what we can do about that."

THAT NIGHT, as they lay in bed, Grace reviewed the Zone 2 holdings of Alabaster Khan. He did own the businesses that Orrin mentioned, but also several others. Particularly several tech firms and security departments. More interesting, it seemed that for the businesses he didn't have direct control of, he still had a hand in their operations. He sat on the board for nearly thirty companies, big and small.

Surely it's in name only, she thought. *No one has the time to run this many companies.*

A familiar name flitted through her files.

Charlotte's Web.

"Hmm."

"What?" Davion looked up from the book open in his lap.

"The man I'm investigating has ties to Charlotte's Web."

Davion closed the book, searching her face. "Who's the man?"

She considered her vow not to talk about sensitive case details with non-investigators. But perhaps Davion would serve as a witness in this case.

"Alabaster Khan. Do you know him?"

Davion's lenscape lit blue with its activation, momentarily obscuring his eyes. She gave him a moment to search the public records for his face. "I met him a few weeks ago. The head of our department was giving him a tour of the building."

"When were you in the building?" she asked. Often he worked remotely. Since the security of the zone's borders could be enforced from anywhere on the network, it wasn't necessary for Davion to remain in Charlotte Web's bio-sealed headquarters in Low Town. This made him more available for Kaiden's schedule. She loved that aspect of his job.

"I don't remember the exact day," he confessed. "But I think Hamper said he bought the company."

Grace searched the public records. Any shift in owner-ship of a business would be listed in the white papers.

She found what she was looking for about five minutes into her search.

Eight weeks ago, Alabaster Khan assumed a 52% share of Charlotte's Web.

"Why would he buy Charlotte's Web?" she wondered aloud.

"Rich dudes have nothing better to do than buy shit."

"Maybe." Or there's more.

Find the truth, Khan had begged.

Davion returned to his book. "You'd better not forget about tomorrow."

"I won't," she said, deactivating her lenscape. "My mom will be here at eighteen hundred."

"Mmhmm." He gave her a sideways glance.

She laughed. "I won't forget!"

He nestled into the pillows. "I know that look. You're getting wrapped up in a case. When you do that, you stop coming home early. You miss appointments. You get obsessed."

She couldn't argue. She tilted her head and snuggled closer to him. "This was the first day. I'm not obsessed *yet*."

Despite her assurances he was still pouting.

She kissed his neck. "I won't forget. We'll have dinner. We'll see the movie."

"I want to go out for a drink."

"We'll go out for a drink," she added. She kissed higher until she reached the space of skin behind his ears.

He shivered. "You'd better not forget."

Lore Duchovny was in her office when she arrived the next morning. He rose from his seat when she entered and did a little salute.

"First things first," she said, setting her koffee on the desk. "You have to relax. You're not going to have time to stand up, salute, or anything else when we're working."

The tops of his ears were already red. "I want to show proper respect to my commander."

"You're respectful. And you're one of the best officers in the precinct, which is why I wanted to work with you."

A shy smile broke through. "Thank you."

Her eyes snagged on a strange object on her desk. "What's that?"

"I don't know, sir. It was here when I arrived."

Grace picked it up, found that it was actual paper. She couldn't remember the last time she'd seen something made of paper that wasn't a book. But this looked like one of the file folders of her lenscape, except it was a pale beige, rigid, and had more sheets of paper inside it.

"Is something wrong?" Duchovny asked.

"Did you see who delivered this?"

"No, sir."

"Have you seen anything like it before?"

"No, sir."

How strange. Why would someone give her a folder with paper in it instead of sending a download cache or ping? It was completely unsecured, not to mention fragile. What if she misplaced it? Damaged it? Or someone unauthorized read it?

For Commander Buteo's Eyes Only

What a ridiculous name for a folder. Yet her eyes flicked up to Lore's.

He held his hands up in surrender. "I didn't look at it. It was already here when I came in."

She opened the folder and looked at the first page. It was a resource management sheet. It listed all the units of a property's consumption. Electrical. Waste Removal. Water.

Water.

Each pinned collection of papers was a different company.

At the bottom of the first page was a hand-scrawled note:

Do the math – H

She stared at the *H*.

H.

Something stirred in her chest. A deep sadness she didn't understand.

"Are you all right, sir?" Duchovny asked.

"I'm fine," she said reflexively. She snapped the folder shut. "Let's go. We're already behind schedule."

LORE PROVED to be an excellent notetaker. He was skilled at compressing all her data, recordings, and case details into a concise summary for the end-of-day cache. Simply bringing him along had already eliminated 99% of her paperwork, on which she could easily spend hours trying to determine what was essential and informative versus superfluous.

His responsiveness was also impressive. When she asked for something, he sent it via ping immediately. He never questioned her orders. When she solicited his opinion, his responses were thoughtful and insightful.

Truly, she'd never gotten on with another agent as well.

So why had this air of melancholy followed her throughout the day?

Sometimes she would stare at Lore and almost wish… for *what?* What was she missing exactly?

He was everything she'd ever wanted in an assistant, and yet his mere presence made her feel a strange, distant loneliness. She could neither rationalize nor understand this, but it was true.

You're just uncomfortable, her mind chided. *You've never been good at asking others for help.*

Perhaps that was true.

Yet when they'd stopped to have lunch between meetings with the Zone 2 commissioner and High Town electorates, she'd found herself thinking, *His eyes are the wrong shade of blue.*

She'd almost burst out laughing.

The wrong shade of blue? Lore was possibly the best assistant in the history of assistant inspectors and her one grievance was that his eyes were the wrong shade of blue?

My mother's right. I'm too hard to please.

She spent the rest of the day making a point to praise Duchovny for every proficiency he displayed. Each exchange was clearly uncomfortable for them both. Grace gave him a reprieve by sending him home an hour before their 17:00 shift ended.

She used the last hour to look at the strange folder again.

Do the math – H

She had in fact done the math for all of the resource tallies. At first pass, nothing was amiss. The numbers were correct. It wasn't until the third pass that she caught the small discrepancy.

The issue was the public data versus that which was found in the paper file.

She checked the companies again, flipping through each page, running the numbers.

"Thirteen companies," she muttered to herself. Her voice echoing softly around the office. "It's off for thirteen of them."

In the public tax records, the water allotment for each company was shown. However, for these thirteen, the number of units used and what was allotted didn't match.

Company	Allotment	Actual Usage
Trinity Trust	86	93
Edgewell Vertical Farms	101	122
Ptolemy Vertical Farms	73	86
Yorkshire Cryogenics	93	142
Mercy General	65	76
Plasticity, Ltd.	35	101
Westside General	77	222
Capricorn Meats	65	98
Habsworth Dentistry	90	134
HCN (Home Carer Net)	76	154
Eversure Transport	100	658
Premier Solutions	49	1164
CyTown Towers, Inc.	724	3,888

She set the page down, her mouth ajar. "Over three thousand units over. Just for CyTown."

Her preliminary tax-record search did nothing to quell her concerns. There was no record that the aforementioned companies paid any extra tax or were otherwise held accountable for their expenses.

She took a cursory glance and saw that Charlotte's Web was allotted forty-two units of water per tax quarter and used only twenty-three.

Not for long, some little voice said.

It didn't help that Alabaster Khan either outright owned or sat on the board of all of the companies.

Was that why Khan was interested in Charlotte's Web? Was it a chance to hide excessive water usage by diverting it through another company's numbers? Given the enormous overuse in three of his companies, he would need a lot more than Charlotte's Web to hide what he'd been doing.

Companies hiding what they're doing.

"This is like…" Her voice trailed off. *Like what?*

She was going to say that this was like a case she'd worked before. But when she pressed her mind, searching her memory, nothing came up. What case had been like this? She couldn't recall.

Her mother pinged her, interrupting her thoughts. <<Gracie, baby, where are you? Davion said you're on your way. Are you?>>

Grace checked the clock and saw she was late. "Shit."

<<I am. Be there soon.>>

HER MOTHER'S idea of cheering up Davion was to flirt with him. Grace saw this herself when she rushed through the front door. She'd hoped she was only imagining the stiff jaw when she kissed her husband's cheek a second later, before taking appraisal of Kaiden's homework situation and reminding everyone they still had an hour before they had to leave for the movie.

The movie turned out to be a romantic comedy about aliens from the neighboring galaxy going on a date night on Earth, only to have everything go horribly, amusingly wrong.

"Don't let that be you!" Kaiden teased as Davion and Grace left them on the corner to go to dinner alone. "Say no to the shrimp!"

"You cut it close today," he said as she turned back, watching her mother guide Kaiden to the arcade down the block.

She squeezed his hand. "I'm sorry. But I made it."

He sighed. "You're right. You did."

She hooked her arm around his waist, squeezed him. He was very ticklish on that side, and as predicted, he jostled into her hip, laughing.

Grace held him close. "For the rest of the night, I'm yours."

He finally softened, his grin radiant. "You'd better be."

She tried to mirror his smile, but it felt tight. For some reason, the right side of her face didn't want to cooperate. "Did you already book our table?"

"You bet." And it was a good thing too, because the Filipino restaurant had a line out the door when they arrived.

They were seated quickly, their drinks delivered promptly.

Grace liked restaurants. The smell of the food, the low hum of conversation. The way the lights sparked in her companion's eyes. It was relaxing to eat this way, slowly and with good company.

Davion was watching her. "I missed you."

Her heart clenched. She reached a hand across the table. "I missed you. How've you been?"

He laughed. "Tired. I feel like Kaiden's waking up earlier and earlier these days."

"Glad I'm not the only one." She smiled. "I thought I was imagining it."

"No. You're not. But I wouldn't trade him for anything."

"Nor I." She ran a thumb over his knuckles. "But…"

"But…" Davion mimicked. "I wouldn't be *devastated* if he stayed the night with your mother more often."

She laughed. "I don't think she'd mind. And sleep is important."

He rolled his eyes skyward. "So important."

She couldn't stand it. When he was being cute like this, intentionally trying to draw her out, make her laugh, it was too much. She leaned across the table. "Kiss me."

"Happily." His lips were feather light, moist enough to stick against hers.

The AI server appeared, her hair pulled into a high ponytail, a cat filter giving her pointed ears and kittenish eyes. "Okay, here we go. Lechon kawali, sinigang, and chicken adobo. Does it look okay? Do you need more rice?"

"This is plenty," Grace said, inhaling deeply. "It smells amazing."

After the server refilled their waters and left, Davion sat up in his seat eagerly. "I feel like I haven't eaten in ten days."

"Let's remedy that then."

Once they'd had their fill, they paid their bill and had the leftovers sent home.

Davion gestured at the bar across the street. There was a couple singing karaoke in the large glass window and others leaning against the bar chatting.

"Let's stay out a little longer," Davion urged, pulling at her hand. "Unless you're tired."

"I'm not tired," she said, almost defensively. "Are you tired?"

He lifted his chin. "I could go all night. I plan to."

Heat spread across her face. "My mother did agree to keep Kaiden until tomorrow."

He laughed. "I'm glad I can still make you blush."

"Two drinks," she said, nodding toward the bar. "More than that and I'll fall asleep before we even make it home."

He tugged her into the pedestrian walk. "Oh, don't worry. I intend to take you home wide-eyed and bushy-tailed."

She snorted. "It's a little premature to be talking about tails, sir."

He cocked his head. "Is it? I thought this was part of the foreplay. Should we pretend to be strangers?"

She arched a brow. "I'm better at that than you are."

"Ouch."

"Last time you lasted two minutes."

"To my credit, you were devastatingly attractive in that white turtleneck. I need more time to get into character."

"What's the penalty if we break character?" she asked.

He considered this. "The first one to break character has a.m. duty with Kaiden for a week. They have to do the oh six hundred request for breakfast and all that."

She smiled. "Deal."

"But I'm going to need time to get into character."

"Take as long as you need," she said, with a mischievous grin. "But I *never* go home with strangers. You'll have your work cut out for you."

"Challenge accepted."

At the door, the AI registered their ages and invited them inside. Across the threshold, the music swelled. It was two women with high-gloss filters dancing vigorously to an upbeat song featuring heavy bass.

"Is this where we get into character?" she asked, giving him a devilish grin. She'd always found this game exciting, no matter how many times they'd played it over the years.

Davion bit his lip. "Yes."

She placed a hand on the back of his neck but resisted the urge to kiss him. She liked the mounting tension.

She released him. "Good luck."

He pushed his way into the crowd, disappearing into the throng of people talking at the back of the bar, somewhere less raucous than the front, near the singing.

Grace aimed for a spot near the middle. Enough space to make conversation possible, but still close enough to enjoy the show.

She found an empty stool and ordered a glacial sunrise. The blue, white, red, and gold drink arrived, and she sipped it slowly while the music stopped and the couple climbed off the stage to enthusiastic applause.

The next group, a trio, seemed to be arguing about

which song to sing. Conversation swelled to fill the music's absence.

She'd had about four sips of her drink when she felt the presence of someone sliding in beside her. She smiled, wondering what Davion's opening line would be.

When she looked up, it wasn't Davion.

A man a few inches taller than Davion was claiming the seat beside her. His hair was black, cutting across his cheekbones. His eyes were a stunning blue. Blue like the exotic ocean waters she often saw in photographs. She wondered if it was a filter.

"Hi," he said, catching her gaze.

Shyness warmed her ears. She hadn't been expecting to talk to a *real* stranger. "Hi."

"I must say, you have a beautiful smile," he said.

The compliment surprised a laugh out of her. "Do I?"

"And that laugh." He looked almost pained as he wet his lips. "It would be wonderful to hear that every day."

"Really?"

Without missing a beat, he said, "Really."

Her face was positively on fire, and it was too soon to blame the alcohol for that, or for the giddy lightness she felt throughout her body, lifting her out of her seat. *Pull yourself together*, she thought. *A beautiful man is flirting with you. Big deal.*

"Thanks." He flicked his eyebrows up, accepting a drink from the bartender, though he was looking at it like he wasn't sure what it was.

Then he was watching her face again. "When I tell you that you're beautiful, you smile and blush."

"I'm pretty sure that's how most people react to a compliment."

"Is it?" He cocked his head. "Because you usually act impervious to my charms. Actually, you seem downright annoyed by them. I thought I'd lost my touch, but they appear to be working just fine in here."

She leaned toward him. "It *is* a bar. I suspect flirtation works best in a bar."

Her knee brushed his.

He flicked his eyes down. "Is that what we're doing? Flirting?"

"Sure, what's wrong with a little harmless flirting?"

The eyebrows stayed up this time. "I mean, I'm always flirting, but I didn't realize it was your style. I'm beginning to suspect I might have had a few things wrong about you."

If Davion showed up now, he had it coming. It wasn't that flirting with other people wasn't allowed in their game. Sometimes it even added flavor to the ruse.

No, he had it coming because he'd been the one to insist they not break character.

And because once Grace had had to cut in to a *fifteen-minute* conversation Davion was having with a gorgeous, bubbly redhead. He later claimed he didn't know how to excuse himself.

The blue-eyed stranger was watching her, a curious expression on his face.

He really was too handsome for his own good. It provoked a strange feeling in Grace—like she wanted to reach out and slap him. Not too hard. Just enough to confirm he was real.

What a strange impulse.

Those eyes...Something about those eyes.

She frowned. "You seem very familiar, Mr...."

"Blue," he said. "You can call me Mr. Blue."

"Like your beautiful eyes."

"You like my eyes?"

Her blush deepened. "I do."

He swore and threw back his drink, finishing it in one

go. "You're killing me, Gray."

Her heart skipped a beat as the music began again. This time two men began a rapid-fire rap.

"How do you know my name?"

He flicked his eyebrows. "Maybe I'm a spy."

The only person who ever called her Gray was Davion.

Maybe this was a test. This man could be one of Davion's coworkers, though she couldn't imagine him saying, "Go flirt with my wife until I get there. See if you can get her to break character."

If this man was a coworker it would explain why he looked familiar, if she'd met him before. And why Davion had not yet arrived to interrupt.

"Why are you talking to me then, Mr. Spy?" She put her head in her hand, rolling her eyes up to meet his. "What information do you need?"

"Actually, I'm just wasting time. I've got Ar—*someone*—running location on me. If he can pinpoint where we are, maybe we can find you."

Grace frowned. What gibberish was the guy spouting?

The man, however, hurried on.

"So, let's play twenty questions." He motioned for another drink. "Not that we'll get through half of them. We can't have more than a couple minutes before the calvary arrives."

She assumed he meant Davion. All right. No doubt he was trying to prove he'd gotten better at the game. Grace was determined to adapt and win.

"Ask away," she said.

"Oh, you want me to start?" He bit his lip. "Okay. Nothing too serious or world-shattering…How about: do you find me attractive?"

What would single Grace say? she wondered. "Very."

"Too easy. Of course you do." He bit his lip. "Would

you kiss me?"

She hesitated. Should she point out she was married or did that count as breaking character? Probably.

"I would kiss you if the conditions were right," she said. *There.* That was vague enough. She hadn't brought up a husband but also hadn't given the impression she would make out with this stranger here and now.

"If the conditions were right, would you do *more* than kiss me?"

"Yes," she said without hesitation. "If the conditions were right."

It was his turn to blush.

He swore and accepted the second drink placed in front of him.

"You asked three questions. Is it my turn?" she asked, playfully arching a brow.

He finished the second drink without stopping, setting the glass on the bar with a hiss. "Why the hell not? Ask away."

She met his gaze over the rim of her drink. "Do you find me attractive?"

He chewed his lip. "Incredibly."

She couldn't help but smile. "Do you want to kiss me?"

"I almost have like twenty times. I'm surprised you've never noticed."

She leaned toward him. "Do you want to do *more* than kiss me?"

His throat clicked. "God, yes."

If he was a coworker, she was torturing him. If he was a stranger, then she was leading him on.

Grace decided to have pity. So what if she had to get up early for a week? Davion deserved a break from the chore anyway.

"In a different world, one where I wasn't here with my

husband, Mr. Blue, I imagine it would be hard to resist you."

"Oh, you do a fine job, don't worry," he said. "It drives me more than a little crazy."

If he was a stranger, the mention of a husband should've upset him, but he didn't even bat an eyelid.

Coworker then.

He looked down into his lap and puffed his cheeks. "I'm going to regret this. You'll kill me if we get out of here and you remember any of this, which isn't certain by the way. They're trying to unravel your mind as we speak. I keep giving you things to hold on to, clues, ideas, things that will keep your mind busy. And Khan's been a big help with his back doors."

Her headache spiked again. "What? What are you talking about?"

"They want to make it impossible for you to survive off the system," he said. "It's an effective way to ensure silence."

She pulled back, pressing her fingers into her pounding head. "I...Oh god."

His hands were gentle on hers. "I'm sorry, Gray. Forget I said that. I think it makes it worse when I introduce new data that's incompatible with the system. I'll have to be more subtle. I need a way to introduce code that looks like theirs. Did the folder work? That was my idea. Oh, and I have another one."

Grace's head pulsed. She could feel her heart beating in her eye sockets.

He took a bamboo napkin from its holder on the bar and pulled a pen from his pocket. Whatever he was writing, Grace couldn't see. She was squinting against the light again, pressing her fingers into her temples, trying to ease the splitting headache blooming there.

Mr. Blue capped the pen and bent forward. She could feel his hot breath and warm lips on her ear.

"Gray, you're in a bar with your husband. You're talking to a handsome stranger. It's a playful exchange. It means nothing. You're enjoying a glacial sunrise. Excellent choice, by the way."

Her headache eased, the spiking pain softening to a dull throb.

"After this you'll go home with your husband and have amazing sex. You'll think of me though. You won't be able to help yourself."

She laughed despite the headache.

"I'm sorry I pushed too hard. I thought I could wedge you out, but you're already too deep. Gray, look at me," he begged. "Ask me another question. It's going to take me a minute to finish this code."

She opened her eyes. "Who are you really?"

Hadn't he mentioned Khan? The folder? She was certain only Lore had seen it.

Was he an informant? What was going on here?

"Why are you talking to me?" she asked.

"Because…" He seemed to search for the words. "I was curious what you were like before. I've seen you laugh and smile more in the last few minutes than…ever. I'd hate for it to stop."

"It doesn't have to stop. I like to smile and laugh." The heat had nearly overtaken her face now. Muscles low in her body were beginning to respond to the alcohol and his voice.

"Do you?" He looked almost sad. "I'll remember that."

She pulled back then. It was his sadness. It was too real. It hit her like a rock in the chest. The throbbing in her head was building again.

His face. She knew this face.

"How do I—"

A commotion at the back of the bar swallowed her words. Officers were forcing themselves into the bar from the rear exit, shouldering their way through the crowd.

"I have to go," he said. "Take this. Maybe it will help us find you. It's been damn near impossible. They have *millions* of pods, and they won't tell us where you are."

He slipped his hand into hers, squeezed. He used the momentum to pull her off the stool and into a kiss. He gripped the side of her face with his free hand. It was deep, hungry, and it set her whole body on fire. Before she could stop herself, she'd snaked an arm up his back, committing to it.

He pulled back, his eyes glazed. He looked ready to kiss her again. Devour her. "I swear to god, I'm going to do that for real one day."

Her brow furrowed. Her head pulsed.

Then he released her, taking his heat and body with him. Leaving her cold as the song began to change again.

She was unsteady on her feet. The world moved at a tilt as she opened the piece of paper he'd slipped into her hand as they kissed. She mouthed the words to herself.

Remember me, written on the bar's napkin with his ink pen.

Resting her weight against the bar, she traced the big *R* and some of the ink came away on her finger.

She looked up, but Mr. Blue—or whoever he'd been— was gone. Officers rushed past her in pursuit.

"Hey!" She reached out and touched a shoulder. "What's going on?"

Commander Adams turned, lifting his face shield so that he could see her. "We have a hacker in the zone. He's penetrated the defense code for the city and threatens border security."

"Why didn't anyone call me?" Grace followed them out onto the street.

A CityRide screeched to a stop in the road. The sound silenced by a sickening thud and a large crack.

A body tumbled across the road.

Grace ran to the man's side and recognized the black hair, the long lashes. But there were no Tahitian-blue waters. Not anymore.

The people on the streets gathered around. The riders climbed from the vehicle, swearing, arguing.

"How in the world—"

"I thought they had sensors and fail-safes! I thought it was impossible for—"

"He must've darted out at exactly the wrong moment. Poor guy."

"This is a lawsuit waiting to happen," Adams said beside her, shaking his head at the corpse as if it had ruined things for everyone. "But at least we don't have to worry now."

"What do you mean?"

Adams pointed at the dead man. "He was our hacker."

Hacker? Was it possible that he'd singled her out because she was the police commander and not because he was Davion's friend?

Grace looked up and found her husband among the crowd. She searched his face for recognition, for pain. If this was his friend or coworker, the accident wouldn't be easy on him.

But Davion didn't cry. He didn't even register the man's face.

Perhaps not a friend. A stranger.

The note in her pocket.

The simple message: *Remember me.*

TWENTY

SHE SPENT NEARLY an hour in the precinct, listening to the panicked assessment of the zone's security. Grace sent Davion home with her apologies. And though he'd insisted that he understood, he was disappointed to have their date end as it did.

The commotion began to die down once it was clear that whatever code the invader had used to break into their zone was gone now. It had self-destructed almost as soon as he died.

Once the junior agents were dismissed, Grace sat down across from Adams at one of the admin tables.

"We have no idea what he was after?" she asked, incredulous.

Adams harrumphed. "These common pirates are hardly organized. They're looking for resources, money. They're not always sure how they will get it, only that they will stop at nothing to do so. Did he really give you no clue?"

"His questions were innocuous," she insisted. "He could've asked me anything about the zone, but he didn't."

She had informed her co-commander immediately that she'd spoken to the suspect at the bar and that perhaps she might have been compromised. She stopped short of detailing the flirtation.

"Still, we need to be careful. It's possible that he has bugged you. Have you noticed any changes in your lenscape or data processing? Did he ever put his hands on you?"

Grace thought of the note in her pocket. Smudged by her fingers and weighing heavy on her heart. But she'd already shown that to Adams. They'd both agreed it was only a bamboo tissue. It came from the bar where they'd sat. It was hardly a weapon.

"He kissed me."

Adams's eyebrows shot up. "The perpetrator kissed you."

"It made sense in the context."

Adams remained incredulous. "It isn't my place to ask about your marriage, but I think we could consider the possibility that the kiss was merely a ploy to plant a device or harvest data of some kind."

Stupid, she thought. *He could be hijacking your lenscape or personal files right now. He could be—*

He's not doing anything, her mind insisted.

"He's dead, but it's possible that he wasn't working alone. These pirates rarely are. We should assume he was willing to sacrifice himself to throw us off his team's tracks."

Her heart clenched.

"I'll submit myself to a full evaluation first thing in the morning."

"Good." Adams was watching her carefully, his gaze heavy on hers. "We have to keep our eyes open. Damage might already be done."

Davion was on the wide steps outside the precinct when she walked out.

She saw him and smiled. "I thought you went home."

He shook his head. "I didn't want to leave you."

"You must be exhausted." She checked the clock on her lenscape and saw it was nearly one in the morning.

He took her hand. "I promised I'd go all night with you."

She frowned. "This is probably not what you were imagining."

"I wasn't leaving without you." Davion reached out and took her hand.

Her heart kicked. She wrapped her arms around his neck, breathed him in. "Then take me home."

They didn't actually make love until the next morning. She'd woken an hour early explicitly for this task, her own form of apology for the wayward result of the night before. An hour wasn't much, but it would leave her time to shower, dress, and make it to work on time.

But there was a problem.

She was kissing Davion, but Mr. Blue kept slipping into her mind, like he'd said he would.

Davion's dark eyes shifted into blue-green waters. And there was a moment, at the height of her climax, as her hips arched to absorb the impact, that she was sure Davion's scent had changed from its deep sandalwood to… What? Water?

Her eyes flew open and she cupped his cheeks. Dark skin. Dark eyes. Long, beautiful braids trailing across her breasts and stomach.

A crushing sadness filled her. It pooled in her chest. She began to cry.

"What is it?" he panted.

I don't know. I don't know but—

Davion felt like a dream. He felt like a mirage that would evaporate before her eyes. Sands that would slip between her fingers and be lost.

Gone. She blinked, her vision blurry.

"Nothing," she said. "I'm fine."

He arched a brow. "Fine? You're crying."

"It's fine. Better than fine." She reached out and pulled him close. "Come here."

THE NEXT DAY at the precinct passed in a haze. She couldn't understand why that morning's lovemaking had left her sad. In between her meetings, debriefings, and paperwork, she kept retracing her steps, examining her thoughts. Was it because it'd been a while since their last time? She'd been as busy with work as he had—and having a child in the house was never conducive to an unrestrained sex life.

But she'd long ago made her peace with those realities. These ideas couldn't account for this new heartbreak. This sense of loss.

Only it didn't feel new, did it? It was like a memory. Thick and ever present.

Had she had a bad dream the night before? She couldn't remember. In fact, she couldn't remember any of her dreams since the one she'd awakened to days ago—the dream of Kaiden and Davion perishing in some sort of auto accident.

Had the accident with Mr. Blue retriggered those fears?

"A bullet and a half and a microgreens sandwich," Duchovny chirped, stepping into the office and placing her drink on her desk. Then he smiled as he slid the sandwich in its cream-colored bamboo wrapper across the tabletop toward her.

She stared at the sandwich. "What happened to the falafel?"

Duchovny froze. "I…Oh, I'm sorry, I thought you asked for a sandwich. It's fifteen hundred. Is it too late for lunch? I noticed you hadn't eaten and your koffee was cold. I—"

"It's fine," she was quick to say. His face was turning red at an alarming rate. "Thank you. It was my mistake. I thought you were going to the falafel truck—"

Like we always do. She stopped short of saying this. Like they always did? Lore had only been her assistant for two days. It was far too soon to have a routine.

"There's a falafel truck?" Lore asked, his brows rising. "I had no idea."

She bit into her sandwich and made a point of declaring it delicious until Duchovny's unease abated.

"We've received the files you requested from eight of the companies," he said, settling into the chair across from her.

A sense of déjà vu washed over her, watching him there, in that chair.

"Show me." She accepted the cache he shared and looked through the notes. She frowned. "These numbers don't match the quarterly numbers reported."

"Yes, they do. At least, they match public records."

Grace accessed and opened the tax reports filed with the zone's tax bureau. He was right. They did match the public records, but they didn't match the numbers left in the folder on her desk. A manila folder, her research had told her. A filing device that hadn't been used since the 2200s.

Was the document made up? Meant to mislead her

while terrorists ransacked her zone's security? Or was it an innocuous practical joke from an attention-seeker?

Or a whistle-blower trying to show you what others refuse to see, she thought.

A rough knock on the door made them both turn. "Come in."

Adams pushed open the door. "We have a name for that hacker."

"The one hit by the auto?" Her koffee stalled on the way to her mouth.

"One and the same. Heron Jane. The son of a famous scientist. These wealthy kids have nothing better to do than play at revolution."

Adams pinged her a file, which she opened.

There was Jane's face. Strong jaw. Ocean-blue eyes. *Heron Jane.*

A chill of déjà vu shivered through her.

"If he tries to reach you—" Adams was saying.

"Reach me?" Grace laughed. "We saw him die in the street. He's not going to reach out to anyone."

"His contacts then, whoever he was working with. He's a very dangerous person."

Heron Jane.

Heron.

H.

She considered the signature again and wondered if the one leading her to investigate these companies was their very own terrorist. If so, what implications did that have? Was it a ruse? Something meant to distract and confuse her so that a dark plot could unfold?

Adams flicked his eyes to Duchovny. "I see you're busy. I'll leave you to it."

Adams shut the door behind him.

"Grumpy," Lore remarked.

"Heron Jane," Grace muttered. "Does that name mean anything to you?"

He shrugged. "No. It's new to me."

That was the problem, wasn't it? The name didn't feel new to her at all.

She searched the public records for Heron Jane but little returned. She found a picture of the scientist mother Adams had mentioned—a beautiful, regal woman with a fierce gaze. She looked like one of the Valkyrie warriors from Kaiden's cultural reports.

H.

It might be a diversion, or a breadcrumb. There was only one way to be sure.

Grace programmed sixteen spyders and sent them into the mainframes governing the companies in question.

It was one thing to report numbers and another to run the metrics internally and report back. If the numbers were fraudulent, Grace's spyders would harvest the data proving so. Perhaps this was a paranoid move. Perhaps she should have let go of the very notion that *H* meant anything at all. That Heron Jane was anyone other than a terrorist bent on destabilizing the zone she worked hard to protect.

If that's true, then the spyders will confirm the public tax records, and that'll be the end of it, she thought.

If she was being honest with herself, that wasn't what she expected to happen.

"Commander," Lore said.

"What's wrong?" The tone of his voice caused her to deactivate her lenscape and look up.

"Your face is very flushed," he said. "Are you feeling all right?"

She activated the mirroring feature of her lenscape and

saw the red cheeks and glassy eyes for herself. She opened the inner temperature gauge.

37.9.

She frowned. "You're right, I have a fever. You?"

His eyes lit blue. "No, I'm normal."

She saw his reflexive move back and nearly laughed. She couldn't blame him.

"Should we…" he began tentatively.

She considered the work pending. This was as good a stopping point as any. With an unchecked fever, it was doubtful she would be much use in the remaining hours.

"We should call it a day."

She accessed the public healthcare network. There were eight doctors available within the hour. She selected one of the physicians whose names she recognized and confirmed an appointment. She had an hour to make it to the office.

"I'll walk you out," Lore offered, and Grace agreed.

As she stood, her head swam with heat.

Fresh air helped. As they crossed the threshold into the open air, she breathed deep.

Grace pinged her mother. <<I have a fever. Are you and Kaiden okay?>>

After a brief pause she replied, <<How bad? Davion too? Kaiden and I are fine. Not a decimal above. We've had a wonderful day today. He's showing me how to hoverskate.>>

A knot in Grace's chest loosened. Kaiden was fine. He wasn't sick. Whatever she had, she hadn't passed it on.

<<I'll keep him for the night to be safe,>> her mother added. <<I promised to teach him how to play mahjong.>>

<<Thank you.>>

To Davion, she wrote, <<I have a fever. Mom is keeping Kaiden for the night. Do you have a fever?>>

<<No fever. Are you going to the doctor?>> was his immediate reply.

<<On my way now,>> she wrote. <<Assuming I don't have the plague, then I'll be home.>>

<<Come home anyway. Plague or no.>>

Again, that well of sadness. What was wrong with her? How could she miss people who weren't gone? Who were perfectly safe and accounted for? It made no sense.

<<Will do. Love you.>>

"Should I wait until your auto comes?" Lore asked, hesitating in the wide plaza outside the precinct. Grace noted the polite distance he kept now. That was fine. Better safe than sorry.

"You go on," she said, waving him ahead. "I'll see you tomorrow."

As soon as Duchovny disappeared into a white City-Ride, she walked east toward the corner of Constantinople and Damascus, where the food truck was. Only when she reached the corner, it wasn't there. To be sure, she circled the precinct and its surrounding block three times. She found a food truck at the corner of Lisbon and Gibraltar, but they didn't even know what a falafel was.

"We only sell pretzels," the girl insisted through the digital window. "With caramel or cheese sauce on the side."

GRACE WAS GIVEN a mask by the AI who took her temperature at the entrance. She accepted it, slipping it over her nose and mouth and activating the air-filtration piece above her nose. Dr. Tove was located on the sixth floor of Mercy General today.

She rode the escalator up and found herself the only patient in a quiet sitting area. The AI attendant marked her arrival and offered her water and a fever reducer, both of which Grace accepted gladly.

After several minutes she was led to the back and asked to change into a gown. The man who came in was older, no less than seventy, with deep wrinkles, thinning gray hair, and small black eyes. But what most surprised her was his use of glasses.

"Good afternoon, Commander," he said with a bright smile. "What brings you in today?"

She recounted her fever for him and ended with, "I recognized your name. I'm pretty sure I've seen you before."

She paused, allowing him to palpate her throat.

Dr. Tove frowned. "You must have a better memory than I. I don't remember meeting you before today."

Grace wasn't offended. She was certain that the doctors of the zone must be incredibly busy, shuffled around as they were.

She forced a smile. "That's all right."

"Are you sure we've met?" he asked gently. "Do you remember where?"

Grace searched her memories. What surfaced was… nonsensical. She had a vague memory of him in a cluttered office filled with books. But she wouldn't have come to his personal office unless it was on a case. More bizarrely, she had a second memory—of Dr. Tove in a pair of mouse ears.

I'm losing it.

"What's your specialization?" she asked.

He brightened. "Fertility. Would you like another child?"

She laughed, but it made her head pulse. "No. The one I have is work enough."

"I'm here if you change your mind."

When the examination was complete, he pulled off his gloves and sighed.

"Commander, you seem perfectly healthy apart from the fever. No swollen glands, no mucus or signs of distress in your lungs. Your heart is strong. It's very possible that we are at the early stages of a virus and you will get worse before you get better."

"If it's a virus, then I contracted it from somewhere."

"Yes," he concurred. "Any close contact with sick persons? Drinking or eating after anyone? Any kissing?"

She was about to say she only kissed her husband and ate and drank after no one. Then the kiss from the bar blazed in her mind.

Heron Jane.

"You can catch a virus from kissing," she said flatly, not even a question but a dangerous realization.

"Yes," the doctor replied patiently.

"Doctor, would someone develop a fever if their lenscape had contracted a virus? Or their personal data storage unit?"

"I am not specialized in neurotech," he admitted. "I would need to consult with a colleague. Can you wait here while I fetch her?"

Grace agreed. A few minutes passed, and the door opened.

"She can see us now." The doctor beckoned her forward. "This way, please."

She was led into a dark room and asked to lie on a table

As she lay in the dark, a woman's voice came through the speakers.

"Hello, Commander. I'm Dr. Monica Richelle. I'm going to take a look at your neurocomponents and see if there are any problems, all right? Please be as still as you can."

"All right," she said, trying not to move, but her panic began to mount.

Jane gave me a virus. He wanted to steal classified files, passcodes, anything that can be harvested to destabilize security. I've been breached.

"I don't see any signs of contamination on any of your neurocomponents," the doctor said. "I can examine the interior data for you, but I see that it is marked as classified and password protected. You would have to authorize my entry and give me the passcode for me to do that examination."

In a flare of paranoia, she thought, *The doctors are in on it. They want to use my passcodes themselves. I shouldn't give them to them.*

"I…" She licked her lips.

"It's possible that a virus could do permanent damage to the neurocomponents if left unchecked."

She felt sweat slide from her temple into her hair. She felt helpless and pinned on this dark table.

"I don't want to do that," Grace managed despite her hammering heart.

After a brief pause, Dr. Richelle said, "That's no problem."

The table began to slide out of the tube, bringing Grace back into the light.

"We will send you home with medicine for the fever," Dr. Tove was saying, stepping from a dark corner. "Stay hydrated, get plenty of rest, and if it gets worse, call me."

TWENTY-ONE

IT DID GET WORSE. Something was absolutely, definitely wrong. Her head was killing her. And the promise to take the next three days off of work and sleep had added to rather than detracted from her anxiety. She had support and that helped. A little.

Her mother agreed to keep Kaiden for as long as necessary, and Davion had wanted to stay home. They spent most of their time in bed. He rubbed her shoulders, her feet. Asked her how she was feeling.

He was militant about making sure she had enough to drink.

She took long, hot showers and ate small meals.

While temporary relief came and went, nothing cured her.

It wasn't only the fever. She was losing feeling in her right arm and the right side of her face. She'd touch her cheek with a pen over and over again, but *nothing*. And when she looked in the mirror, she thought she saw scarring. Faint, yellow, beneath the clear complexion of her skin.

Davion assured her this wasn't true. That her face was perfectly fine.

"It's the fever," he said, guiding her back to bed. "You're over thirty-eight degrees now."

In addition to the light hallucinations, she was remembering things that Davion did not.

"What do you mean Mom bought you a Boi?" he said, laughing, one night over dinner. He'd made her soup, trying to get her to eat it with minimal success. "Why in the world would she do that when I'm right here?"

Why would she do that? her mind echoed. *Why would she do that?*

She went to the closet and opened it, but it wasn't there.

Then there was Kaiden's room.

Once she looked into it and it was empty. All his toys and furniture were gone. All his drawings taped to the wall evaporated. His rumpled sheets and clothes vanished.

She'd begun to cry, and Davion found her like that, crumpled outside their son's bedroom door, sobbing.

Then she'd blinked and everything was back again.

"I'm losing my mind," she said once she could draw enough air into her lungs.

Calling Kaiden just to hear his voice, to talk to him over a ping, had only helped for a few minutes. The absolute dread in her chest didn't abate.

"He's safe," Davion assured her, kissing the top of her head, rocking her. "Keep reminding yourself it's the fever. None of this is real. It will pass. The doctor said that it will pass. Come to bed."

She did sleep, finally, and woke sometime after sunset.

The room was thick with twilight. She heard the television in the other room and the sounds of the ChefMate's arm working in the kitchen.

He's not out there, she thought. *Kaiden and Davion aren't there, because they're dead and—*

It hurt. She blinked back tears. She couldn't understand the loneliness inside her. The deep well of loss. She had no reason to feel that way. She was lucky. Luckier than most.

She'd had more happiness in the years of her marriage and motherhood than some have in their whole lives.

"It's only a fever," she said, pressing her hands into her wet eyes. "A fever—it will pass. It will pass. It has to pass."

The mattress sank beneath someone's weight.

She blinked past the tears and recognized the man sitting on the edge of her bed.

"Heron," she said. She blinked again, but he didn't disappear. "I saw you die. I saw that CityRide hit you. And you gave me this fever."

"I did," he said.

"What is it? C. auris? Is it going to kill me?"

"I hope not," he said. "I wanted to find you, but they have you hidden in the Towers. They're pulling the same bullshit they pulled with Range. That you went in willingly. That you're too emotionally fragile to be disturbed. Khan has been a big help. Did you know he coded CyTown with his brother before they sold it to the Pendam family? He's been helping me move in and out without detection. No more messy exits."

"I don't know what you're talking about."

He nodded, sad. "I've missed you. It's been a long two weeks. But we're close. They're doing a real doozy on you. Alabaster wants what's in your head."

She thought of Dr. Richelle's innocent "I need your passcode for this."

"The doctors are terrorists?" she asked. It sounded

absolutely ridiculous. Of course they weren't. None of this was real. The fever was ravaging her mind.

I must be dreaming, she thought. *This is just another fever dream. It means nothing.*

This idea relaxed her.

"We didn't complete our questions game," he said, placing his chin in his hand. "Do you want to continue?"

She adjusted her head on the pillow. "Okay."

"I'll go first. Where did you meet me?"

"In a bar."

"*Bannnn.* Wrong. Think about it."

She tried, and the headache began to return.

"Don't give up. The code I wrote links the VR to your stored data. Where did you meet me for the first time?"

A mist-like dream rose in her consciousness of Heron standing in front of a reception desk. Heron chatting with a pretty receptionist. Flirting. Smiling.

"We were…" she began, unsure of herself.

"At the precinct?" he pressed.

"No, not at the precinct. We were…" She pushed harder. She saw the sign, heard the AI announce her name. Remembered holding up her arms so that the AI could scan her biometrics and give her access to the building. "At Viscosity."

Heron's face lit up. "Yes! What else do you remember? Anything about Khan?"

Viscosity. She was sure she'd never been to Viscosity in her life. Why in the world would she have a memory of meeting this man there?

And Khan? What about Khan?

There was something about ravens. About a woman with a tiger. Dragons swimming in the sky above the atrium in the…Trinity Music Hall and…and…

"Orrin Khan is the CEO and founder of Trinity Trust."

Heron sucked his teeth. "Wrong Khan, but we'll come back to that. Who takes care of your mother?"

"Lenorie Range." She saw Lenorie's face in her chair. Saw Heron standing beside her. Lenorie was…asking about her brother because…because…

"Trent was taken."

"Tristan," Heron corrected. "Tristan Range. Taken where?"

The headache was nearly unbearable now. The pounding in her temples intensified.

"Hurry, Gray. We're so close. Where was Range taken? Who took him?"

She saw two gleaming towers covered in rose gold, reflecting the haze of the afternoon sun.

"CyTown. They took him to CyTown."

"And where are you?" He seemed desperate, fixated on her face as if he were reading it like a screen. "Where are you right now?"

She tried to sit up, to look around the room.

"No," he said, tapping the side of his head again. "Where *are* you?"

Where am I? Where am *I?*

She saw the glow of a medical occ-mod, the hand it belonged to but not the face.

"I'm…"

He lay down beside her. He stretched himself long, pushing a hand into her hair. "Who took Tristan? Who took you?"

She shivered at his touch.

She should stop this. This dream wasn't nice.

"You kissed me," she whispered. "Why?"

"I'll tell you when you wake up." He frowned, pushed back her hair. It was delicious, his fingers in her hair.

"Gray, you have to wake up. You have to *want* to wake up. It's not easy, and I know you want to stay here, but please. *Please try.*" His eyes flicked to the door. "We're out of time."

As soon as he said it, she heard feet on the steps.

"I have to go. Keep trying. Don't give them anything and don't give up."

Heron went to the closet and opened it.

She laughed. Where was he going? There was no exit in her closet. She wasn't even sure a person could fit in there with all of her and Davion's clothes. Mostly Davion's clothes.

But the closet door closed.

She rose from the bed, opened the closet, expecting to see Heron—that name was getting more and more comfortable in her mind—squeezed in among the clothes and mechanical racks.

But there was no one.

She pushed aside pants and shirts. Nothing.

Her bedroom door opened.

It was Davion, frowning. "What are you doing?"

"He's gone," she said, marveling. "How did he do that? Is it because he's dead?"

Davion's smile only deepened as he touched her head. His hand was ice cold compared to her face.

"You're burning up," he said. "You need to drink some water and get back in bed. I'll call the doctor."

"It was only a dream," she told him.

"Right," he said, pulling back the covers and helping her inside. His eyes were lit blue with his activated scape. No doubt he was calling the doctor as promised. "Just a dream, baby. Now go back to sleep."

They weren't sweet dreams that followed. They were nightmares.

Dr. Tove with his graying hair and a scruffy gray beard flashed. He was leading her into the dark.

Don't trust him, her mind screamed. *Turn around!*

Meanwhile, conversations grew, swelled, and bled around her.

Sometimes she heard Davion's and Kaiden's voices.

Other times she heard voices she didn't recognize.

"We could increase the sedatives, but it's already too high. It'll disrupt the reality and simply put her in a coma."

"That's preferable to the alternative," a man countered.

Doctors, she thought. *Discussing my care. My fever must be too high. I must be in some sort of unresponsive state.*

"Mommy," Kaiden said. "Mommy, I miss you. Mommy, don't go."

I'm not leaving, baby, she thought. But her voice didn't comply. Her mouth and throat remained dry. *I'm not going anywhere.*

"Gray," Davion said. "Stop this. Come home now."

Stop what? How in the world could she stop a fever? Why was he mad at her?

Cold hands were on her face.

"Grace," the voice said. It was stern. It cut through the chaos. "Grace, can you hear me?"

She knew this voice.

"Grace, you have to wake up."

The man shoving the *Remember me* napkin into her hand. It was Heron's voice.

Ungloved fingers glowed red.

"Who took you?" Heron asked. "Who took you to CyTown Towers?"

She saw the old man again. The gray hair and scruffy face. The sadness in his eyes. A name floated to the surface.

"Dr. Tove. Dr. Ezekiel Tove."

The relief in Heron's voice was palpable. "Yes. That's right."

"I can't," she begged. The dreams, the images, kept swelling and collapsing onto themselves too quickly. She felt sick. She felt like she was going to puke. "I—"

"You're close," Heron said. "Dr. Tove asked you to come to CyTown—why?"

Why? Why?

"He asked me to come to CyTown..." Her mind groped for the threads in the dark, combing black waters for anything solid. Anything whole. "Because he wanted to give me evidence."

"For?" She realized now that Heron held her up on her feet. They were in the Soul Grove. They were looking at the trees filtering dappled sunlight across their skin. There were two trees in front of her. They flickered, coming into and out of focus.

"I can't," she begged. "I can't look. Heron, please."

"Dr. Tove," he said again. "What did he want to give you?"

The soul trees had moving screens on them. She could almost see the faces. Almost recognize who must be buried there.

On one tree were the faces of Davion and Kaiden. Kaiden grinning, laughing, wrapping his arms around his father's neck. Davion's face. His dark eyes shining. His bright white teeth, smile eternal.

Beside it another tree. In this one, Heron was calling her name.

He was speaking to her. "Grace, please. Please try. Tell me about Dr. Tove!"

She looked back and forth between the two screens. Davion and Kaiden. Heron.

Pick one, a voice whispered. *Choose your life.*

No. No…

"Dr. Tove!" Heron screamed through one screen.

In the other, Kaiden had begun to cry. "Mommy, don't go! Please don't leave me!"

"Gray, don't," Davion yelled. "I need you!"

"Why did Tove take you?" Heron begged. "Please remember."

She reached for his face. Her fingers brushed the screen over his pleading lips.

Something clicked.

"For…the CyTown Case. He put me in the rig!"

"Arjun, now!"

TWENTY-TWO

GRACE CAME UP SCREAMING and she didn't stop. Only a vague part of her mind noted Heron's hands, pulling her out of the rig, and Arjun doing something to the back of the machine. Or was he only standing there?

She didn't care. *Couldn't* care. Her knees hit the floor.

"Breathe," Heron said, his voice barely audible over the sound of her own screaming.

She found it impossible to draw a breath. All the air was leaving her. It kept leaving her, and across the cinema of her mind all she could see was Davion, Kaiden. Dying again.

Leaving her again. And again.

"She's turning blue," Arjun said.

"I can't get her to take a breath."

"Knock her out," a man said. "Quick, before she destroys her own mind."

"I'm sorry," Heron muttered as a soft light began to grow in the periphery of her vision. "I'm so sorry."

And he sounded it too.

Black rose up like a wave and crashed over Grace. The darkness was complete.

When Grace woke she first registered the cream-colored walls. Then the doorframe, open to show the landing beyond. She knew this comforter. This lamp fixed to the wall. She sat up and her head whirled. She crashed back to the pillow with a groan.

"Take it easy."

Her double vision cleared and she saw Heron leaning over her.

He looked nothing like the handsome man she'd seen inside the simulation. This Heron was a wreck. His hair was everywhere. The purple bags under his eyes were deep and puffy. His eyes red. The scruff on his jaw thick.

"What the hell happened to you?" she asked.

"I haven't slept in a while."

"How long is a while?"

"Seventeen days."

"Seventeen days?" she marveled. Her fingers found the IV stint in her arm.

"That's how long you were gone." He ran a hand through his hair. The grease in it shone in the light. "I thought I'd lost you."

Lost me. She thought of Davion, of Kaiden. Of Lore Duchovny as her assistant. But their faces were already fading into the backdrop of her mind.

Now they felt like dreams and she herself waking from a long sleep. It had been the same going in, hadn't it? That side had felt real and this life but a dream.

Was that all reality was? What your mind chose to accept and reject given one's vantage point in space?

"What took so long?" she asked. "Seventeen days seems—"

Her voice broke. Not from emotion but because of how dry it was. There was no moisture in her mouth.

Heron snorted. "They hid your body. I couldn't just walk in and get you. Once you were in, you were *in*. If I couldn't wedge you out of the system, when I pulled the plug it would've killed you."

He reached for a large glass of water on the side table. "Drink this."

When she ran her tongue over her lips, they felt like peeling paper.

She drank half the glass before Heron snatched it back. "Not too fast. You'll throw it up again."

"Again?"

"You've been in and out of it for two days. Every time you forget that we talked before. This is the first time you've asked cogent questions though, so that's good. I'm hoping the memory loss is only a temporary side effect."

Memory loss. Her panic spiked and she rushed to access the memory bank files in her lenscape.

Heron must've known what she was doing. His face hardened into a mask of sorrow. "We think the reason your mind accepted that reality so easily is because they used your own memories. They recreated the world you knew to be true from before the accident."

Grace tried to access file after file after file but got only error messages.

"They corrupted the files when they harvested them to reconstruct your reality. They were converted to match CyTown's data and can't be converted back. Everything they used is gone."

"My memory bank—"

Heron shook his head. "I asked a technician to

examine your implant to see if it could be fixed, but she said that they'd have to remove all of the software, the lenscape, both chips, and the cranial node. She said the cranial node removal at your age was too risky. It could cause permanent damage or even kill you."

"You had someone examine me?"

"Oh god, yes. Doctors, technicians. When you came up screaming and didn't stop I was terrified you were going to die of shock. The constable insisted that you be examined. You were in a hospital for a whole day before they let us bring you home."

Her mind frantically searched, trying to prove that what he was saying was wrong.

No. It can't be. It can't be all gone. Not all *of it.*

"But I remember the IED. The winter parade," she said.

"The world they made for you was based on your life before the accident. Only what they used is lost."

She finally found a file that would open. It was the night of the winter parade.

All she had left, was her last night with her family. The terrible memory of their deaths.

"Everything good is gone."

Tears sat in the corners of his eyes. "I'm sorry I wasn't there when Tove came. I thought I should give you space. That was stupid. From the moment you got the Egg Island invitation, I should've known they were planning something. That they would strike the second you were alone."

She remembered him on the steps outside the administration building. She remembered being cross and short with him. Him walking off into the crowds and leaving her to catch an auto home.

"It was my fault. I trusted him instead of calling you in to come with me. That was incredibly stupid."

"I'm glad you didn't," he said. "Or I might've been in a pod with you, and then where would we be?"

His weak smile was far from convincing.

What a contrast this worn-out man was to the one she'd seen…in a bar? God, why did it fade so fast?

"I think you kissed me," she said.

His lip hooked into a crooked grin. "I don't know what you're talking about."

"Was that how you introduced the code so you could find me and separate me from the CyTown mainframe?"

"No." He laughed, a weak sound. "The code was in the napkin. *Remember me?*"

Her mind tried to conjure the image of the napkin. It wouldn't come.

"Lore was my assistant," she said.

"Oh yeah. How'd he do?"

"He was good. He listens better than you do."

The laugh was real this time. "Noted."

"We were working on a case about…" She searched for the details. "Water."

"You got my file."

H.

"What was that about?"

"I wanted to give you something your mind could work on, something that would keep you *you*. You're at your best when you're working."

"The case wasn't real?"

His eyebrows shot up. "Oh no, it was real. I have a lot to tell you. About all of that, Khan, CyTown, and things about Davion, too. But I'm dead tired. I'll bungle it if I try now."

Grace looked at the deep purple under his eyes. At his dark jaw. The stubble was sparse. She didn't think Heron could grow a full beard even if he wanted to. But he also hadn't had the energy or motivation to shave in a while.

"Come here," she said, patting the covers beside her. "Lay down before you drop."

"I don't want to impose."

"Heron, *lay down.*"

He didn't protest a second time. He slipped his socked feet under her comforter and plumped the pillow under his head.

She had a lot of questions, but they could wait. Neither one of them was worth anything right now. She expected Heron to fall asleep immediately. Her eyes were already growing heavy themselves.

But Heron's eyes were open. They were searching her face. "I hope you don't regret…don't regret my pulling you out."

"I was kidnapped," she said.

"Yes, but you were so happy with them. You were smiling. You were laughing. There was a minute where I almost believed their lies: that you'd turned yourself in willingly. That you'd wanted to be integrated because you missed them and it was either integration or suicide."

"Is that what they said?" If so, there was going to be a lot of confusion and a lot of explaining to do once she recuperated.

He nodded, his eyes drooping closed. "Fortunately, I was able to convince Lore that you were in real danger. We've been taking turns guarding your house."

"Who's here?"

"I'm not sure," Heron said. "Lore's been recruiting. Only people loyal to you. People he trusts."

His voice dropped away. His breathing evened out. Grace was desperate to talk more, to get a handle on this strange world that she'd returned to, to understand what was happening—what *had* happened.

"Wait, Heron."

"Mmm," he groaned.

"How were you able to get into my CyTown. To see me and talk to me like you did?"

"I added an anti-VR packet into your software when I uploaded the pre-CyTown cache."

For a moment, Grace only blinked at him. She couldn't for the life of her remember what he was talking about.

"I added a bunch of updates so that you could piggy-back into CyTown with me to interview Range. Do you remember?"

"Vaguely."

"It occurred to me when I made that cache that if Tristan could be kidnapped and forced into CyTown, so could we. But I must've gotten the coding wrong because it didn't keep you aware like I thought it would. It was supposed to keep you rooted to *our* reality, knowing you were in CyTown."

Grace wondered if her desire to see Kaiden again, to hold him, smell him, kiss his cheeks, had been too much of a draw. And yet…

"I think you were able to pull me out because I wanted out. I wanted…" She tried to adjust her legs under the covers, but they weren't cooperating. They were heavy and sluggish.

To let go? To lose them again?

Admitting it felt like fresh betrayal, like she'd turned her back on her child, willingly. Her husband, who'd she'd vowed to love as long as there was breath in her lungs.

Grace's voice broke. "How could I *want* to let go? I must be the most depraved, most wretched, sick—"

"No." Heron reached out and pulled her close. "No,

you're not. The only thing wrong with you, Gray, is that you want to *live*. You want your life, no matter how tragic and messy and imperfect it is. You want *your* life and you want to *live* it."

And he was right. He was right.

"I got that memory bank when I found out I was pregnant. I'd wanted to remember everything. The first time he was placed in my arms. The smell of him. The…the…"

And now it's all gone.

The dam broke inside her and she collapsed into sobs.

"I'm sorry," he said again. And again. Until they both fell asleep.

TWENTY-THREE

A SOFT KNOCK on the door made Grace look up. It was Arjun, standing in the doorway, one hand on its frame. He lifted a tray of food. "Any chance I can get you to eat something?"

Assuming he meant the plural *you*, she said, "He's sleeping."

Heron still lay on the bed beside her, his face placid on her pillow. A soft snore escaped him.

"He sleeps like the dead," Arjun said, and put the tray on her lap. "And he's long overdue."

Grace sat up, positioning herself against the pillows. She was ravenous.

"I thought you might be starving," he said. "I can't imagine not eating for almost three weeks."

She tried to remember how they fed CyTown residents. Intravenously, she was sure.

"I hope my stomach can keep it down." She was more than a little self-conscious about how she might look right now after weeks in a pod, having lived off of a liquid diet and fever dreams.

He seemed to read her thoughts. "I've seen worse. And I remember what you look like when you're well."

She unfolded her napkin and put it across her lap. Her hands shook.

"Muscle weakness," he said. "Imagine what it's like for those people who've been in there for years. They're supposed to use electricity to keep the muscles stimulated, but I can't believe it replaces actual use."

Grace lifted the piece of toast and took a bite. It was like heaven with butter and goberry jelly spread on top.

"I went with something simple to see if you can keep it down. There's crackers too, if the bread is too much. I was worried about the jelly."

"You didn't have to do this." Her heart clenched. "Thank you."

Arjun watched Heron sleep, a soft expression on his face. "I'm glad he found you."

Grace's heart kicked. If Arjun noted her rising panic, he made no sign.

"I've worried about Heron for a long time. He's a brilliant guy. Absolutely brilliant."

Grace managed a weak laugh. "Don't tell him that or it'll go to his head."

Arjun smiled. "But he had no focus. No way to channel all of his gifts and abilities into a useful, productive outlet. Until he met you. This job has been good for him. *You've* been good for him."

Grace thought about how Heron came alive when they were solving a case together. How he loved to tease out the details, craft plans. He was far from orthodox and made her skin crawl with his out-of-the-box schemes, but there was no denying that Arjun was right. Heron was brilliant.

Her face burned.

Arjun politely didn't point this out. "I thought he was

going to kill himself trying to get you out. I've only seen him do that once before. Run himself down like that."

"Next time, stop him." Grace took another bite. "I'm not worth it."

"He disagrees." Arjun didn't smile. "So do I. Besides, if you think I can stop him once he has something in his head, you're mistaken. Heron is relentless when he wants something. He's been that way since he was a kid."

"I keep forgetting that you knew him as a kid. Davion too?"

Arjun turned the box of crackers between his hands. "We met him on a mission with Dr. Jane. Did he ever tell you how they met?"

"I-I don't know. I've lost—" *Everything.* "My memories. I had everything stored in a memory bank, but CyTown corrupted the files and now I can't access them through my lenscape."

"You don't need your lenscape to remember."

"I can't—"

"You're relying on your head," Arjun said. It was firm but gentle. "What does your heart remember?"

"I don't…I can't…"

"You didn't get the memory bank until…?"

"I was pregnant."

"So what do you remember of your childhood? Of your parents? Of meeting Davion? Of how you fell in love?"

"I—"

"Try," he urged. He opened the box of crackers and put a few on her plate now that the toast was gone. "It can't hurt to try."

Her childhood?

Glimpses at best. What formed were more like emotional imprints. Grace running through Whitman Park with her parents not far behind, kicking blossoms up with her feet. Sprawled on her bed, reading books about detectives and heroes and women with capes.

The flu. Of her father never leaving her side, his low, steady voice as he told her funny stories. Every time she woke, they were there with soft words and a cool rag for her brow.

Of learning she'd been accepted to the academy and her dream of becoming an inspector would come true. How she'd run through the house, pinging her parents, demanding they read her acceptance letter at once.

How one day she'd been sitting in a café window, talking to her best friend, Joanne, when a man walked by. He passed once, did a double take. Smiled at her. Waved through the window.

"He's not looking at me," Joanne had said, nudging Grace's legs with her own. "Say hi."

"Are you nuts? *No.*"

And despite her bout of shyness, she'd seen him again in a bookstore not a week later. Both pretending not to see the other, shy smiles on their faces. Her own cheeks red.

Then a third time in a Low Town apartment, at a mutual friend's birthday party.

"We have to stop meeting like this," Davion had said, taking a spot beside her against the wall.

"Okay." She'd pretended to leave, only to turn around smiling. "Kidding."

Then another memory. The details weren't clear. The room was a white haze, the doctors were masked. But a warm, slick body was laid on her chest. The most beautiful raisin she'd ever seen. A knife through her heart when he began to cry.

Davion's warm hand sliding into hers. His words: "You did good, Mama."

"I—" She choked. She looked up and found Arjun's half-smile. "I remember when Kaiden was born."

Tears slid down her cheeks.

"See. They're still there," he said. "They always will be."

TWENTY-FOUR

HERON WAS STILL ASLEEP, snoring softly beside her, when voices woke Grace. She slipped quietly from the bed, shuffling forward in the dark and opened the bedroom door.

"I understand that!" a man hissed. "But if we don't tell her immediately, Alabaster will go public. He's wanted to from the start! It's the only way he can run her out of the city, which is what he wants to do, I tell you!"

On the landing, Grace saw three figures below. Arjun, in a fresh shirt, his long hair pulled back in a low ponytail. Lore with bags under his eyes thick enough to rival Heron's. And that was…

It took a minute for the name to come to her. Orrin Khan.

"Tell me what?" Her voice was still paper thin and raspy, but it had improved much in the hours since she first woke.

"Commander," Lore breathed. "We didn't mean to wake you."

"You didn't," she lied, and pointed a thumb at her bathroom rather than explicitly state why she'd gotten up.

"I need to speak with you," Khan said. "*Urgently. Please.*"

"Let me use the bathroom and I'll be down."

Grace splashed cold water on her face, smoothed her hair into a bun, and brushed her teeth. The dark circles were still there, and it was strange to see the scars again after weeks of seeing herself unblemished.

Realizing she'd done the best she could, she met the men downstairs.

Arjun put tea biscuits and a cup of hot tea on the table in front of her.

"Where is your partner?" Khan asked.

For a terrible moment, Grace thought he meant Davion. Her mind was still doubling, struggling to bring itself fully to this reality.

But then Arjun said, "He needs to sleep."

"Never mind," Orrin said, waving his free hand. The other held his own tea. "I can start without him."

Grace caught Lore's eyes, and he forced an embarrassed grin.

"You've more color in your cheeks," he assured her.

Grace thanked him but had no need to run her lie-detection program to know he was only being nice.

Khan rubbed the furrowed skin between his brows. "I've had a lot of time to think about how to tell you this, and I think it's best if I tell you in two separate stories. At the end, you'll see how they match up."

Grace took a biscuit from the tray, too hungry to hide it.

"First, there's the reason why my brother wants you out of the way."

"Alabaster," she said, now remembering the name.

"Yes. He would kill you outright if he could, and he's certainly tried. But he would've settled for imprisoning you in CyTown for the rest of your life."

"Why?" she asked.

"Apart from the fact you cannot be bought or sold, unlike everyone else in this zone?"

"I can't be bought," Lore said.

"No?" Khan said, turning an incredulous glare on Lore. "There isn't a price for making sure your daughters arrive home from school today?"

Lore blanched.

Orrin softened. "We all have a price. There's no shame in it. The only problem is that Grace has already paid hers, and Alabaster knows this. She has nothing to lose."

I wouldn't be so sure.

Grace revisited Heron's kiss in the bar. How real it had felt. His face in the Soul Grove screen. Her deliberate choice to return for…what? This life? Or him?

She caught Arjun's eye and her face burned.

"Her position in the zone. Her credibility. Her reputation as a hero protects her. That is why he wants to tell everyone what Davion did and hopes Grace goes down with him."

Lore's eyes widened. "What did Davion do?"

Both Khan and Arjun looked to her. They weren't going to tell this story for her.

"Davion was forging visas and smuggling families in from the outer zones. He was stealing from companies to fund their living and travel expenses."

Lore blinked. "He told you this?"

"Not until after he'd died." She stopped short of saying Heron had been the one to deliver Davion's last recorded message.

Lore turned on Khan. "How can Alabaster blame her for that? She didn't know."

"That wouldn't mean diddly squat to the public. They'll hear conflicting sides. They'll doubt her ignorance at best, her cognitive ability at worst. They'll say things like, 'If she couldn't see the devil in her own home, how in the world can she be trusted to—'"

Grace pinched her eyes shut. "Enough. I get the point. He wants to discredit me so that I can't tear down his companies over water rights. Is that it?"

"That's part of the second story. We'll come back to water rights."

Grace shoved another biscuit in her mouth.

"Every step of the way I've argued you should be left alone. I campaigned for you to be admitted into Egg Island, hoping it would offer you some measure of protection. Members don't attack other members, or at least we've vowed not to."

"That's why you looked the other way, because your brother is a member."

Orrin rolled his eyes. "Of course. We founded it together. And its evolution and direction have largely been a war between our two wills, but that's neither here nor there."

Arjun discreetly put six more biscuits on the plate as if Grace couldn't see him do it.

"Thank you," she said out of the side of her mouth.

"You're welcome."

Lore took a biscuit for himself.

"But he only plans to honor his end of the bargain—"

"Which is not killing me?"

"Yes." He adjusted himself in his seat. "If *you* intend to honor the no-attack rule yourself."

Grace frowned. "Why wouldn't I?"

Khan sighed. "Because of the second part of the story I'm about to tell you."

No one spoke, and as expected, Khan immediately filled the silence.

"Zone 2 has a water shortage because of misuse by many of its companies. The calls to donate your water shares don't go to the storm-torn zones—they go to corporations here in this very zone. Documents are falsified to report only usage within the limits allotted—"

"That's fraud!" Lore exclaimed.

Khan barely glanced at him before pushing on. "And they acquire and consume smaller companies so that they can manipulate their water numbers as well. Even the kidnapping and imprisonment of thousands of CyTown residents is a quest to expand his water margins, as higher residency means higher allotment. That's why he was doing all he could to silence and control voices like Mr. Range's and increase recruitment."

"Is he working alone?" Grace asked.

"My brother is responsible for these hostile takeovers, but he isn't alone, no. There are many who believe what he believes, those who feel the corporations should have more power, and they're willing to manipulate the government and the people to support them, convincing them that what is good for the corporations is good for the people. It's not!"

"Why tell me about the water?" Grace asked. "Your company will be sanctioned along with his."

"Because he has to be stopped and I can't do it. I've never been able to outmaneuver him in all my life. Whenever I've gone against him, I...Heaven, I can't. He's my brother." He rubbed his forehead, and for the first time

Grace saw a very tired, very old man. "But if he isn't stopped the entire zone will go bankrupt. Our aquifers will not last forever. Men like my brother think that will be someone else's problem. Let *them* save the world, he says. But who is this mythical *them*?"

It was a good question.

"This is our problem. *We* must act. But I don't know how we'll manage it. The way our borders are created, we've locked ourselves up tight in these little cells. This is great when we've got something to protect, but once our resources run out, then what? We will be locked in the empty pantry. Don't you see?"

Déjà vu washed over her. Had he told her this before somewhere? At the party, maybe? In the CyTown simulation?

"To be clear, you're saying that I was admitted to Egg Island because Alabaster hoped I would not prosecute him for the water?"

"Admittance is done by vote," Arjun said gently. "You and a few others would've also had to agree to bring her in."

Grace met Khan's eyes. "Why did you want me to join EI?"

"I invited you out of fear." He squeezed his kneecaps with his palms. "CEOs in boardrooms around the zone sat up and took note when you destroyed Peters."

"I didn't—"

"You destroyed him. His company incinerated overnight. And we all noticed."

"He was firing thousands of people and not reporting it. He left them homeless, hungry, without protection so he could expand his profit margins." Grace wasn't going to apologize for taking down Viscosity.

Khan held up a hand. "I'm not saying what he did was right. I'm only saying that it was impossible to overlook."

"And your brother was furious," Lore said.

"Absolutely. He saw Grace as the threat. He wanted her gone. Our compromise was her admittance into Egg Island. He's under the illusion she can be controlled if she is 'one of us.'"

Arjun was watching Khan closely. "Tell her."

Khan only nodded.

"When I found out that your husband was stealing money from my company, I had no intention, *none whatsoever*, of harming him. But my brother sits on the board of my bank. He knows everything that happens within its walls. He heard about the theft. Then he discovered that someone was smuggling people into the zone, that the thief was stealing not only our money but our water. He was furious."

Grace's heart sped up.

"When he discovered it was your husband, I begged him to leave it alone. 'Look the other way,' I said. 'If you kill him, she'll never stop.'"

Her heart pounded in her throat. "Are you saying…?"

She couldn't finish.

"He set out to kill her, too, to kill all of us," Lore murmured, astonished. "That *bastard*! A lot of people could've died!"

Khan nodded. "I know. I know. This is why I've been afraid to come forward and tell you the truth."

Grace's breathing was shallow. Her face hot. Her heart hammered like a war drum.

Say it, she thought. *Just say it.*

"I suspected he would try something, and instead of telling you, of warning you directly or protecting your family—or hell, even turning my brother in—I was a coward. I called on Adams instead. Asked him to make you more aware. I took unnecessary and gratuitous side channels to protect myself, my companies, and my brother."

His eyes were bright with tears now.

"I protected myself, and my brother," Khan said in a trembling voice, his lips wavering. "And because of that, your husband and your son are dead."

TWENTY-FIVE

GRACE CROSSED one leg over the other and met the constable's eyes. "My husband, Davion, forged visas and stole money from several corporations. One of them was Trinity Bank, and Alabaster Khan ordered two IEDs to be set at the precinct during the last winter parade. He is responsible for the death of my son."

The constable's hand, which had been holding a koffee en route to their mouth, wavered. "*What?*"

Grace had arrived thirty minutes before the scheduled hearing with Pendam and the Khans in order to make this statement to Ezra.

As quickly as she could, she recounted everything she'd learned about Davion since waking up in the hospital after the winter parade explosion. Everything that Khan had told her in her living room only four days before.

"Grace. Dear god." The constable sat down on the edge of their desk, their legs visibly shaking. "What are you going to do?"

"I'm not sure. If I challenge him outright, then my ability to investigate the water rights will be impossible.

That could cost more lives. And throwing him in prison won't bring my son back."

"But you want justice?"

"Of course," Grace hissed. "I want him to *rot* for what he did."

Her face felt as if someone held a flame up to it.

The constable massaged their forehead. "Where is your assistant?"

"Outside." Grace had asked Heron to wait on the steps. She'd wanted to know the minute Pendam and the Khans arrived. Also, it would help to give the constable the impression that Heron was ignorant of the situation, should this conversation turn another way.

"And you didn't know what Davion was doing before he died?" the constable repeated for the third time.

"This is why I asked you to turn on your lie-detection program," she said calmly.

The constable only nodded to this.

"This is a hell of a mess, isn't it?"

Grace took this to be a rhetorical question.

"If you call Dr. Tove in here, he can tell you how Davion helped his family enter the zone," she said.

The constable startled. "Dr. Ezekiel Tove is dead."

Grace's heart kicked. "Since when? How?"

"Apparent suicide eight days after you were kidnapped. The wife and children are missing. We presume they've left the zone."

At least the constable was calling her abduction what it was. That was promising. But the news of Tove's death still made her heart flinch.

The constable pressed their fingers into their temples. "I told you that you needed to be careful."

"I know," Grace said. What else could she say?

Finally, the constable looked up and met her gaze.

"What are you going to do? If you challenge Alabaster this will get ugly. He'll fight you screaming into the grave. I'll fight like hell for you, but Grace, you could still end up on the Midnight Train. Terrorism is a serious charge."

Grace wasn't worried about herself. She was worried about Heron. If they began to dig too deep, they might discover he wasn't an inspector at all. Then what would happen?

Heron pinged, <<They're here.>>

Grace relayed the message. "Can I have a few minutes alone with Alabaster in the mediation room before we begin?"

Their mouth unhinged. "What if he attacks you?"

"He won't."

They scoffed. "You don't know that."

"I do," she insisted. *For the same reasons I haven't murdered him outright.*

The constable pointed at the door. "Five minutes then. God help you."

THE MEDIATION ROOM was overcooled and spacious. There were chairs on either side of the large desk. Grace was already sitting at a table when Alabaster appeared. He was tall, his long white hair trailing down his back. He wore head-to-toe black.

He looked down his long nose at her. "You wanted to see me, Commander Buteo?"

She gestured to the empty seat across from her. "Sit."

He arched a brow but didn't object.

He crossed his legs and settled his back against the seat. "I assume my brother has spoken to you."

Grace had no intention of letting this man control the conversation.

She laced her fingers and put on her best interrogator face. "I am new to Egg Island, but I believe the custom is that members work to resolve their issues out of the public eye. Is that correct?"

A spark of hopefulness flashed in his eyes. "Yes."

"For example, in our situation, I should forgive your attempt to *imprison* me in virtual reality, and in exchange you will pay all taxes owed on the water you've stolen and have a five-year ban on acquiring any more companies. You *will* adhere to the water restrictions placed on your enterprises."

"That seems unfair."

"Hmm." She tapped her chin. "And yet it was my *life* you were trying to end."

"Nonsense. I wanted to *give* you the gift of your family. I understand their loss has been detrimental for you. What was your sweet boy's name? Kaiden?"

Rage flashed through her. She didn't want her son's name uttered by those lips. She kept her face neutral, breathing slowly in an attempt to keep the heat from creeping into her face.

He just wants to know if I know he's responsible. She wasn't going to give the game away so easily.

When she trusted herself to speak, she said, "Will you agree to these terms or not?"

He arched his brows. "If I don't, I suppose you'll destroy my companies one by one, like you did poor Getty Peters'?"

Grace only grinned.

I'm going to do more than tear down your companies, she thought, keeping her smile bright. *I'm going to take everything from you. Like you took everything from Kaiden.*

Alabaster rolled his eyes. "Fine. What are a few million dollars to me? I'll agree to these terms."

Grace called Heron and the others into the room. To Alabaster she said, "Smart move."

GRACE AND HERON were seated on the constable's left. Pendam and Alabaster took seats on the right. To everyone's surprise, Orrin Khan pulled out the chair on Grace's left, the one between her and his brother, and sat down.

The constable arched a brow at this but said nothing.

"Arden Pendam and Alabaster Khan, you are charged with kidnapping Commander Grace Buteo and with forcing her entry into CyTown residency. How do you plea?"

"Not guilty," Alabaster Khan said immediately, looking down his imperial nose at all of them.

"Not guilty," Arden Pendam echoed, with a thin veneer of smugness hiding his concern. His fear was on much greater display than Alabaster's.

The constable turned to Grace. "Are you willing to testify against these men and affirm the charges against them?"

"No," Grace said.

All heads—except Alabaster's—turned toward her, the shock evident on each face.

"With conditions," she added.

"Grace, you can't—" Orrin murmured.

Beneath the table, Grace nudged his knee, doing her best to keep the movement imperceptible. Orrin fell silent immediately.

Alabaster let out a sharp, surprised laugh. "Let's hear these conditions, dear Commander."

The constable's eyes remained on hers. "Commander, if you waive the right to a trial—"

"I understand." Grace met their eyes. "Would you like to hear my conditions?"

The constable frowned. "Go on."

"First, I want it circulated widely that I entered CyTown of my own volition for a temporary stay. I wanted to say goodbye to my husband and son properly in a way I hadn't been able to do before, given the unexpected circumstances of their deaths. Make it clear that all previous rumors are inaccurate, spread by gossipmongers, and that this is the official story."

The constable's lips twitched with a suppressed smile. "This story will best be sold by yourself. Perhaps a public briefing to assure everyone who's been worried about you?"

Now Grace was trying to suppress a grin. "Excellent idea. I'll schedule it for this evening."

Alabaster shared none of their humor. "Anything else I can do for you, Commander Buteo?"

"The sixteen companies I've outlined here will be audited for their resource management, and should it be found that their allotments are exceeded for any reason, those companies will pay any outstanding tax immediately, as well as an underpayment penalty."

Grace waited for all those present to accept the ping with the listed companies. Their lenscapes flicked blue.

"I agree to Trinity Bank, Capricorn Meats, and the vertical farms of which I am the primary holder," Orrin said at once.

"CyTown is on here!" Pendam protested. "Why do I have—*Ow!*"

The table jumped, and Grace thought she saw Alabaster's leg sliding back into its original position.

"With the exception of those my brother owns, and

Mr. Pendam's CyTown Towers, I see the other eleven are mine."

The constable was watching him now. "Do you agree to the audit, Mr. Khan?"

With a labored sigh he said, "I do."

"Mr. Pendam?" Ezra prompted.

Managing to sound like a sulky child, Pendam said, "Yeah, whatever."

His nose still upturned, Alabaster asked, "Anything *else* I can do for you today, Commander?"

"Only one more thing. There can be no more soliciting for a citizen's water shares through the information bulletins until the matter is fully investigated and we can confirm exactly where that water is going. You own Premier Solutions, the media company who creates and distributes the bulletins, don't you, Mr. Khan?"

Now Khan was properly furious, his jaw working. "You want me to stop sending out bulletins zonewide?"

"No," she said. She looked him dead in the eye. "I simply want you to stop asking people to divert their personal water shares to your companies."

"Fine." He stood. To the constable he said, "Are we done here?"

"I will reevaluate this matter in thirty days to confirm that all mediation requests have been met, including the bulletin," Ezra said, their arms crossed. "Do all parties accept?"

"I do," said each of the three men in turn.

Pendam and Alabaster left without looking back. Both the constable and Orrin lingered, but it was Orrin who voiced her own concern.

"I hope you know what you're doing," he said to Grace.

"It will slow the water leak and give us time to assess the real danger."

It will buy us time, Grace thought.

Khan squeezed her scarred arm. She barely felt it. "I meant about justice for your family. This was your chance to formally charge him. I was ready to testify to—"

"It's all right," Grace shushed him.

"But—"

"Nothing I could've done today would bring Kaiden or Davion back," she said. "All that would've happened was a large, ugly investigation. And we might've lost our chance to solve the water crisis."

Her compromise with Alabaster wouldn't solve all of their problems, true, but as she'd crafted these conditions, she'd thought of Lore in her living room. Lore with his wide, earnest eyes as he told Orrin, *We could've all died!*

That had driven her decision to seek compromise more than anything. If she got herself killed or exiled now, what would happen to them? To Heron? To Arjun or her mother? To Lore and his family? Or to all the families that Davion had saved?

As angry as she was, she didn't want his death to be for nothing.

What they had needed most now was time, time to find their next move. And she'd won them that at least.

The citizens of Zone 2 had no idea how close they were to the edge of ruin.

She had to think of them first.

Orrin rubbed his brow. "Enforcing the tax will not change the fact that the water is drying up. He will pay more because he can, but you can't buy what doesn't exist! The zone will run out of water and we'll starve! We'll die and—"

"*Breathe.*" Heron patted Orrin Khan on the back.

"Give Grace some credit. She's an excellent problem-solver."

"But your son," Orrin said again.

"Water first. Then justice."

He searched her face, but Grace remained firm.

"All right." Khan's shoulders slumped. "If you're sure."

On the steps outside, after watching Khan and the constable disappear into their autos, Heron turned toward her at last.

"I meant what I said. You'll solve this."

She looked over the boulevard, at the autos gliding down the wide avenue. At the throngs of people walking, laughing, blissfully unaware of the black clouds on the horizon.

"I hope you're right."

TWENTY-SIX

GRACE STOOD on the steps of a small apartment with a fruit basket in her arms. She'd knocked for the third time before wondering if she should leave the basket and go. Then the door opened.

Lenorie's nose and cheeks were red, her eyes tear-stained.

"Hi," Grace said tentatively. "I just wanted to give you this. I don't have to stay if this is a bad time."

"No, please," Lenorie said, waving her in. She took the basket. "Thank you. This smells amazing."

"I think it's the goranges."

Heron had helped her pick out the grief basket, claiming that the goranges—a hybrid of grapefruit and oranges—were good for depression. Grace hoped he was right.

"Do you want one?" she asked, putting the basket on the counter.

"No, I just ate. But please help yourself."

Lenorie pulled a plate from the cabinet and used a

large blade to slice one of the goranges in half. She brought it to the coffee table but didn't eat it.

"How do you like your new place?" Grace asked as the woman sat down on the blue sofa beside her. "The plants are beautiful."

A wall of plants adjacent to the window sparked in the morning light. Grace counted thirty-six at first glance before a second-level transport vehicle cut past the large picture window and broke her concentration.

"It's very cozy." Lenorie pushed her hair behind her ear. "The insurance replaced almost everything. I'm only missing a couple of things."

"If you need anything else, let us know," Grace said.

Lenorie nodded, but her gaze was distant. "It's just strange. Him being gone."

Grace's heart flopped. "I'm sorry."

Lenorie shook her head, her gaze falling to her lap. "It's not your fault. You went and got him, and that's what counted."

When they'd pulled Tristan off the CyTown programming, he had a stroke and died within two hours.

"I know he'd rather be dead than in that place, but…" She wrung her hands. "It's just hard. He's gone. He was the last person I had."

Grace placed a hand on her shoulder and squeezed. "It'll get easier."

"Will it?" Lenorie looked up, fresh tears rolling down her cheeks. "You'd know, wouldn't you? God, I hope you're right."

Grace's own tears welled. "I'm sorry we weren't fast enough."

Lenorie hugged her, hard. "You believed me and you tried. It's all I wanted."

They both knew this was a lie.

Grace stood beneath the trees of the Soul Grove, watching her husband's and son's faces light up with laughter on the embedded screen. Kaiden's arms were tight around his father's neck. There was more peace in her heart than there'd been the last time she'd come here. Last time, her anger for Davion had been fresh, nearly alive.

Now she understood.

Or she was beginning to understand. Concessions had to be made when trying to save others. She didn't miss them any less, but understanding helped.

The sound of footsteps made her turn and look up the narrow path between the trees.

It was Heron, with a bouquet of stargazers resting in the crook of one arm.

He hesitated on the path. "I didn't know you were here. Should I come back later?"

"No," she said. "Join me."

Grace moved aside so that Heron could put his bouquet in the vase holder buried in the forest floor. They were beautiful there, the starburst of color against the lush green.

This was the first time Grace had seen Heron's bare feet.

When Heron took a seat beneath the tree, Grace did too. The grass was soft under them.

For a while they sat in silence, the sunlight dancing along their skin.

Grace tilted back her head to welcome the breeze cutting across her face.

"I just came from Lenorie's."

Heron's brow furrowed. "How is she? I feel bad about Tristan."

"Me too." She ran a hand through her hair. "She'll make it. She just needs time."

"I have something for you," Heron said.

His clothes rustled, and Grace peeked open one eye. From inside his coat he pulled out a small black device. It looked a lot like the screens embedded in the soul trees in front of them.

"It's crude compared to your embedded memory chip," he explained. "But I thought this was better than nothing. I loaded it with all your memories from your memory bank account. You can search it with the touch-screen the way you could in your head. You just have to touch these buttons."

He gave her a demonstration of the device's abilities. With a few taps, he'd pulled up a memory. It was an innocuous conversation with Lore. She wondered if he'd seen any others while loading the device.

He handed it over.

"Thank you." She thought of Arjun's memories lesson and her heart clenched. "Arjun's a good guy."

Heron's brows arched, clearly confused by the change in topic. "He is."

She told him about Arjun bringing her the tray of food shortly after she woke. It was easier than talking about memories.

Once her story ended and the silence stretched out again, she said, "I'll give you some time alone with him."

She began to rise, suspecting that he wanted to visit Davion on his own like she had.

His hand shot out and grabbed hers. "Don't go. Stay."

Heat trailed up her arm. Her skin was electric under his fingertips, but he didn't let go.

"Okay," she said, and took her place beside him, about three inches closer than she'd been before. Now she could feel the heat from his body. Smell the cologne along his throat.

"Do you want to talk about it?" she asked. It was evident he had something to say. It was only a matter of whether or not she was the right audience.

"Honestly…" He ran a hand up the back of his head. "Davion was…He was…"

He chewed his lip. "He meant a lot to me, and obviously I'm sad that he's gone. But sometimes I'm not as sad as I should be, because if he wasn't dead I'd never have had the chance to—I'd never have had the chance to come here and meet you and do this exciting work and—" He puffed out his cheeks and sputtered his lips. "God, it sounds worse aloud. I'm going to stop now."

"It's all right. You can say it." She knew already where this would go. Her rabbiting heart was warning enough.

He rubbed his forehead with his fist. "I'm not as sad as I should be because I'm…I'm happier than I've been in a long time. Maybe ever."

But was that because of her, or the work?

"I don't think he would be upset about that," she said.

"He would if he knew that I wanted—" His mouth snapped shut.

"What do you want?"

Grace thought of her last moment in CyTown. The treacherous moment where she'd hung between the two realities, the two trees in the Soul Grove of her mind.

She could've chosen Davion and Kaiden. She could've stayed there and, well, not lived exactly, but she could've stayed. Someone could argue it wasn't living.

That she'd only chosen Heron because it meant choosing reality.

Yet if she'd had the same choice to make three months ago, she would've stayed with Davion and Kaiden, even if they were figments of her mind.

"What do you want?" she asked again.

"To be totally honest…" He swallowed. "You."

Her heart dropped into the pit of her stomach. If he'd met her gaze then, she thought that might be it. It would be all over for her.

But he didn't. He looked up the aisle between the trees as if looking for something in the distance. She waited for him to fold, to turn it into a flirtatious joke. But he didn't do that either.

"It's very thoughtful but I can't accept your gift." She handed over the memory device he'd given her.

Had he given it to her right after she'd returned from CyTown she would've taken it, but now she understood how much she'd used her old memories to limp through her life. They'd been a crutch. True, Kaiden's were too painful to touch, but Davion's memories had prevented her from trying to bear her own weight again.

It was time to let go. This seemed as good a time as any.

His brow lines knit tight together. "I'm sorry if I—"

No. An apology wouldn't do.

"You can hang on to it for me," she said. "Maybe I'll want it someday, when I'm ready."

"Okay, but…" He tapped the device against his hand. His face shifted, falling into its usual casual flirtation. "About what I said—"

"Stop." She didn't want him to cover his feelings with jokes. She pushed a strand of hair behind her ear. "To be totally honest with you, Mr. Blue, I want you too."

It was the truth she hadn't allowed herself to consider for weeks. But it was impossible to ignore now that she'd stood in the Soul Grove of her mind and had seen her choices clearly.

And she'd chosen Heron. She'd chosen the future, not the past.

A nervous laugh escaped her. "And I'm confused about that. Not only because of Davion, but there's still Arjun. He's a good guy. You need him."

"I need you too," he said, searching her face.

Grace hadn't forgotten what Arjun had said about Heron as an inspector. How the work was good for him. It was good for her, too. Through it, Heron and Grace were united in a way that she'd never managed with Davion.

"My feelings are reciprocated," he said, staring out into the grove. He placed a hand over his heart. "That's nice."

She rolled her eyes. "There's also the fact that you flirt with anything that moves. I don't know if I can handle that as a serial monogamist."

Heron sat up, and they were almost shoulder to shoulder, facing each other. "I suppose with everything going on in the zone and our lives, it's hard to say where we'll be tomorrow, let alone next week, next month, or year…"

"Right," she agreed.

He cocked his head and met her gaze. "We could let things happen naturally and see where we end up?"

"Yes, that."

She slid her arms around his neck. Smelled his throat, the lobe of his ear. Felt his body stiffen in surprise, then soften completely against hers.

"Is this okay?" she asked.

He pressed a hand against her lower back, holding her close. He was steady. Warm. "More than okay."

· · ·

Enjoying Grace's story? It continues in book three *The City Outside*

Did you enjoy this book? You can make a BIG difference.

I don't have the same power as big New York publishers who can buy full-spread ads in magazines, and you won't see my covers on the side of a bus anytime soon, but what I *do* have are wonderful readers like you.

And honest reviews from readers garner more attention for my books and help my career more than anything else I could possibly do—and I can't get a review without you! So if you would be so kind, I'd be very grateful if you would post a review for this book.

It only takes a minute or so of your time, and yet you can't imagine how much it helps me. It can be as short as you like, and whether positive or negative, it really does help. I appreciate it so much and so do the readers looking for their next favorite read.

So please leave a review today.

Thanks.

Kory

GET YOUR FREE STORY TODAY

Thank you so much for reading *The City Within.* I hope you're enjoying Grace's story. If you'd like more, I have a free, exclusive 2603 story for you. See Heron, Arjun and Davion meet for the first time during one of his mother's scientific expeditions and learn more about how dangerous the outerzones are.

You can only read this story by signing up for my free newsletter. If you would like this story, you can get your copy by visiting ➜ www.korymshrum.com/thecitynewsletteroffer

I will also send you free stories from the other series that I write.

Please add me to your address book so my emails aren't marked as spam. Once you sign up, check your email and make sure you received the story okay. Can't find it? Email me at ➜ kory@korymshrum.com and I'll take care of it.

As to the newsletter itself, I send out 2-3 a month and host a monthly giveaway exclusive to my subscribers. The prizes are usually signed books or other freebies that I think you'll enjoy. I also share information about my current projects, and personal updates (like pictures of my dog). If you want these free stories and access to the exclusive giveaways, you can sign up for the newsletter at ➜ www.korymshrum.com/thecitynewsletteroffer

If this is not your cup of tea (I love tea), you can follow me on social media in order to be notified of my new releases.

ACKNOWLEDGMENTS

Writing and releasing two books at once was a new challenge for me! Coupled with the fact that my mother died in July of this year means that I needed more support than usual. And to my surprise, I got it.

Special thanks to my first readers: Kimberly Benedicto, Kathrine Pendleton, Angela Roquet, and Monica La Porta. They gave me a good idea of what was and wasn't working as I crafted this new, exciting world.

Then came the professional help: the lovely Toby Selwyn did a great editorial job. Christian Bentulan's cover is awesome and Alexandra Amor, my wonderful assistant, helped with formatting (among many other things).

Last, but not least, my street team swept in the act as final cleanup crew. Shoutout to Larry Fletcher, Holly White, James Slater, Chris Christoforou, April Hardin, Phyllis Cazares, Dorkas, Chris De Francisci, Stan Hutchings, Melissa Izquierdo, Denise, Carmela Chateau, Valerie Ranne, Margaret Young, Rosemary Kenny, Mark Roberts, Murf, Fiona Agnew, Terry Monk, Rosemary Swierczewski,

Kalynda Schock, Darryl, April, Debra Fortune, Victoria G. and Valarie Moss for their proofreading efforts!
I appreciate your hard work so much.

Dying for a Living series
Dying for a Living
Dying by the Hour
Dying for Her: A Companion Novel
Dying Light
Worth Dying For
Dying Breath
Dying Day

Shadows in the Water: Lou Thorne Thrillers
Shadows in the Water
Under the Bones
Danse Macabre
Carnival
Devil's Luck
What Comes Around

Design Your Destiny Castle Cove series
Welcome to Castle Cove
Night Tide

2603 novels
The City Below
The City Within
The City Outside

ABOUT THE AUTHOR

Kory M. Shrum is author of the bestselling *Shadows in the Water* and *Dying for a Living* series, as well as several other novels. She has loved books and words all her life. She reads almost every genre you can think of, but when she writes, she writes science fiction, fantasy, and thrillers, or often something that's all of the above.

In 2020, she launched a true crime podcast "Who Killed My Mother?" under the name K.B. Marie, sharing the true story of her mother's tragic death. You can listen for free on YouTube or your favorite podcast app.

When not writing or producing her show, she can usually be found under thick blankets with snacks. The kettle is almost always on. When she's not eating, reading, writing, or indulging in her true calling as a stay-at-home dog mom, she loves to plan her next adventure. (Travel).

She lives in Michigan with her equally bookish wife, Kim, and their rescue pug, Charley.

Learn more at www.korymshrum.com